DONOR

Other Titles by Ken McClure

DONOR

Ken McClure

Polygon

First published in Great Britain by Simon & Schuster Ltd, 1998

This edition published in Great Britain in 2010 by
Polygon, an imprint of Birlinn Ltd

Birlinn Ltd
West Newington House
10 Newington Road
Edinburgh
EH9 1QS
www.birlinn.co.uk

ISBN 978 1 84697 162 4

British Library Cataloguing-in-Publication Data
A catalogue record for this book is available
on request from the British Library.

Typeset in Adobe Garamond by Palimpsest Book Production Ltd,
Falkirk, Stirlingshire
Printed in Great Britain by Clays Ltd, St Ives plc

Charity shall cover the multitude of sins.

I Peter 4:8

PROLOGUE

Amy's room was cold; the heating had been turned off. Outside, snow was falling from a white-grey sky and the view from the window was blurred as a slight breeze caught the flakes and threw them silently against the glass. There was no rattle of raindrops or hammering of hail. This was as it should be, thought the woman who stood there looking out. The weather was showing proper respect. The whole world seemed quiet; it was holding its breath.

There was a distant hubbub from the people waiting downstairs but that served only to accentuate the silence in a room that had so often been alive with childish laughter. Ostensibly everything about the room itself was the same as it always had been. The pink wallpaper, the Disney curtains, the toys, the dolls, the picture of the boy-band on the wall. Amy's pyjamas lay on the pillow, neatly folded in a little square parcel; her colouring books were stacked on a bedside table with a box of pencils on top; but none of them would be needed again.

There would be no more brightly coloured pictures of jungle animals for her father to admire before telling her bedtime stories, no improbable pink giraffes or mauve tigers. Red birds would no longer fly off into green sunsets and Jack would not be slaying the giant again to childish sighs of relief. Amy was dead. She lay in the little white coffin in the middle of the room.

The hospital had given special permission for this. It was unusual for the bodies of patients who had undergone postmortem examination to leave the premises. They were usually taken directly to the hospital mortuary to await collection by appointed undertakers on the day of the funeral. But Amy's mother had dug her heels in and insisted that she be allowed home for the last time. She didn't know why she'd done it and she suspected the authorities had only given in to avoid a prolonged scene with a grief-stricken woman. She only knew that, as she continued to look out of the window, it seemed right. Amy was going to start her last journey from her own room.

Jean Teasdale's face was expressionless, her eyes distant. There were no tears; she had cried herself out. She barely acknowledged the fact that a hearse was drawing up outside the house, its wheels silenced by the snow. A few moments later the sound of the hubbub downstairs increased as the door behind her was opened and then faded as it was closed again.

'It's time, Jean,' said her husband softly.

'What was it all for? Tell me that,' she asked without turning.

'I wish I could,' came the whispered reply.

'Seven years of life and then nothing. Snuffed out. What a waste, what a stupid, pointless waste.'

Frank Teasdale put his hands gently on his wife's shoulders and kissed the back of her head lightly. She didn't turn round but she reached up her right hand to rest it on his.

'It's time to be brave,' he said.

'It's stupid, I know, but I can't help worrying about all that snow out there.'

'What about it, love?'

'I keep thinking . . . when they put Amy in the ground . . . she'll be cold.'

Frank Teasdale lost the battle with his emotions; and he had been doing so well up till that moment. Tears flooded down his cheeks and his shoulders heaved with the effort of trying to maintain a masculine silence. Jean finally turned away from the window and they held each other tight as they sought solace; but in this situation none was possible.

Frank broke away, pulling out a handkerchief and blowing his nose as he fought to find composure again. 'We'd best be getting downstairs,' he said. 'Get this over with. People have come from the hospital.'

Jean nodded. 'That's nice,' she said.

They paused together by Amy's coffin and rested a hand on the lid for a moment in a silent gesture of farewell. Frank looked at Jean; his eyes asked the question. She nodded in reply. They went down to join the mourners, passing between two of the undertaker's men who were waiting at the foot of the stairs.

'All right if we go up now?' asked one.

'Yes,' replied Frank without looking at him.

Amy's coffin was taken from the house and gently loaded into the hearse, to be surrounded by flowers from friends and family. They looked strangely incongruous against the snow, a splash of colour in a black-and-white world. Frank Teasdale found himself mesmerized by them; he kept staring at them through the windscreen of the car behind as he sat in the back with his arm round Jean. It was impossible not to draw analogies: beautiful, ephemeral things there for only a moment in the great scheme of things before withering and dying. He thought, it will soon be Christmas.

The next hour or so saw Frank and Jean Teasdale support each other through their daughter's funeral service and subsequent interment in the churchyard of St Mungo's, their local church, although neither had seen the inside of it since Amy's christening. They clung to each other as if afraid to let go even for a moment. It was almost a relief when the first shovel of earth hit the coffin lid and Amy could now exist only in memory.

Frank had started to guide his wife back along the path to the car park when she suddenly stopped. He felt her arm become rigid and looked up to see what had caught her attention. A woman was standing in the trees off to the side. She was wearing a raincoat and headscarf but Jean had recognized her.

'It's that nurse,' she said. 'It's that damned nurse. Why won't she leave us alone? Why must she go on spreading her poison?'

Frank could sense his wife becoming distraught. He tried to calm her, before taking a step towards the woman in the trees. The woman made an apologetic gesture as if to indicate that he needn't move; she had not meant to cause trouble. She moved back until she was out of sight.

'She's gone,' said Frank, returning to his wife's side.

'Why does she persist?' demanded Jean.

He looked sadly back to the trees. 'I really don't know,' he said.

ONE

'Who can tell us where we get bread from?' asked Kate Chapman. There were eighteen children sitting in front of her. She smiled as a forest of eager young hands went up and enthusiasm filled their faces. She loved teaching, especially at primary school. For her there was something magical about introducing children to the voyage of discovery she firmly believed education should be. She took her early navigational responsibility seriously. Not for her the cynicism that said these would be the surly teenagers of tomorrow, the bus-shelter vandals, the lager louts, that each new generation was more spoilt than the last. Kate simply could not see beyond the innocent little faces that currently vied for her attention.

'Kerry?'

'Please, Miss, a baker, Miss.'

'Good, Kerry. Now, who's going to tell us how the baker makes our bread?

No hands went up this time.

'Come on, what does the baker use to make the bread?' coaxed Kate.

A little boy, wearing glasses with one lens blanked off to encourage a lazy eye, put his hand up tentatively then withdrew it. He did this several times with furtive glances to the side as if afraid of making a fool of himself.

Kate sensed his dilemma. 'Yes, Andrew,' she said encouragingly. 'Come on, have a try. What do you think the baker uses?'

'Is it flour, Miss?' asked the little boy, putting his head to one side and then putting the end of his pencil in his mouth.

'Well done, Andrew. It's flour.'

He flushed with pleasure.

'Now, what kind of man makes the flour that goes to make the bread?'

Kate glanced behind her at the colourful pictures that lined the wall. She looked directly at the one showing a windmill with a red baker's van standing outside it.

Several hands went up as excited children got the clue and made the connection.

'Yes, Annie?'

'A miller, Mrs Chapman.'

'A miller,' agreed Kate. 'Well done, Annie. Now then, what does the miller need to make the flour?' She looked along the rows of children as they struggled to come up with the answer. The expressions on their faces were such that she could almost hear their minds working. But she frowned when she came to a pretty little blonde girl in the second row. She felt a sudden wave of concern. Amanda clearly wasn't concentrating on the question. Her eyes were dull and distant and her face was pale with a suggestion of moistness on her forehead.

'Are you feeling all right, Amanda?' she asked.

The child did not respond and the class murmured uneasily.

'Amanda?' repeated Kate.

The little girl turned her face towards her but still seemed distant.

Kate went over to her and put her arm round her shoulders. 'What seems to be the trouble?' she asked. She bent her knees, sat on her heels and smoothed the child's hair back from her forehead. She let her hand rest there for a moment. Amanda was burning up.

'Oh dear,' Kate soothed. 'You're not very well at all, are you?'

Kate now had a problem. Amanda was not only one of her pupils; she was also her daughter. There was therefore no option but to pass the buck to a third party. Sandy, her husband, a medical lab technician, was on duty at the local hospital and there was no one else she could call on for something like this. They had only moved to Bardunnock a few months before and were still at the settling-in stage.

Kate stood up in front of the class and said, 'I'd like you all to draw me a picture of what you think a miller might look like while I have a word with Mrs Jenkins. Any questions?'

'What's wrong with Amanda?' asked Tracy Johnson, the local postman's daughter.

'She's not feeling very well,' replied Kate. 'I think she's got a bit of a cold coming on.'

Please God that's all it is, thought Kate, as she picked up Amanda and hurried along the corridor to throw herself on the mercy of the head teacher, Isa Jenkins.

Isa Jenkins was teaching her own class. Kate looked through the one clear pane on the half-glass door and caught her attention. She saw Isa instruct her pupils to get on with something before coming outside into the corridor.

'What's up?'

'It's Amanda. She's not well. I think she may be coming down with flu.'

Isa put her head on one side to look at Amanda, who was resting her head on her mother's shoulder. 'Poor wee mite,' she said. 'You don't look well at all, do you?'

Amanda responded by putting her thumb in her mouth and nuzzling into her mother's shoulder.

'I'm awfully sorry about this—' began Kate but Isa stopped her. 'Nonsense,' she said. 'I'm sure we can work this out together. What do you want to do? Take her home or over to the medical centre in Colbrax?'

'I think maybe home,' said Kate. 'I'll put her to bed and keep an eye on her for a while. She's got a bit of a temperature but it could subside as quickly as it came on. You know what kids are like.'

'I should by now,' Isa smiled. She had been a teacher for thirty-two years.

'I really hate doing this to you,' said Kate, 'but—'

'Nonsense,' insisted Isa. 'I'll commute between classrooms until the bell.' She looked at her watch. 'It's only another hour and a half. No problem. What are your lot doing?'

'They're drawing a miller.'

'Right, off you go.'

'Thanks, Isa, I'm indebted to you,' said Kate, finding another reason for liking the life in Bardunnock.

At six o'clock Kate was in the kitchen when she heard Sandy's car come round the bend at the foot of the hill and labour up to the tight right-hand turn into the drive of the cottage. The car was a green, eight-year-old Ford Escort they had named Esmeralda.

'Where's my princess?' Sandy Chapman called out as he opened the door. He paused to wipe his feet on the coarse mat before stepping inside. For once his call was not answered by the sound of running feet and laughter. Kate emerged from the kitchen, drying her hands. 'Your princess isn't very well, I'm afraid. I had to bring her home from school this afternoon.'

Sandy stooped to kiss Kate on the forehead and put his arm round her shoulder before asking, 'What's the matter?'

'I thought it was just a cold but now I'm not so sure. I thought I'd wait till you came home before I called the doctor.'

Sandy nodded, now looking worried. He climbed the stairs to Amanda's room and pushed open the door. Amanda's head didn't move on the pillow but her eyes looked up at him.

'Hello, Princess,' said Sandy softly.

Amanda didn't reply. Her gaze drifted off to the window but her focal point was miles beyond.

Sandy's head nearly touched the ceiling in the upstairs rooms of the old cottage and his shoulders almost filled the doorway. He sat down on the floor beside Amanda and rested his elbow on the bed. 'Poor Princess,' he said. 'Have you picked up some nasty bug?'

He ran his fingers lightly along his daughter's forehead and felt the film of moisture on her pallid skin.

'I think we are going to call Dr Telford to give you some medicine to make you well again.' He looked at Kate meaningfully and she got the message. She left to telephone while Sandy continued to talk to Amanda.

'Tell Daddy where it hurts. Is it your tummy?'

Amanda shook her head slowly.

'All over?'

A nod.

'Have you been to the bathroom today?'

'Can't remember.'

'Can you remember what you had for lunch?'

A blank look.

'The same as the other children?'

A nod.

'You didn't eat any of the berries off the bushes in the garden did you, Princess?'

A slow shake of the head.

'Well you cuddle in now. The doctor will be here soon and he'll make you all better.' Sandy put Amanda's teddy bear beside her and tucked in the covers.

'What do you think?' asked Kate when he came downstairs.

Sandy shrugged. 'Same as you, I guess. I want to believe it's just a cold or flu but I think it'd be as well to get a qualified opinion.'

Kate put her head against his chest and he wrapped his arms round her.

'Oh God, I hope it's nothing serious,' she said.

'We're probably worrying unnecessarily,' said Sandy, but he glanced at his watch and asked, 'Did you get any idea how long the doctor would be?'

'The receptionist thought about half an hour. He still has a couple of patients to see at evening surgery.'

There wasn't enough room in Amanda's bedroom for all three of them to crowd in, so Sandy stayed downstairs while their GP examined Amanda and her mother provided reassurance by holding her hand. Sandy stood looking out at the garden while he waited.

There was no escaping the unease he felt, despite knowing that nine times out of ten a parent's fears were unfounded. The chances were that the doctor would come downstairs joking with Kate, tell them that there was nothing to worry about and accept their apologies for calling him out unnecessarily.

He recognized that the nature of his job at the hospital tended to distort his view of how much serious illness there was around. Was it the same for policemen? he wondered. Did they see crime and potential criminals everywhere they looked? He heard Amanda's door open and turned round to look up the stairs. Dr Telford came down first, with Kate behind. They were not joking.

Sandy knew George Telford through his job. General practitioners in the area were encouraged to participate in the care of their patients while they were in the district hospital.

'What do you think?' asked Sandy.

'I'm not happy with her,' replied Telford, looking concerned. 'I think we should take her into hospital overnight and run some tests.'

'Have you any idea at all what's wrong?'

'I've an idea her kidneys aren't working properly,' replied Telford. 'I could be wrong but I think we ought to run some biochemistry on her. Can't do any harm.'

'I suppose not,' said Sandy. Kate had come over to stand beside him and he had his arm round her shoulders.

'Has she shown any sign of having trouble with her waterworks in the past few days?' asked Telford.

Sandy looked to Kate, who shook her head. 'None at all,' she said. 'She's been as right as rain.'

'Well, a thorough examination at the hospital should put our minds at rest.'

'What hospital were you thinking of?' asked Sandy.

Telford looked thoughtful. He said, 'I'm trying to decide whether to take her in to the district hospital for overnight observation or maybe have her taken directly up to the Sick Children's Hospital in Glasgow.'

'She doesn't seem to be in too much discomfort,' said Kate, hoping to influence the decision in favour of the local hospital. That would be more reassuring than having Amanda taken off to Glasgow.

'True,' agreed Telford. 'That's what we'll do, then. We'll take her over to the district hospital and have some preliminary tests done.' He looked at his watch and said, 'I suppose at this time it'll mean calling out the duty technician in the lab. That's not you this evening, is it?'

'Not tonight,' replied Sandy.

'I'll stay at the hospital tonight,' said Kate. She knew from Sandy that on occasion the parents of young children were permitted to stay over in a guest room at the hospital.

'Good idea,' replied Telford.

It was just after eight thirty when Kate turned to Sandy and said, 'You must be starving. You haven't had anything to eat.' They were waiting in the small side room outside the ward while Amanda was settled by the nurses.

'I'm not hungry,' replied Sandy.

'Me neither.'

'What do you think?' she asked anxiously.

There was no need to ask what she meant. Sandy said, 'I think she's got worse in the last hour.'

'It could just be the upset at coming into hospital.'

'Maybe,' conceded Sandy, but he sounded far from convinced.

'Why don't you go on home?' Kate suggested. 'There's nothing you can do here. I'll be here for her if she wakes in the night.'

Sandy nodded as if only half considering the suggestion. 'I think I'm going to pop along to the lab first to see if Charlie got the specimens okay,' he said. 'Maybe I'll hang around until he's got the results. If they seem okay I'll go on home. You will call me if anything changes?'

'Of course,' replied Kate. 'And don't stand over Charlie. You're an interested party, remember.'

Sandy nodded; he kissed Kate on the forehead and turned to go.

The district hospital lab was situated in a small brick building, separate from the main building and hidden behind a row of conifers that bent in the wind as Sandy left the warmth of the hospital and walked down the path towards it. He got intermittent glimpses of the lights on in the building as the lower branches of the trees separated. Icy raindrops started to pepper his face as he turned into the shelter of the ivy-covered porch outside the lab. The door was locked. He fumbled in his pocket for his key but discovered that he'd left it at home. He rang the night bell and a few moments later the door was opened by a short, dark-haired, studious-looking man wearing a white lab coat with a green plastic apron over it. His dark-rimmed glasses seemed too large for his round face, giving him the look of a wise old owl.

'Evening, Charlie,' said Sandy as he stepped inside and closed the door behind him.

Charlie Rimington smiled and said, 'I had a feeling I might be seeing you when I read the label on the specimens. How is she?'

'Not good, but it's always hard to tell with kids. How are the tests coming along?'

'Up and running. I take it you're going to wait?'

'If you don't mind.'

'I've got kids too, remember.'

The insistent bleep of an electric timer distracted them and Sandy turned off the machine he was standing beside. He'd done this a thousand times before for other people's children's samples. It had never felt like this.

Feeling awkward because it was Rimington's duty shift and not his, he stood back to allow Rimington to open the loading cage and extract the specimen tube. He saw the ward label on the side of the glass: 'Amanda Chapman'. It made the hollow feeling in his stomach worse.

Rimington tore off the print-out from the machine and sat down, pencil in hand, at his desk to read it, using the pool of light from an anglepoise lamp. Sandy stood at his shoulder feeling impatient but fighting hard to hide it. After thirty seconds of silence he could stand it no longer.

'Well?' he asked.

'No signs of infection and no toxic substance present,' said Rimington.

'But?' said Sandy anxiously.

'All the signs . . . suggest sudden renal failure.'

'Jesus,' said Sandy, gripping the bench and letting his head fall forward. He remained like that for a few moments before asking, 'What are we talking here? Mild?' He took the analysis sheet from Rimington's hand and read the results for himself. 'Jesus,' he repeated. 'We're talking dialysis.'

''Fraid so,' agreed Rimington.

Sandy stood by while Rimington phoned the result through to the ward. There was no question about it: Amanda would have to be transferred to a hospital with a dialysis unit, and the sooner the better. The district hospital did not have this facility. It would have to be Glasgow after all.

A knot of fear formed in the hollow space in Sandy's stomach. He was worried sick about Amanda but he had to be strong for Kate's sake. Then there were the logistics of the transfer to be worked out. Kate could go in the ambulance with Amanda, while he drove up to Glasgow in Esmeralda so that he and Kate could get back, whenever that would be. He couldn't see that far ahead.

Charlie Rimington said, 'Don't worry about the lab. Andrew and I can cover for you. Take as much time as you need.'

'Thanks,' said Sandy, turning to leave. 'I appreciate it.'

Outside, it was now raining heavily. Sandy was soaked by the time he got back up to the hospital. He paused just inside the door to wipe the water from his face and push his wet hair back from his forehead before entering the ward.

Kate was talking to George Telford, who was telling her the

13

results of the tests. There was anguish on her face. She saw Sandy arrive and came towards him.

'Oh, Sandy,' she sobbed.

Sandy took her in his arms and held her tight. 'Come on now, Kate,' he encouraged her. 'She's going to be okay. We just have to get her to the right place.'

'Dr Telford says she has to be transferred tonight,' said Kate.

'It's for the best,' said Sandy.

'But how will we—'

Sandy put his finger on her lips. He said, 'Let's just take everything one step at a time. You travel in the ambulance with Amanda. I'll drive up. Then, when we've heard what the doctors in Glasgow have to say, we'll decide what's best.'

Kate nodded and wiped away her tears.

'Come on now,' soothed Sandy. 'Let's be strong for Amanda.'

Sandy had to fight against recurrent feelings of disorientation as he followed the ambulance on the road to Glasgow. He was having difficulty in coming to terms with just how quickly everything in their lives had been turned upside down. Only a few hours before he had expected to be watching television with Kate in front of the fire in their cottage while Amanda slept safely upstairs in her room. Now here he was heading north through driving rain on a dark night, with Amanda seriously ill in the vehicle in front and Kate in a terrible state. He wanted it to be a bad dream. In a moment he would wake up and find he was in bed at home with absolutely nothing amiss. Ahead, the ambulance pulled out to overtake a heavily laden lorry in the nearside lane of the dual carriageway. Sandy did the same and hit the wall of spray coming from the lorry's wheels. He turned the wipers up to maximum speed. This was no dream. It was a nightmare.

Kate and Sandy sat on a bench in the hospital corridor while Amanda underwent further tests. They stood up when the doctor who had been dealing with her came out and introduced himself.

'Mr and Mrs Chapman? I'm Dr Turner.'

'How is she, Doctor?' asked Kate.

'She's pretty low at the moment but I should stress that she's not in any danger. There's just been a build-up of toxic substances in her blood because of the kidney problem. Once we clear these away she's going to feel a whole lot better, I promise you.'

'Any idea why she went into renal failure?' asked Sandy.

'Impossible to say at this stage,' replied Turner. 'But there are a lot of tests we still have to do over the next few days.'

'Is there a chance that this was just a one-off problem?' asked Kate.

Turner displayed the unease of a man being asked to provide an encouraging answer he knew he couldn't give. 'I . . . I don't really feel that's likely,' he said.

'So you think she'll need further dialysis?' said Sandy.

'It's early days yet, but in all honesty I fear so. That's usually the case.'

Sandy felt his spirits sink and his limbs become heavy. The chances were that Amanda was going to need regular dialysis from now on unless . . . He shut out thoughts of what might lie ahead and tried to confine himself to what was going to happen tonight.

'Is it okay if we stay?' he asked.

'Of course,' replied Turner. 'But if you'll take my advice you'll go home and get some rest. She's in good hands.'

'But what if she should need us in the—'

Turner shook his head. 'We're going to keep her well sedated. Come back tomorrow. We'll be able to tell you much more after we've carried out some more tests.'

Reluctantly, because all Kate's instincts said that she should stay near Amanda, Sandy and Kate took Turner's advice. It was a thirty-mile drive back to Ayrshire but the roads would be quiet in the early hours of the morning and the rain had settled down to a drizzle rather than the earlier downpour. They didn't speak much as they walked to the car down the wet cobbled lane at the side of the hospital. They were both preoccupied with their own thoughts and could think of nothing encouraging to say to each other. A black cat that scurried off among the dustbins seemed to be the only other living creature in the darkness of the night.

The house was cold when they got in; the heating had switched itself off some hours ago. The coldness added to the feeling of quiet and emptiness that met them.

'Are you hungry?' Kate asked as Sandy knelt down to light the gas fire in the living room.

'Not really. But I could use a drink.'

Kate poured them both a whisky. They sat on opposite sides of the fire. They hadn't yet taken their coats off.

'Everything's been going too well,' said Kate. 'Something like this was bound to happen.'

Sandy looked at her questioningly.

'You get your job, then I get mine. We find the cottage in the perfect village. Everything has been going just too smoothly. It had to stop.'

'Nonsense,' said Sandy softly. 'That's a very Scottish thing to say.'

'We're very Scottish people,' replied Kate.

'That doesn't mean we have to subscribe to the "Weary Willie, we'll pay for this somehow" philosophy.'

'I suppose not,' agreed Kate with a wan attempt at a smile.

'Anyone found enjoying themselves will be dealt with severely,' mimicked Sandy in severe Presbyterian minister tones.

Kate's smile grew broader. She got up from her chair and said, 'I'll make us some toast. We've got to eat something.'

Neither of them managed much sleep. Both were relieved when it was time to get up and busy themselves. They phoned the hospital and were told that Amanda had had a comfortable night and that it would be best if they waited till early afternoon before going in. By then the doctors would have the results of the tests they planned for Amanda and should have something concrete to tell them.

Kate phoned Isa Jenkins to tell her what had happened and that she would not be at school today.

'Don't worry about it,' said Isa. 'I rather thought that might be the case. The wee soul didn't look well at all. I took the precaution of calling one of the supply teachers over in Ayr last night and warning her she might be needed today, so everything's under control.'

Sandy called Charlie Rimington at home and was given similar assurances. 'Nice people,' he said when he put down the phone. Kate nodded.

'Dr Grayson and Dr Turner will see you now,' said the nurse who put her head round the door of the waiting room. Sandy and Kate followed her a short way along the corridor and were shown into a small, sunny room where the two men were sitting. Both got up when Kate and Sandy entered, and Grayson was introduced to them as the consultant in charge of the renal unit.

'She's looking better this morning,' said Turner with a smile to Kate, who was looking anxious.

Kate nodded. 'Yes, she is.'

'She had a good night's sleep, which I dare say is more than either of you two did.'

Sandy nodded his agreement.

With the pleasantries over, Grayson got down to business. He was a man in his mid-forties with thinning grey hair and a pepper-and-salt moustache. His dark suit looked expensive and appeared to have been made to measure with millimetric precision. The cuffs of his white shirt showed one centimetre on both sides and his gold cuff links seemed to rest at precisely the same angle on the table as he sat with his hands clasped in front of him. His shirt collar seemed to ride a little high and looked distinctly uncomfortable to Sandy's way of thinking but it was the perfect foil for the dark university tie that hung below. The overall impression was of a man precise in all things.

'Frankly, the news is not good.'

Sandy felt as if he had been hit by a train. He swallowed and looked at Kate, who seemed to be reeling too. He took her hand and squeezed it.

'Amanda's renal failure is quite severe, though we can see no reason for it. She has responded fairly positively to dialysis, although not as well as we expected. As regards prognosis, I think we should be looking at dialysis as a way of life well into the foreseeable future.'

Sandy rubbed his forehead. Grayson didn't fool around with dressing up what he had to say. His worst fears were being confirmed at an alarming rate.

'Can I ask what you do?' continued Grayson.

'I'm an MLSO at Dunnock District Hospital,' said Sandy. He looked to Kate to see if she was going to reply for herself. She was looking down at her shoes. 'Kate's a teacher,' he added.

'Good,' said Grayson. 'Then, thinking ahead, I feel we should be considering a home dialysis unit for Amanda when one becomes available. You're both obviously quite capable of dealing with its demands.'

Sandy raised his right hand slightly. It was a gesture designed to slow Grayson down. He was reeling from the onslaught. 'You said, "foreseeable future",' he said. 'What exactly does that mean?'

'It means that Amanda will need dialysis until such time as a kidney transplant becomes available for her.'

The word 'transplant' seemed to have put Kate into shock. She sat with her eyes wide, staring at Grayson as he spoke.

'A transplant,' repeated Sandy slowly.

'Yes.'

'It's that serious? But how? When? I mean, how long?'

'Far too soon to start talking about that,' replied Grayson. 'We've lots more tests to do.' He looked distracted, and almost before they could respond he had made his excuses and left, leaving them alone with Clive Turner.

Turner seemed more sensitive to their feelings and almost embarrassed at Grayson's manner. 'I know what you must be thinking,' he said softly, 'but these days kidney transplants are very common and very successful.'

'But you need a suitable donor,' said Sandy.

Turner nodded. 'True, and that's where the waiting comes in. Amanda will be tissue-typed and her details entered on an international register. As soon as a match comes up we can get the organ and do the surgery.'

'How long?' asked Kate. Sandy barely recognized her voice.

Turner shrugged uncomfortably. 'It could be some time,' he said.

'Weeks? Months? Years?' Kate persisted.

'It could be a year or so,' admitted Turner.

Sandy looked at Kate. He couldn't remember ever having seen her look so unhappy. Her world was collapsing around her.

TWO

The convoy of three official vehicles accompanied by a police car swung through the gates of the Médic Ecosse Hospital in Glasgow and came to a halt at the entrance. Their drivers opened passenger doors and stood by respectfully as the eight occupants got out and waited around like camels at an oasis. They orientated themselves with their surroundings, straightened their ties and fidgeted with the buttons of their jackets until the official welcoming party emerged through sliding glass doors to greet them. The smiles were all on the welcoming side.

Leo Giordano, administrative secretary of the Médic Ecosse Hospital, part of the Médic International Health group, stepped forward and shook the hand of the junior minister from the Scottish Office, Neil Bannon. Giordano was tall, dark and good-looking with an olive skin that implied Mediterranean ancestry, although he himself was second-generation American. Bannon was short, ginger-haired and running to fat. He had recently grown a moustache in the mistaken belief that this would lend gravitas to his presence. Unkind observers thought it made him look more like a second-hand-car salesman than ever.

Bannon and Giordano had met on several occasions during the planning stages of the hospital and now exchanged a few pleasantries before Giordano commenced the formal introductions. These were dealt with quickly in deference to the drizzling rain and icy wind and the bowed huddle moved inside.

'I thought we might have coffee first before getting down to business. It'll give people a chance to get to know each other.'

Bannon nodded his assent without enthusiasm or comment and

followed Giordano across the carpeted entrance hall to a long, low-ceilinged room with large picture windows looking out on to a formal garden. At this time of year the garden displayed all the starkness of winter in northern climes. Bare branches criss-crossed a grey sky and moss crept along stone paths, flourishing as nothing else could in the damp and cold. As a centrepiece, it boasted a lily pond with, at its head, a sculpture clearly influenced by ancient Greece. The hunting figure seemed pathetically far from home.

Coffee was brought in by waitresses carrying silver trays and wearing pale pink uniforms with the Médic Ecosse logo on them.

'It's no bloody wonder they're in financial straits,' whispered one of the visiting party, a local Labour councillor. 'This isn't a hospital, it's a bloody gin palace. Look at it! Carpets everywhere, air-conditioning, tailored staff uniforms. Hospitals shouldn't be like this.'

'On the contrary,' replied his colleague. 'You may prefer Victorian slums smelling of disinfectant and echoing to the profanity of Saturday-night drunks, but frankly I happen to believe that all hospitals should look exactly like this, and the sooner they do the better.'

'Privatization, you mean,' sneered the councillor. 'Fine for the rich, but what about the rest of us? Tell me that. And what about the chronic sick and the mentally ill? Who's gonna look after them?'

The second man clearly had no heart to enter an old argument all over again, particularly one there would be no resolving. He put a stop to the tack they were on with a raise of his hand. 'All right, I know the words of the song. Let's not sing it this morning.'

'I'll tell you one thing,' said the councillor. 'If they think I'm going along with any plan to sink any more taxpayers' money into this monument to privilege unconditionally, they've got another think coming. We were promised that this place would be self-sufficient within twelve months and making a handsome profit within eighteen. We were promised jobs and rates money to improve the district and here we are, three years down the line, and they're

21

looking for handouts again. It's offensive. The public just won't bloody well stand for it.'

The councillor moved off, to be replaced by a member of Bannon's personal staff who had overheard what had been said.

'I don't know about you but I'm not sure I can see an alternative,' said the newcomer. 'Having committed twenty-seven million to the project already, we can hardly write it off and walk away. Apart from anything else, the opposition would have a field day.'

'Quite so, but I remember the noise they made at the planning stage. They said it would never happen. They said there was more chance of setting up a distillery in Riyadh or a pork-pie factory in Tel Aviv, but up it went, an exclusive private hospital in the very heartland of the Glasgow Labour Party. Ye gods.' The man smiled at the recollection.

'It was only high unemployment in the building trade that swung it in the end. The prospect of losing a major building project was just too high a price to pay for the sake of anyone's prejudice,' said the official.

'Principles have a habit of becoming "prejudices" when there's money involved,' said the man.

The official smiled. It was a worldly-wise little smile. The smile of someone who knew the game and how to play it.

'How bad is the trouble they're in?'

'If you ask me, it's nothing that couldn't be solved with a bit of judicious marketing. Business has been a bit slower in appearing than anticipated and there's a good chance that Médic International the parent company, are trying it on. They think the government can't afford to let the hospital go to the wall with all the attendant publicity and loss of jobs, so they're making a play for more public investment instead of underwriting the problem themselves. Rumour has it that Bannon's hopping mad.'

'So why has business been slow? Why didn't all these rich folk and their families materialize to receive the best medical treatment money could buy?'

'Hard to say. Maybe they prefer to go to London for their triple by-passes and hip replacements,' said the official. 'Down there they can always have their food sent over from the Dorchester and nip out to Annabelle's for the odd alcohol-free lager when they start to feel better.'

The man smiled at the allusion to religious abstinence. 'But I understand it's different when it comes to transplants,' he said. 'Médic Ecosse has already built a reputation as one of the finest transplant hospitals in the country.'

'No question,' agreed the official. 'And James Ross is acknowledged as one of the best transplant surgeons.'

'I met him at a reception once,' said the man. 'Nice chap. Unusual combination, brilliance and niceness.'

'I understand his research output is also phenomenal. His publication list in the journals is the envy of many a university department. Maybe the prestige thing will carry some weight in the decision.'

'I think we're about to find that out,' said the man as he saw the Scottish Office minister and the administrative secretary start to move off. A tall man who had been standing beside them moved off too and the question was asked, 'One of yours or one of theirs?'

'His name's Dunbar. He's up from London,' replied the official. 'Don't ask me why.'

The man in question was Dr Steven Dunbar, tall, dark-haired and dressed in a dark business suit that suggested a good London tailor. His tie told of a past association with the Parachute Regiment and he had dark, intelligent eyes that were constantly looking and learning. His mouth was generously wide, giving the impression that he was about to break into a grin, although he never quite did.

He had been sent by the Home Office, or more precisely a branch of the Home Office known as the Sci-Med Inspectorate. This comprised a small group of investigators with varied and wide-ranging skills in science and medicine. They were used by central government to carry out discreet investigations in areas outside the usual expertise of the police.

Although the police did have certain specialist branches, like the Fraud Squad and officers trained in the dealings of the art world, it was generally acknowledged that there were large areas of modern life where their understanding of what was going on was sadly lacking. Sci-Med inspectors provided an expert interface. It was their remit to investigate reports of possible wrongdoing or unusual happenings and establish whether or not there might be a problem deserving more detailed investigation. Dunbar was one of their medical specialists.

As discretion was important when dealing with the sensibilities of often powerful and influential professional people, Dunbar's credentials had not been announced. He was officially present as a London civil servant attached temporarily to the Scottish Office, where only Neil Bannon had been informed of his true mission.

Dunbar had been treated politely but coolly by his hosts since his arrival the previous day. This hadn't worried him. He was used to working on his own as an outsider. He preferred it that way. The fewer people he had to confide in the better. It made his job easier. The perfect mission was one where he arrived at the job, found out what he wanted to know and left again without anyone realizing what he'd really been doing. No one liked having a snooper around, particularly when, as it often turned out, there was no real problem to investigate.

Keeping an investigation secret was perhaps the most difficult aspect of Dunbar's job but it was also probably the most important. Any suggestion of incompetence or malpractice brought out the worst in the medical profession. No other section of the community did a better line in self-righteous indignation or closing ranks. He had to be awfully sure of his ground before breaking cover. At this early stage he had only the unsubstantiated allegations of two former nurses at the hospital to go on. He would need a lot more than that before revealing who he was and why he was there.

Dunbar settled himself into the well-upholstered chair in front of his name card on the oak table. He poured himself a little water from the crystal decanter and sipped it as he watched the others take their places. The thickness of the carpet made it a strangely silent operation. He knew little of the circumstances that had brought the visiting party to Médic Ecosse, only that the hospital was in some kind of financial trouble and was requesting more government help. His masters had seen it as an opportunity to get him inside the hospital unannounced. It had all been a bit of a rush. He had had a minimal briefing from the Scottish Office and had also managed to pick up snippets of what had been going on through listening to conversations outside while people had been having coffee. He thought he knew who the important players were, so now he was going to observe the in-fighting and blood-letting he suspected might ensue.

James Ross, consultant surgeon and director of the transplant unit, was one of two senior members of the Médic Ecosse medical staff present at the table. The other was Dr Thomas Kinscherf, medical director of the hospital, urbane, smiling and generally very much at home in dealing with people. Ross was seated opposite Neil Bannon, listening politely to what was being said around him and smiling at intervals. An occasional glance at his watch betrayed a slight impatience for proceedings to begin.

Ross was a pleasant-looking man in his early forties, of average build and with fair hair swept back from his forehead. His skin was smooth and tanned and he wore frameless glasses with large, square lenses. He looked like a man at ease with himself, self-confident, successful in his chosen career and with nothing left to prove to anyone. His suit was conservatively dark but he wore a pink bow tie with matching handkerchief in his breast pocket. The typical, give-away flamboyance of the surgeon.

The admin secretary, Giordano, was exuding charm as he spoke to the Scottish Office contingent. Any word uttered by the visitors claimed his rapt attention, any suggestion of humour brought a large grin and a hearty laugh. It was clear that the Médic Ecosse people were on their best behaviour. The day was all about good public relations.

'Shall we begin?' asked Bannon. He was one of the few people not smiling.

Giordano brought the meeting to order and requested that the 'financial parameters for debate' be established. This translated into the reading of finance reports both from Médic Ecosse's accountants and from the financial officials of the Scottish Office team.

When they had finished, Bannon looked round the table at the gloomy faces and said, 'Gentlemen, I think we should cut the Gordian knot and come straight to the point. It's quite clear that this hospital cannot continue functioning unless it receives an immediate injection of cash. It's a question of where this cash is going to come from.' He paused. People round the table exchanged glances. 'I understand that Médic International feel that they're not in a position to invest any more at this time. This leaves public money and, frankly, this too is quite unthinkable at a time like this when we're urging restraint on public spending and cutting back on even essential services.' He paused again to let the buzz die down before continuing. 'But there again, the alternative is equally unpalatable. The hospital would have to close down, with the loss of money already invested and the accompanying human cost in terms of jobs. This leaves us, as our American cousins might say, between a rock and a hard place. Personally I think it would be an absolute tragedy if an almost brand-new, state-of-the-art hospital with a world-class medical staff had to close its doors, but these are the bare facts.'

'Not to mention politically embarrassing and bloody expensive for the Tory party,' muttered the Labour councillor.

'If it's so state-of-the-art and world-class, why is it losing money?' asked a distinguished-looking man who, unlike the others, favoured a light-coloured suit. He was a representative of a major Scottish insurance company which had invested at the outset in Médic Ecosse.

'We feel it's a problem we can deal with,' replied Thomas Kinscherf. 'We simply don't have enough patients at this moment in time.'

'Why not?'

'It appears that would-be clients still prefer London hospitals, although we believe that with the right marketing this problem can be overcome. It's just a geographical thing that we didn't consider seriously enough at the outset and still haven't taken the appropriate steps to remedy.'

'There are plenty of patients not more than a mile from here,' interjected the councillor. 'It's just that they don't have the money to pay for all this fine treatment.'

'I think we've been through all that,' said Bannon rather testily. 'The hospital's being run as a business for foreign clients who bring money into this country. It's a service industry, just like hotels and theme parks. There's nothing wrong with that. It benefits us all in the end.'

'Not if it doesn't actually make any money.'

'It will, sir,' interjected Kinscherf. 'We just need a little more time.'

'And a lot more public money,' added the councillor.

'Frankly, there is no question of further unconditional funding,' said Bannon. 'Our people have carried out an in-depth analysis of the figures from each department and come up with projected figures for the next three years. Based on these we will be prepared to offer funding at a suitable rate of return but with conditions attached.'

Giordano and Kinscherf exchanged glances. Neither man was smiling any more.

Bannon continued, 'Our money people have highlighted a certain problem area which we'd like to see dealt with. In fact, we would insist on it.'

'I'm sure we would be willing to consider your findings,' said Giordano.

'We are disturbed at the very low profit margin being shown by the transplant unit,' said Bannon.

James Ross looked surprised. He shifted uneasily in his seat. 'Are you suggesting my department doesn't pull its weight?' he asked. His surprise was obviously shared by many at the table.

'Far from it,' replied Bannon, 'Your unit is clearly a success story. Unfortunately, at the moment, it's the only one.'

'So why pick on us?'

'Frankly, and not to put too fine a point on it, it's more of a medical success than it is a financial one. Your overheads seem uncommonly high.'

'We have to do our best for our patients,' said Ross, taken aback. 'Transplant surgery is an extremely expensive business in terms of both equipment and staff but our results are second to none.'

'And this is reflected in the fees charged by the hospital,' countered Bannon. 'No one is disputing your expertise, Doctor. The excellence of your department is why you've been so successful in attracting custom. As I understand it, the survival rate shown by your patients is extremely good.'

'Quite outstanding,' interjected Giordano.

'So what is it you want from me?' asked Ross. 'I can hardly cut staff.'

'It's not a case of cutting staff, Doctor. The money is coming in to your unit but investors don't seem to be seeing the returns they should from it. We have pinpointed the problem as being your very high research-budget costs.'

Ross seemed to search for words before replying calmly, 'My contract states that research funds at an agreed proportion of income will be made available to me. That's why I agreed to come here in the first place.'

'We understand that,' said Bannon. 'But if more public money is to be found to support the continuation of Médic Ecosse, this arrangement simply cannot continue.'

'But my research programme is absolutely vital to me if we are to go on increasing our knowledge and improving patient care,' Ross appealed.

'I understand how you feel, Doctor, and it does you credit but this is not a research institute, it's a commercial enterprise. It's a private hospital and it's a business. It treats sick people. It treats them and then charges them accordingly. It's that simple. The universities and research councils provide funding for research. Médic International and its co-investor, Her Majesty's Government, do not.'

'But my contract—'

'I think if you re-examine the exact wording of your contract, Doctor, you'll see it states that the percentage of funding you refer to is only valid if other departments in the hospital are doing equally well.'

'I don't think I understand,' said Ross, leaning forward slightly in apprehension. He looked to Giordano and Kinscherf for support.

'Your agreement for research funding is that fifty per cent of net profits from your unit be returned to you to carry out your research programme,' continued Bannon.

'Exactly,' said Ross.

'But,' said Bannon, holding up his index finger, 'only if the receipts from the transplant unit amount to no more than twenty per cent of the total income of the hospital. As it is, income from your unit currently amounts to sixty per cent of profits.'

Ross slumped back in his seat and looked towards Giordano. Giordano was whispering to the Médic Ecosse accountant by his side but his expression told everyone the question. The nod he got in reply told everyone the answer.

'But any adjustment in line with these figures would effectively bring my research to a halt,' said Ross, obviously upset.

'I'm sorry, Doctor,' said Bannon. 'But I repeat, this is a hospital not a university.'

'In that case, gentlemen, I may have to consider my position very seriously,' said Ross, gathering his papers together.

There was general discomfort at the way Ross was being singled out by Bannon. Everyone bar him seemed to realize that Ross was the hospital's main asset. Without Ross and the transplant unit the hospital would be doomed to closure anyway, but the government side seemed determined to take a hard line.

Dunbar, as an outside observer, could only assume that the Scottish Office, riled by rumours of Médic International trying to put something over on them, had decided to take a tremendous gamble. He suspected that the ultimatum was really a bluff and they would back down if it looked as if Ross was going to resign. As Ross was head of the unit he was interested in, he was keen to see how things were going to turn out.

Bannon watched Ross prepare to leave the table before saying, 'Doctor, I sincerely hope that you'll find it possible to continue performing the marvellous feats of surgery you've been doing over the past few years.'

Ross acknowledged the words with the merest hint of a smile. He had obviously been totally unprepared for what had happened. He cleared his throat and asked, 'Is there any room for compromise in the figures?'

'I'm afraid not,' replied Bannon.

Ross swallowed, then rose from the table, 'If you'll excuse me, gentlemen,' he said. 'There are things I have to do.'

Bannon said, 'Believe me, Doctor, if there was some way we could continue funding you we would. I know how strongly you feel about your research and it does you credit. I urge you not to make any rash decisions. Things might be very different should this hospital start to give returns worthy of its potential.'

The Labour councillor, sitting opposite Dunbar, leaned across and whispered to him, 'Bloody hypocrite. They don't give a damn about research. Profit's the only thing that lot understand.'

Dunbar smiled at the man's volte-face in now defending Médic Ecosse, but he took his point. Ross did seem to be getting a raw deal. He could feel the tension round the table. People knew how high the stakes had gone. It was like watching a high-roller at the roulette wheel.

'Would there be any other conditions?' asked Giordano as Ross left the room. He said it tongue-in-cheek, clearly expecting a negative reply.

Bannon took the question at face value. 'Yes,' he replied. There would. We'd like to do something about the public perception of the hospital. There will be deep resentment at further public funding of a private institution, whatever the circumstances. If we were to reach agreement and the public were to inject yet more cash into a facility that for the most part they have no access to – even if it is just for long-term business reasons – I think Médic Ecosse might have to make some kind of popular altruistic gesture in return.'

'Some kind of public relations exercise you mean?' asked Giordano.

'If you like. I thought perhaps you might consider offering free treatment to a reasonable number of Scots NHS patients who would benefit from your highly specialized equipment and professional expertise.'

Giordano had recovered his cool. He smiled and said, 'Minister, I think that's a splendid idea. We've taken a few patients in the past when approached, but I think I can safely say we would have no objection to taking a few more. It's always good publicity for us.'

'Good. I think our friend here should be pleased with that too,' said Bannon, looking towards the Labour councillor.

The man shrugged and said, 'If I had my way we'd be taking over the whole damn shebang and using it for the good of all the people.'

'And running it on hot air, no doubt,' said Bannon.

'Anything else?' asked Giordano.

'One last thing,' said Bannon. The room fell silent again. 'We would like to have one of our people on-site, as it were. A sort of overseer of things in general.'

'Another public relations exercise?' asked Giordano quietly.

'You could say that,' agreed Bannon. 'Our man would be here to monitor the prudent application of taxpayers' money.'

'An accountant?'

'More than that. We would like him to have access to all aspects of the hospital's administration, including files and records.'

'Are you suggesting this man should have some kind of executive authority?' asked Giordano.

'No executive authority,' said Bannon. 'Just cooperation from you and the staff.'

'In that case, I don't see a problem.'

'Good,' said Bannon.

'Do you have someone in mind for this role?' asked Giordano.

Bannon gestured towards Steven Dunbar and said, 'Dr Dunbar would be our man on the ground.'

Dunbar smiled and nodded. He watched the reaction of the Médic Ecosse people: their smiles were uncertain.

'So there we have it,' said Bannon. 'The big question now is, do we have a basis for agreement?'

There were no dissenting voices, but everyone knew how much now depended on James Ross, and he was out of the room.

'Why don't we adjourn for lunch?' suggested Giordano. 'The food here is very good. I don't think you'll have any complaints.'

'I never thought Bannon would have the balls to try something like that,' said the man in front of Dunbar as they went out of the room.

'Bloody criminal, the way they treated Ross,' replied his companion. 'Do you think they're going to get away with it?'

'I rather think that's up to Ross. Without him they're just another hospital.'

'Or five-star hotel.'

'D'you think he'll resign?'

'Depends on how much they're prepared to back-pedal on the research cuts. He might feel obliged to move on as a matter of pride. It's not as if he couldn't work elsewhere. With his reputation he could get a position almost anywhere in the world. If you ask me, the Scottish Office are playing a losing hand here.'

'No change there, then.'

'I wonder why Ross came here in the first place,' mused the first man. 'If it's research he's really interested in, you'd think he'd have gone to one of the big medical schools.'

'Good point,' agreed the second.

'Mind you, it could have been the food,' said the first admiringly.

They had reached the dining room and were looking at what was on offer. Tables groaned under the sumptuous buffet that had been prepared for them.

* * *

32

Lunch was over by two o'clock. The meeting was scheduled to reconvene at two thirty, and both sides used the interim to discuss matters among themselves. Dunbar picked up what he could while circulating, coffee cup in hand. He fended off questions about his proposed role with skill and humour, saying that it was too soon to talk about such things. As yet no agreement had been reached.

As the meeting seemed set to reconvene he saw Giordano, who had been deep in conversation with Ross, move away and Bannon, looking distinctly nervous, walk over to take his place. He wondered if Bannon was beginning to have second thoughts about his intransigence. He positioned himself within earshot of the two main protagonists.

'Nothing personal in this, Ross, you understand,' said Bannon with a half-hearted attempt at a smile.

Ross gave him a look that suggested that politicians were akin to something he might find occasionally on his shoe. 'Of course not,' he said flatly.

'I do appreciate how important your research work is to you, Doctor, and that you'll probably need more time to consider your position, but I just wondered if perhaps you've come to any kind of decision yet in your own mind?'

'Yes, Mr Bannon,' replied Ross. 'I've made my decision.'

THREE

As the days became weeks, the strain of constant travelling up and down to Glasgow, and guilt over excessive time taken off work, began to tell on Kate and Sandy.

'I'll have to resign,' said Kate as they drove up to see Amanda on the Friday of the third week. 'It's not fair on the school.'

'I'm sure they understand,' said Sandy.

'I'm sure they do too, but it's too much of an imposition on them. They're bound to be feeling the strain and they're far too nice to say so themselves. I'll have to make the decision.'

'Maybe you're right,' conceded Sandy. He didn't feel so bad because, although his two colleagues were covering for him during periods taken off in the daytime, he was taking on more evening duties to compensate. Both Charlie and Andrew had young families, so they were quite happy with the arrangement. Kate was not so happy. It meant that she seldom saw Sandy in the evenings.

'I thought we'd have had her home by now,' said Kate. 'They said at the outset she'd probably be home within two weeks and we'd just have to travel up on dialysis days. I think something's wrong. In fact, I'm sure something's wrong and they're just not telling us.'

Sandy glanced out of the corner of his eye at Kate in the passenger seat. She was biting her lip and nervously interlocking her fingers as she stared at the road ahead without giving the impression of seeing anything.

'No doubt Grayson will tell us,' he said. 'He's not one for gift wrapping anything and Clive Turner did say he wanted to see us today.'

'Do you think our marriage will survive this?' Kate asked suddenly.

'Of course it will,' replied Sandy, taken aback by the question. He took one hand off the wheel and reached over to squeeze Kate's hand. He felt her grow tense. 'What brought that on?'

'We were always so close,' said Kate. 'But now things seem different. You don't even tell me what you're thinking most of the time.'

'We're both under a lot of strain,' he said. 'Too many other things on our minds, I suppose. I never knew continual worry could be so exhausting. It's like being an overwound spring.'

'If that's all it is.'

'Of course it is.'

'I don't want this to drive us apart,' said Kate.

'It won't,' said Sandy supportively. 'We'll soon get Amanda home and then we'll get back to being just as we were.'

'Apart from the dialysis.'

'We'll even get used to that in time, and when we get a home set-up it'll be practically no bother at all. You'll see. It'll become part of our routine. So much so that we'll hardly notice it.'

Kate smiled weakly and looked across at him. 'I don't know what I'd do without you.'

'Come on, love,' said Sandy. 'I need you every bit as much as you need me.'

'We have a problem,' announced Grayson with characteristic bluntness as he spread his notes on his desk and moved his glasses to a more comfortable spot on his nose to read them.

'What sort of problem?' asked Sandy. His skin tingled in fear and anticipation. It was as if his every sense had suddenly been heightened. He was aware of every raindrop running down the window behind Grayson's head as he waited for him to begin.

'Truth to tell, we're not very sure ourselves,' said Grayson. 'Amanda's blood is becoming contaminated almost as quickly as we clean it. She's been requiring much more dialysis than we anticipated. We thought things would settle down after a fortnight or so, but that's not been the case, I'm afraid. We think it may have something to do with a tissue-degradation problem in her kidneys.'

Tissue degradation! The words echoed round and round in Sandy's head. 'You mean her kidneys are breaking up?' he asked. His throat was tight and it showed in his voice. He had to swallow.

Grayson shrugged and said, 'That's our theory at the moment. Of course, we'll have to wait until we get a full histology report before we can be absolutely certain.'

Sandy felt that he was listening to a garage mechanic tell him what was wrong with his car, rather than a doctor pronouncing on his daughter's condition. What made a man like this become a doctor? It wasn't the first time he had wondered this same thing. His job had brought him into contact with a number of people in the medical profession who he felt lacked any basic compassion for the sick. They didn't see people in front of them, only cases, intellectual challenges, problems to solve, games to win or lose in the struggle to advance a career.

'I take it this means that we'll not be getting her home in the near future?' said Kate.

'Out of the question,' said Grayson.

Kate looked down at the floor and clasped her hands, twisting her fingers as she listened to Grayson continue.

'The fact is, I'm sorry to say, that Amanda is one of these patients for whom dialysis just isn't good enough. It isn't working. She really needs a transplant.'

'Or she'll die,' said Kate in a flat monotone.

There was an agonized silence in the room before Grayson said quietly, 'That is a possibility, I'm afraid.'

Sandy saw that Kate had stopped fidgeting. Her hands lay still in her lap and her face was perfectly calm. It unnerved him. He reached across and laid his hand on top of Kate's. They were ice-cold. The tightness in his throat still made talking difficult but he asked Grayson, 'Surely there must be some kind of priority given to such cases?'

'Of course. Amanda will be given urgent status on the transplant register,' agreed Grayson.

'What does that mean in practice?'

'It means that she will be allowed to jump the queue if a suitable organ should become available, but of course we'll still be constrained by considerations of tissue type. The organ has to be a good match for her.'

'What about us?' asked Kate.

'I was about to suggest that,' said Grayson. 'It's possible that either you or your husband might prove to be a suitable donor and we'll certainly check your tissue type, but I don't think you should bank on this. It happens less frequently than people imagine. A brother or sister would be a better bet and a twin would be ideal, but of course Amanda is an only child.'

'So if neither of us matches her type we'll just have to wait and hope?'

'That's about the size of it.'

'How much time have we got?'

'Impossible to say, I'm afraid,' replied Grayson curtly.

'Doesn't it concern you at all?' said Sandy, his patience with Grayson's apparent callousness finally giving out.

'I beg your pardon?'

'Our daughter's plight. Aren't you concerned – as a person, I mean?'

'Of course I am,' replied Grayson, obviously flustered by the question.

'You could have fooled me,' replied Sandy flatly but Kate put a restraining hand on his arm to stop things going any further. He and Kate got up to go.

Clive Turner, who had been silent throughout, followed them outside. 'I'm sorry,' he said when the door had closed behind him. 'Dr Grayson's a bit of a cold fish. I'm sure he means well, but he doesn't always come across that way.'

Sandy nodded. 'How soon can we be tested for tissue type?' he asked.

'We can do it before you leave,' replied Turner. 'But as Dr Grayson said, I don't think you should build your hopes too high.'

Sandy's look suggested that this was the last thing he wanted to hear.

'Look, why don't we all go and get some tea?' suggested Turner. 'There's something I'd like to talk over with you.'

Sandy's first inclination was to decline the invitation but he changed his mind when he saw that Turner wasn't just being polite or mounting a damage-limitation exercise on behalf of his boss. The man looked as if he really did have something to say. 'All right,' he said. 'I think we could all do with some.'

The visitors' tea room smelt of strong tea and plastic. The tall windows looking out on to the courtyard were misted over, thanks to a tea urn with a faulty thermostat which bubbled constantly and sent wafts of steam up into the air. Here and there a cleared patch on the glass permitted views of the rain speckling the puddles in the courtyard below. At Turner's suggestion, Sandy took Kate across to one of the red-topped tables and sat down with her while Turner got the tea and brought it over on a brown plastic tray. There was a slight hiatus while he righted the cups in their saucers, placed them around the table and poured out the tea. As he sat down, he said. 'This must be a nightmare for you.'

'It all happened so quickly,' said Sandy, searching for something sensible to say in reply. 'She was as right as rain one moment and then suddenly she's in here and . . .'

'She's dying,' said Kate.

Turner's silence was worse than anything he could have said at that moment, thought Sandy.

'What was it you wanted to speak to us about?' he asked, determined to end the silence.

Turner rested both forearms on the table and leaned forward as if to impart a confidence. 'We have to think ahead about what to do for Amanda if neither of you should prove to be a suitable donor.'

'I thought we'd just have to wait,' said Sandy.

'I don't know how you'll feel about this,' said Turner, 'but I thought there was one possibility we might explore together for Amanda. It's only a possibility, mind you, and it might come to nothing, but I think it's worth considering.'

'What is?' asked Sandy.

'We had a circular from the Scottish Office recently concerning the Médic Ecosse Hospital here in Glasgow. Apparently, because of some political agreement reached between the hospital and the government over funding, they're taking on a number of NHS patients recommended to them for specialist treatment. They've done this occasionally in the past but it was only out of the goodness of their hearts. Now it's been put on a more formal basis. I suppose it's still a PR exercise but the fact remains that a patient accepted by them under the new scheme will be treated as one of their own patients and completely free of charge.'

'How does this affect us?' asked Sandy.

'It just so happens that Médic Ecosse has a world-renowned transplant facility.'

'You mean you think they might accept Amanda as a private transplant patient?'

'As far as I could see, there was no qualification about what kind of patient could be referred to them. If a case could be made out that a patient would clearly benefit from their expertise or facilities, then the criterion for referral would be met. That, I have to say, may be wishful thinking on my part but on paper there's no bar.'

'Do you think Amanda would benefit from such a referral?' asked Sandy.

'I think . . .' Turner paused as if considering his words carefully. 'I think that Amanda might conceivably get her transplant quicker at Médic Ecosse than here in the unit, and in her case time is of the essence.'

'But how, if there's an international register and a waiting list?' asked Kate.

Turner paused again, then said, 'I suspect there may be several international registers, not all of them available to NHS-funded hospitals.'

'I don't think I understand.'

'I'm afraid that where there's any kind of demand there's always a supply based on currency rather than need,' said Turner. 'The international trade in donor organs is no different from any other commodity in short supply.'

'How awful,' said Kate.

'But even if that were so,' said Sandy, 'surely they couldn't admit to that and accept Amanda on those grounds?'

'No indeed,' smiled Turner. 'But in addition, and this is important, they have the most modern dialysis equipment available anywhere in the world. I think a case could be made out that Amanda would benefit greatly from that alone. What she needs most right now is time. The Médic Ecosse unit could give her that. If they can come up with a kidney for her too, so much the better.'

'How do we go about asking Médic Ecosse?' asked Sandy.

'The referral would have to come from here. I'll speak to Dr Grayson if you like.'

'Would you?' said Kate, gratitude obvious in her voice.

'Maybe I shouldn't have rattled his cage,' said Sandy ruefully. 'I was pretty rude.'

'Don't worry about it,' said Turner. 'He's too thick-skinned to have taken it to heart. He'll have put it down to your being upset. Insensitive people always put it down to a misunderstanding on someone else's part. I'll get back in touch as soon as I've talked to him. Why don't you go up and see Amanda for a while, and I'll get in touch with the lab about tissue-typing you before you leave. It's a simple procedure.'

Sandy stood up and shook Turner's hand. 'We really appreciate this,' he said.

'Let's hope something works out,' said Turner.

Turner left and Sandy waited for Kate to finish her tea. She was taking her time, trying to compose herself. She didn't want Amanda to see that she had been crying. 'What do you think?' she asked as she put away her handkerchief and smoothed her hair back.

Sandy gave a long sigh as if suddenly releasing the tension he had been under. It was as if Kate's question had acted as a relief valve. 'I don't know what to think,' he confessed. 'I feel numb. Everything seems to be happening at such a rate that I can't keep up. I keep wanting to yell out, "Stop! Just a minute! Let's all sit down and talk things over. This wasn't meant to happen to my family. There's been some kind of terrible mistake. It's not really our daughter who's supposed to have this thing." But it is happening and time's ticking away. I'm scared.' He looked Kate in the eye.

She swallowed, before reaching across the table and taking his hand. 'So am I,' she whispered.

Sandy shook his head and said, 'You know, I can't believe it. I'm reduced to sitting here praying that some private hospital is going to take my daughter on as a charity case. Me! Ex-treasurer of the university Labour Club, veteran of a hundred campaigns to defend and support the NHS. Jesus! What a fake.'

'You're just a father trying to do his best for his daughter,' said Kate softly. 'There's no shame in that.'

Sandy shrugged, not convinced. 'Let's go see her,' he said.

They both broke into broad smiles as they walked into the room where Amanda lay, but the smiles were window-dressing to hide their worry. Amanda looked very ill. She had the distant look in her eyes that Kate had first seen on the day she fell ill. Her skin was pale, and she seemed slow and feeble in her movements. 'I want to go home, Mummy,' she said as Kate gave her a cuddle.

'I know you do, darling, but you're not well enough yet,' crooned Kate. 'But it won't be long. All the boys and girls in the class send their love. They've sent you this card and look, they've all signed it.'

Amanda looked but her distant expression didn't change.

'Dr Turner says you've been a very brave girl,' said Sandy but he was inwardly appalled at how weak Amanda appeared. There was hardly a flicker of spirit about her, despite the fact she had been dialysed that very morning. He tried not to think about it but logic insisted that he recognize that the chances of a suitable donor organ coming up in time must be remote.

Turner reappeared and ushered them out into the corridor to say, 'I managed to see Dr Grayson and he has no objections to a formal request being made to Médic Ecosse. He's left it up to me to take care of the paperwork so I'll get on to it right away.'

'We're very grateful,' said Kate. This was echoed by Sandy.

'In the meantime, the lab people are ready for you, Nurse here will take you down.'

'Do you really think she's going to come through this?' asked Kate as they drove home. 'Honestly?' Her voice had taken on a flat quality that Sandy hadn't heard before. It unnerved him a little. He and Kate were finding out a lot about each other that they hadn't known before the crisis. Sometimes he felt it was like being with a stranger. He knew false optimism wasn't an option, even if he could have managed it; and that was in some doubt. 'I honestly don't know,' he said quietly. 'But if there's a God up there, and he listens to hopes and prayers and knows just how much we both love her, then she'll pull through.'

Kate squeezed his arm and said, 'You know, I'm finding it difficult to know exactly what to hope for. I don't think we can count on a miracle that will make Amanda's own kidneys better, and Grayson and Turner were less than optimistic about either of us proving a suitable donor, so where does that leave us? Hoping that some other child with the same tissue type will die soon? Are we really hoping for a fatal accident to happen to someone else's child?' She broke down as she said it and searched for her handkerchief. 'I'm sorry,' she said.

'I think in the first instance we should be hoping that Médic Ecosse says yes and agrees to take her on as a patient,' said Sandy. He wanted to put his arms round her but had to concentrate on his driving. 'If they really have better dialysis equipment, as Turner says they have, Amanda should start to look and feel better very quickly. That in turn would help us to feel better. As for the

42

kidneys, let's leave all that up to fate and the doctors. What do you say?'

Kate nodded and blew her nose.

Back at the Children's Hospital in Glasgow, Clive Turner was filling in the paperwork required by Médic Ecosse for patient referral with fee waiver. He was using Amanda's case notes as a source of information. The further he got into it, the less likely he felt it was that Amanda would be accepted as a patient. He should have thought of that before he said anything to the Chapmans. You didn't need a medical degree to see that Amanda was a bad risk publicity-wise, and he could sense from the questions that this was what the free-referral scheme was all about. Médic Ecosse needed some good publicity after all the bad stuff it had received from a local press keen to expose it as a facility for the rich, with all the emotional fall-out that that entailed. People were quite happy to embrace the notion of hotels for the rich, cars for the rich and a host of other things that went with having money, but when it came to health care some special egalitarian principle surfaced. Woe betide the politician who didn't – outwardly at least – bend the knee before that particular totem.

Common sense said that Médic Ecosse would be looking for patients they could mend or cure quickly and send on their way, preferably with press cameras waiting outside as they left the premises on the arms of delighted relatives. Prejudice against the hospital could be fought with proof of expertise. People respected learning and ability. But, as far as Turner could see, there was nothing to be gained in taking on risky cases who might die. That sort of concern was best left to Mother Teresa.

He became more and more despondent as he thought it through, especially when he realized that this was why Grayson had agreed so readily to his suggestion that they try for a referral. Grayson didn't want a failure on his books either. He wished he'd never mentioned this to the Chapmans. He had unwittingly raised their hopes and now feared that they would soon be dashed. He wondered if a direct personal approach might help. Maybe talking to someone at Médic Ecosse would be better than just submitting an application form. Concluding that it could do no real harm to try, he picked up the phone and called the Médic Ecosse Hospital. The lines were all engaged.

Turner sat with his finger on the phone rest, watching the raindrops run down the duty-room window for a couple of minutes before hitting the re-dial button. This time it rang.

'I'd like to speak to someone about your new NHS patient free-referral scheme.'

He was put on hold. He continued watching the raindrops chase each other down the window-pane, to the strains of Mozart's *Eine kleine Nachtmusik*.

The music was interrupted and another female voice came on the line. Turner repeated his request for information.

'I can send you out a form, Doctor. You just fill it in, giving the patient's details and why you think a referral would be of benefit, and send it back for consideration by the relevant office.'

'I already have the form,' said Turner. 'I guess I want to speak to someone in the relevant office about my patient.'

'One moment, please.'

More raindrops. More Mozart. Outside in the corridor a child was crying as its mother scolded it over some misdemeanour.

'This is Leo Giordano, administrative secretary of Médic Ecosse. How can I help you?'

Turner explained about Amanda and wondered about her chances of admission to Médic Ecosse.

'We don't usually take on transplant patients for free,' said Giordano. 'For obvious reasons. We're talking big bucks here.'

'Does that mean never?'

'No,' replied Giordano hesitantly. 'I wouldn't say never but, frankly, transplants are awfully expensive and our hospital is not in the best financial position it's ever been in. You may have heard.'

'I was rather afraid you were going to say something like that,' said Turner. 'But really our main problem with Amanda at the moment is that she's not responding well to dialysis. The machines you have up there are much more efficient than ours. Putting her on one of those might give her the extra time she needs while she waits for a donor match.'

'I see,' said Giordano. 'I take it she has no brothers or sisters?'

'She's an only child,' replied Turner. 'We're checking her parents' tissue types, but of course the chances aren't good.'

'So we're talking about a kid who might not make it any other way?'

'Yes.'

'There's a very real chance that she might not make it here either,' said Giordano.

'Of course. Look, Mr Giordano, let's level with each other,' he said. 'It doesn't make any political or commercial sense for you to say yes to Amanda. I'm asking you purely on humanitarian grounds. She's a lovely kid with a couple of real nice people for parents. I'd like to see them all get a break simply because they deserve it.'

'I appreciate that,' said Giordano, 'and thanks for being honest with me. But the final say is not up to me. In this instance we'd have to put the request to our medical director, Dr Kinscherf, and, of course, to Dr James Ross, who's in charge of the transplant unit.'

'Would you at least do that?' asked Turner.

'Sure,' agreed Giordano. 'If it were up to me I think I'd say yes right now. I think it's good if the local hospitals can help each other out. The trouble is that if we at Médic Ecosse so much as ask for the loan of a pint of blood it hits the headlines as the scandal of NHS blood subsidizing the rich. You know how it goes.'

'Yup, I know.'

'In the meantime, why don't you send over the paperwork anyway? It's as well to be prepared.'

'Thanks. I'm grateful.'

'Think nothing of it. Hope it works out for you and the kid.'

Turner put down the phone and tapped his pen end over end on his desk. He'd done his best; he just wasn't convinced it was going to be good enough. He finished filling in the form and signed it. Grayson as head of unit would have to sign it too before it could be submitted. He looked at his watch. Grayson would have left by now. He'd get him to do it in the morning. He was about to put away Amanda's case notes when the lab form listing her tissue type caught his eye. He moved over to an adjacent desk with a computer terminal on it and logged on to the International Donor Register. He had checked availability that morning but there would be no harm in checking again as he had the details in front of him. He entered Amanda's details then requested a search for a match.

DEGREE OF HOMOLOGY? requested the computer.

80 PER CENT, entered Turner.

. NEGATIVE.

Turner punched in, 70 PER CENT.

NEGATIVE.

Turner logged off. Maybe tomorrow. 'Tomorrow and tomorrow and tomorrow,' he murmured as he left the room and returned to the ward.

Sandy looked at his watch and whispered an expletive. The traffic had been heavy on the way back and road works on the dual carriageway had reduced a five-mile section to single-carriageway with no overtaking.

'Are you going to have time for something to eat before you start work?' asked Kate.

''Fraid not,' he replied. 'I'll just drop you at home and then get on up there. I'll have something later when I get home.'

'I'm sure Charlie won't mind if you're half an hour late,' said Kate.

'Normally no,' agreed Sandy. 'But it's one of his kids' birthday today. I said I'd be on time.'

Sandy dropped Kate at the foot of the hill leading up to their cottage, at her suggestion, and drove on up to the district hospital. He was only five minutes late.

FOUR

It was Sunday evening. Steven Dunbar took the airport bus from Glasgow Airport into the centre of the city. Outside it was dark and it was raining. That and the general gloominess of the dark Victorian buildings – made to seem even blacker by the rain water – did nothing to inspire good feelings in him. He was due to begin his attachment to the Médic Ecosse Hospital on the following morning.

It was something he certainly wouldn't have bet on when he'd heard the Scottish Office contingent refuse to modify in any way their demand for swingeing cuts to James Ross's research budget. Their intransigence had come as a complete surprise to almost everyone at the meeting. In retrospect it had been embarrassing that the Scottish Office had not seen fit even to make a token gesture in the interests of making the negotiations seem genuine. The feelings and work of an eminent surgeon had been of no importance at all.

Dunbar had fully expected Ross to tender his resignation and, in doing so, set off a train of events that would have led to the closure of the hospital and a backfire of the whole gamble, but it hadn't happened that way. Instead, and to everyone's surprise, Ross had acceded to the Scottish Office demands, taking it philosophically and saying simply that he understood the awkwardness of their position and the financial constraints they were operating under.

Dunbar supposed that some kind of behind-the-scenes deal between Ross and the Médic International group must have been done to retain Ross's services and to avoid closure of the hospital, but there had been no official acknowledgement of this or of continuing research funding for Ross from an alternative source. Ross had simply stated that, as a doctor, he felt obliged to carry on with his work at Médic Ecosse. He had a waiting list of patients he felt responsible for and couldn't let them down. It would be business as usual as far as the transplant unit was concerned.

It was clear that the Scottish Office people had pulled off a major triumph in the re-negotiation of terms of their involvement at Médic Ecosse. The look of surprise and relief on Bannon's face when Ross had swallowed his pride and acceded to what he must have thought were impossible demands was only fleeting but Dunbar had seen it. Now it wouldn't be known if he had ever intended to back off at the last moment. The injection of more public funds into the hospital would now be offset by the much more favourable terms of the agreement and by greater public access to the Médic Ecosse facilities. Even the Labour opposition at the meeting had been forced to concede that it was a good deal.

As part of the agreement there was, of course, his own secondment to Médic Ecosse as the government's man on the ground, the overseer of public funds. His masters' subterfuge had worked well. He was now in place to begin his investigation.

Sci-Med's involvement had been precipitated by a complaint from a staff nurse who no longer worked at the hospital. She had maintained that there had been something improper about the treatment a transplant patient had received at Médic Ecosse some five months before. The young patient, Amy Teasdale, had died after rejecting the kidney she had been given during what was thought to be, at the time, a routine transplant operation. The staff nurse, one Lisa Fairfax, maintained that there had been a serious mix-up resulting in her patient being given the wrong organ. She was unable to be more specific, stating only that the subsequent rejection had been so severe that no other explanation would suffice. In other circumstances her claims would almost certainly have been dealt with at local level but what had caught Sci-Med's attention was the fact that a similar complaint had been lodged only months after the hospital opened, almost three years before and again by one of their nursing staff.

That time Sister Sheila Barnes had said much the same thing after a young boy in the transplant unit rejected the kidney he had been given. She had subsequently resigned in protest at what she saw as being ignored by the authorities, who had interviewed her but refused to take her claims seriously or to mount an internal investigation. She had maintained at the time that the authorities were keen to dismiss her complaint because they feared the bad publicity would damage the new hospital. Sister Barnes had never retracted her claim. She had intended to press for further investigation, but shortly afterwards had contracted cancer and had had to abandon her campaign. She was now in the terminal stages of her disease, a resident at The Beeches, a hospice for the terminally ill down at Helensburgh on the Clyde coast. She and her allegations had been largely forgotten until Staff Nurse Fairfax made her own complaint and Sci-Med's computer had drawn attention to the similarity as part of its collating programme.

All reports of allegations of wrongdoing in British hospitals were recorded, filed and collated on the Sci-Med computer, however trivial they might seem. Most of them were indeed trivial, usually disgruntled patients making unfounded accusations, or staff with grudges against their employers making equally spurious allegations. But occasionally the computer picked up something that might otherwise have been overlooked. This time it had noted the remarkable similarity between the two nurses' allegations. Both women maintained that their patients had rejected their transplant because they had been given the wrong organ. Now one of these women was currently dying of cancer and the other, Staff Nurse Fairfax, had been dismissed from her post.

Dunbar checked into his hotel near the city centre and found it pleasantly anonymous. It was also warm, which was a bonus because he was feeling chilled. Scotland always seemed to be three or four degrees colder than the south of England, where he lived. He had noticed this again as soon as he had stepped off the plane. The raw dampness of early March made things worse. He threw his briefcase on to the bed and walked over to the window to look down at the traffic moving slowly below in the wet city streets, their lights reflecting in the puddles that were proliferating as the storm drains struggled to cope.

After a few minutes he closed the blind and turned away. He picked up the phone, called room service and asked for a large gin and tonic, some chicken sandwiches and a pot of strong black coffee. After that he would have a warm bath before getting down to reading through his notes and deciding on a plan of action.

As he lay in the bath with the water lapping just below his chin, Dunbar closed his eyes and wondered about James Ross's decision to stay on at Médic Ecosse. Ross was by all accounts a popular man, a brilliant surgeon and a highly regarded researcher in his field. But, although clearly dedicated to his patients and well liked by his colleagues, he was still a human being and therefore subject to the laws of human nature. Dunbar set great store by these laws and recognized them as the driving force behind almost everything that happened in society. Very often he had to pick away at various levels of veneer applied by clever, self-seeking people in positions of power but always, underneath, the same rules applied, whether it was on the factory floor or in the boardroom, the operating theatre or the accounts department.

Ross was a proud man – he had every reason to be. He was also a surgeon with the typical extrovert tendencies of the profession. Timidity and surgery did not go hand in hand. Self-doubt had no place in the operating theatre. According to Dunbar's rules, it didn't befit such a character to lose face in public as Ross had done. The humiliation of having such savage cuts applied to his research funding with not the slightest suggestion of compromise should have pushed him into a dignified resignation, but it hadn't.

Of course, it might have been the thought of his colleagues losing their jobs if the hospital closed that had weighed so heavily on him. Being single-handedly responsible for the closure of a hospital would be a heavy burden for anyone to bear. The man, of course, might also be a saint and therefore outside Dunbar's rules.

He supposed it would be easy enough for him to check on alternative sources of research funding once he had access to the accounts at Médic Ecosse, and he would like to know if a deal had been struck behind the scenes with Médic International; but that still wouldn't answer his question about why Ross had acted out of character. That was the more important thing.

Having been thinking about Ross, Dunbar decided to go through his notes on the surgeon as soon as he was out of the bath. He didn't intend going out again or even downstairs in the hotel, so he just pulled on a sweater and jeans and didn't bother with socks or shoes. He sat cross-legged on the bed with his papers spread out in front of him, the bedside lamp angled to provide light.

James Ross's career to date had been nothing short of outstanding, with prizes and awards punctuating his progress from medical school in London through appointments at a succession of top hospitals both in the UK and the United States. Early on in his studies Ross had been transferred to a leading medical school in New York, where he had been admitted to a programme that had enabled him to do a PhD at the same time as his medical degree. His research for his doctorate had been in immunology. This explained his intense interest in transplant research, thought Dunbar, and his high standing in the scientific community as well as the medical world.

Many doctors played at being researchers, but the days of significant discoveries being made by candlelight in the ward side room had long since gone. Those times had largely disappeared with frock coats and brass, monocular microscopes. To succeed in the extremely demanding and competitive world of medical research in the late twentieth century, you had to be a trained researcher to start with, with all the background knowledge that that entailed. Ross was just such a person. The fact that he had obtained both a PhD and a medical degree concurrently suggested that he was exceptionally gifted intellectually.

He could, of course, still be a lousy administrator, thought Dunbar. There were lots of intellectually gifted people who ended up in charge of university departments when they didn't have the managerial capacity to run a pie stall. If Ross was an ivory-tower researcher, it was conceivable that the running of his unit might suffer but, again by all accounts, this was not true. The transplant unit at Médic Ecosse was regarded as one of the most successful in the country and Ross was no absent-minded professor. He was very much a hands-on leader, not at all the sort of man to preside over a unit where a patient could mistakenly be given the wrong organ.

There was some information on Ross's personal life in the file. He had been married to an American woman, a radiologist he had met while working in Boston, but things hadn't worked out and they had divorced four years ago after three years of marriage. There were no children. His ex-wife had returned to the States, where she had since remarried. Ross lived alone in Glasgow in the penthouse flat of a modern block of flats in Kelvingrove, although he made frequent working trips to Geneva as a clinical consultant.

In the year to April last, Ross had earned £87,000. He drove a two-year-old '5' series BMW and was a member of two clubs. He held an honorary senior lectureship at the University of Glasgow on account of an agreement to deliver a series of four lectures a year on immunology.

Attached to the file were reprints of four of his most recent research publications. One dealt with something called 'Immuno-preparation'; the other three were on the possible use of alternative species as donors of organs for human transplant. Dunbar put them aside to read when he had more time. They'd probably demand a deal of concentration. Immunology and transplant surgery were a far cry from his own area of medical expertise, which was field medicine.

* * *

The only son of a Cumbrian schoolmaster and his music teacher wife, Steven Dunbar had grown up in the Lake District, in the small village of Glenridding on the shores of Ullswater. He'd studied medicine before completing two residencies, one in Leeds in general surgery and the other in Newcastle in Accident and Emergency. It was around this time that he'd started to question his motives for entering medicine and begun to consider other options. He felt as if he'd been on a treadmill since leaving school. Teachers and parents had been delighted at his success in gaining entry to medical school and he'd been swept along in the approval and pleasure of others. None of them, including himself, he had to admit, had ever considered if he really wanted to be a doctor. It wasn't until a friend suggested he think about the army that his future had taken shape.

He opted for the rigours of life in the Parachute Regiment and had been extensively trained, first as a soldier and then in field medicine. The next few years brought all the physical challenges he could have ever dreamed of as he served with units of the regiment and occasionally on secondment to Special Forces. It was, though, a lifestyle that couldn't continue indefinitely, and when the time came for him to stop he knew and accepted it. The big question had been what to do next.

The army ran courses for officers returning to civilian life but Dunbar wasn't included. He was a doctor; it was assumed he'd be returning to medicine in civvy street. Luckily, he had confided in a fellow officer that he had no wish to continue in medicine, for a while at least. This had led to a suggestion through a friend of a friend that he might be suitable for a job with the Sci-Med Inspectorate. Now, after four years with Sci-Med he felt settled and content.

No two assignments were ever the same; each was demanding in its own way and, being concerned exclusively with problem areas in medicine, he was obliged to keep abreast of the latest advances in his profession. His readiness to move to assignments at a moment's notice was part of the job, wherever they happened to be in the UK.

The only real drawback to his lifestyle was that he was seldom in one place long enough to establish relationships. At thirty-five he was still unmarried.

Dunbar flipped open the slim file on Amy Teasdale. She had suffered almost continual renal problems from birth. Various treatments had been tried in a variety of hospitals while she waited for a suitable organ to become available, but her condition had deteriorated until, after a period of particularly severe illness, she was admitted to Médic Ecosse. The team there managed to stabilize her long enough for a suitable donor organ to be found.

Unfortunately the story had not had a happy ending. Amy's body had rejected the organ almost immediately, despite the computerized match being good in terms of tissue compatibility. A copy of the Médic Ecosse comparator sheet was included. Cause of death was given as severe immune response to the presence of foreign tissue, despite satisfactory *in vitro* compatibility. As the compatibility rating of the donor organ was given as 84 per cent, Dunbar thought Staff Nurse Fairfax's complaint that Amy had been given the wrong organ did not sound too convincing.

He turned to the file on Lisa Fairfax herself. In view of what had gone before, it was possible that the nurse's claim might have stemmed from her having been deeply fond of young Amy Teasdale and correspondingly upset by her death – always an occupational hazard for staff in children's wards. She obviously believed that the immunological reaction she had witnessed in her young charge had been caused by the child receiving an incompatible organ, but her reaction could have been inspired by grief and the inherent need to explain away an emotionally unacceptable happening.

Despite assurances from the hospital authorities that there had been no mix-up and that Amy had received an entirely compat-ible kidney, as shown by lab analysis, Lisa Fairfax had persisted in her claims and she and the hospital had parted company. It looked like a classic case of a nurse allowing herself to become too involved with her patient, thought Dunbar.

He closed the file. It seemed straightforward on paper, although the question of why Staff Nurse Fairfax had persisted with her allegations until Sci-Med became aware of them puzzled him. People did tend to make wild claims and accusations when they were deeply upset, but after a period they usually recovered and, in many cases, were embarrassed about things they had said under stress. Maybe he should arrange a meeting with her, to see if there was more to her than had come through in the report.

He looked to see if there was any more about her and found a one-page personnel file. It included her address and some background material, including the fact that she had worked for three years as a theatre nurse and for a further three specializing in transplant patient care. This made Dunbar think again. He had been ready to dismiss her as emotionally vulnerable, but perhaps he was wrong. You accumulated a lot of nursing experience in six years. Lisa Fairfax must have seen a lot of transplant patients come and go in that time. He decided that, in fairness, he would definitely have to arrange a meeting.

The file on Sheila Barnes's complaint was skimpy. A young patient named Kenneth Lineham had, like Amy Teasdale, died after rejecting a transplanted kidney. The organ had been deemed highly compatible with his own tissue type but, again like Amy Teasdale, he had undergone immunological rejection of the organ after the operation. Sister Barnes, like Lisa, had maintained that there had been a mix-up somewhere along the line and he had been given the wrong organ. A preliminary investigation of her allegation failed to find any evidence of this and she had resigned in protest.

Dunbar could certainly understand why the Sci-Med computer had drawn attention to the situation. The two nurses had made almost identical claims about two different patients almost three years apart, and both were experienced transplant-unit nurses. But, it had to be said, there was a total lack of scientific evidence in both cases. The women's assertions seemed to have been based on gut feeling and very little else.

Dunbar wondered if there had been any other cases of apparently severe immune rejection in patients receiving organs classed as perfectly compatible by lab testing. This was something he could check on the computer. He had access to the main Sci-Med computer through the IBM notebook he carried with him. All he needed was a convenient telephone line, and the hotel was equipped with telephone points for modem connection.

He logged on to the London computer through his access number and password and started asking questions about kidney-transplant records. There were plenty of them; kidney transplant had become an almost routine operation over the past few years. He had to narrow down the data available to that pertaining to unsuccessful transplants in the last two years. Asking the right questions was always the key to a successful computer search. Having access to all the data in the world was no use at all unless you knew exactly what to ask.

A lot of thought had gone into the systems design of the Sci-Med service. He further narrowed down the information to patients who had died within two days of their operation, as had Amy Teasdale and Kenneth Lineham. He then asked how many of them had been given kidneys with an 80 per cent compatible rating with regard to host tissue. The answer was none.

Dunbar stared unseeingly at the screen for a few moments. He was thinking about the result. Only two patients in the UK in the last three years had died within two days of their operation after receiving highly compatible organs, and both had been patients at Médic Ecosse. Coincidence? That couldn't be ruled out, he supposed. Two wasn't a large number, maybe statistically insignificant. Perhaps there were more cases just outside the 80 per cent compatibility figure. He asked the computer the same question with a less stringent figure on compatibility, reducing by first 5 then 10 per cent. The two Médic Ecosse patients were still the only ones. He then looked at cases in which the patient had died within the first month after transplant. There were ten, and without exception there had been other circumstances involved in their deaths. The two Médic Ecosse deaths remained out on their own. They were a puzzle.

FIVE

In the morning Dunbar asked at the desk about his hired car and was told that it was already in the car park. He signed the relevant documents and was given the keys to a dark blue Rover 600Si. It was just after nine. He thought he would let the office day begin before he added his presence to it. He arrived at Médic Ecosse Hospital a little before ten and made himself known at Reception. A pleasant woman in her late thirties, smartly dressed in a dark suit and pristine white blouse that successfully conveyed the impression of cool efficiency, said he was expected. If he cared to take a seat someone would be with him shortly.

The someone in question turned out to be a short, dark-haired young woman, also wearing a business suit, who introduced herself as Ingrid Landes. Her gaze was confident and direct, her handshake firm.

'Come with me, and I'll show you to your office, Dr Dunbar. Do you have a car?'

'Yes.'

'You'll need this.' She handed him a hospital parking permit, already inserted in a clear plastic holder for fixing to the windscreen, adding, 'You've been allocated space seventeen round the back of the building. It's clearly marked.'

'Thank you,' replied Dunbar, impressed by the efficient way he'd been met and welcomed. He was even more impressed when he was shown into a well-appointed office, tastefully furnished and equipped with just about everything he could possibly need, including a computer and fax machine.

'Will this be all right?' asked Ingrid.

'Absolutely.'

'Now, can I get you some coffee while you decide what you want me to do? How do you like it?'

'Decide what I want you to do?' he asked.

'I've been assigned to you for the beginning of your stay with us, to help you settle in. But if that doesn't meet with your approval I'm sure we could just—'

'No, no,' interrupted Dunbar. 'It's just that I didn't expect assistance. This is a very nice surprise.'

She gave what he saw as a superior little smile and said, 'Good. And the coffee?'

'Black. No sugar.'

She left the room and Dunbar sat down behind the desk. He wondered about her and why she had been assigned to him. He hadn't requested secretarial assistance. Had she been detailed to keep an eye on him, or was it just a case of creating a good impression, an apple for the inspector? Maybe he was being too suspicious. For the moment he would keep an open mind.

Ingrid returned with coffee and laid it down on the desk. The smell told him it had been made with proper ground coffee. There was only one cup.

'You're not having any?' he asked.

'I'm trying to cut down,' said Ingrid with a smile that showed uneven teeth. 'I was drinking too much of the stuff. It made me jittery. I've changed to Perrier.'

'Then why don't you get yourself a Perrier and then you can tell me about the hospital? After that perhaps you can show me around? I'd like to get a feel for the place.'

Ingrid went out again. Dunbar got up and walked over to the window. The carpet pile felt uncomfortably deep. It reminded him of walking on the beach and how sand stole your stride pattern. His window looked out on the unremarkable main square in front of the hospital. The central area was grid-lined for parking; the road running round it was double-yellow-lined and one-way. Traffic coming in through the gate was directed to the left and brought round clockwise to pass the front doors.

As he looked towards the entrance, a long, black stretch-limousine turned in through the gates and followed the road arrows to glide silently to a halt at the steps leading up to the main door. The tint on the windows of the car was so dark that the glass almost matched the gleaming paintwork. It was impossible to see inside. The registration plate was foreign. Dunbar guessed it might be in Arabic but the angle he was looking down at made it difficult to tell.

Ingrid returned while he was watching the arrival below, and joined him at the window.

'Our Omega patient has arrived,' she said.

'Omega patient?'

'Big money. A whole wing has been reserved for her.'

The front doors of the car opened below and two men got out. Both were of Middle Eastern appearance although dressed in western clothes. The driver was wearing uniform. The other, a thickset man wearing a suit of light-grey shiny material, looked all around with eyes hidden by reflecting sunglasses before resting his hand on the rear door handle. He kept his other hand inside his jacket.

'What on earth?' murmured Dunbar.

Ingrid did not comment.

Having decided that the hospital and its environs posed no threat to the occupants of the car, the man in the grey suit opened the rear doors and four people got out. All were wearing Arab clothes. There were three women and one man. One of the women was obviously the patient; she was helped by the others through the front doors.

As they disappeared from sight, Dunbar craned his neck to get a better view of the rear of the car but didn't manage to pick up any more information.

'Do you get many Omega patients?' he asked.

'Not as many as we need, apparently,' replied Ingrid with a subdued smile.

Dunbar saw the joke and smiled too. 'I take it she's not here for an ingrowing toenail?'

'I really don't know,' replied Ingrid. 'Patient confidentiality is very important. The staff here operate on a need-to-know basis. It's strict company policy.'

'Of course.' He wondered if she really didn't know. She struck him as being something more than an admin assistant.

Two more vehicles drew up behind the limo, one an unmarked van and the second a Renault Espace carrying six more people who got out and saw to the unloading of the van. Dunbar guessed that the chests and trunks comprised the Omega patient's luggage. The man in the grey suit took charge of the operation. Ingrid and Dunbar turned away from the window.

'Who do you normally work for?' asked Dunbar.

'I'm on Mr Giordano's staff.'

'Are you sure he can spare you?'

'It was his idea that I be assigned to you.'

'It was very good of him to spare you; he must be a very busy man.' Dunbar looked for signs of unease in Ingrid as he spoke; he thought her eyes might give away the fact of an ulterior motive, but he saw nothing. Either it's all above board, he thought, or Ingrid Landes is a very good actress.

'Can I ask what sort of work you normally do?' asked Dunbar.

'General PA work for Mr Giordano and liaison between the various units of the hospital.'

'You know why I'm here, I take it?'

'You're a watchdog, sent here by the government to protect their latest investment. A sort of guardian of the public purse.'

'Near enough.'

'So how can I help you get started?'

'I'd like to see staff lists for the various units, salary sheets, monthly accounting figures for the last six months, details of any outstanding bills, details of advance bookings for hospital care and services.'

'I think we anticipated most of these things. You'll find copies of the relevant computer files on disks in the top drawer of your desk.'

Dunbar slid open the top drawer and found an ID badge with his name on it and a plastic wallet containing four floppy disks. He smiled and said, 'I'm impressed. You seem to have thought of everything.'

'We try,' said Ingrid. 'The people who come to this hospital are used to the best. They expect it as of right so that's what we try to give them.'

'Do you like working here?'

'Absolutely,' she replied, as if it were a stupid question. 'We take a lot of criticism for being private, but we're good – no one denies that. The doctors, the nurses, even the porters and cleaners, are hand-picked. When everyone knows that, there's a certain pride about the place, an *esprit de corps* if you like. It makes people want to do their best. It's not like British Rail, where all the employees feel anonymous and end up not giving a hoot about the passengers. It's different. It's nice. It's the way things should be.'

Dunbar nodded. It didn't seem likely that he would be getting any tittle-tattle or scandal from Ingrid Landes. He decided to press her a little to see how strong her loyalty was.

'It's a very artificial environment,' he said.

She took the bait. 'How so?'

'The very fact that it's a private hospital means you can pick and choose your clientele. That makes things a lot easier, don't you think?'

'I don't think we pick and choose. We take anyone who wants to come here and—'

'Can afford to.'

'That's unfair. Many of our patients are covered by health insurance, something they elect to pay for. It's their choice. I see nothing wrong in that.'

'That still doesn't make you a proper hospital.'

'I don't see how you can say that,' said Ingrid, annoyance creeping into her voice.

'You're not obliged to provide services you don't want to. You don't have an A&E department, you don't treat VD, you're not interested in AIDS, TB, or any infectious disease come to that, and as for Alzheimer's or any kind of mental disorder, forget it. Médic Ecosse wouldn't want to know.'

'It's true we don't handle everything,' she agreed defensively, 'but we do have one of the best transplant units in the country.'

'Indeed you do,' said Dunbar with a grin, 'and one of the most loyal staff members.'

Her eyes widened. 'You were testing me!' she exclaimed.

Dunbar raised his eyebrows slightly and pursed his lips in a display of innocence. Ingrid broke into a smile. 'What a thing to do,' she said.

'Are all the staff as loyal as you?'

'I should think so. The working conditions here are very good, the pay's well above the going rate and the holidays generous. Maybe I shouldn't be saying this to you. You'll probably put all that into reverse,' laughed Ingrid.

'Fear not,' smiled Dunbar. 'I don't have any such powers and I do appreciate that if you want the best you have to pay for it. So you never have staff problems or problems with disgruntled employees?'

Ingrid frowned as she thought. 'Not that I can recall,' she said.

Dunbar maintained an encouraging silence.

'Well, there was one, come to think of it,' said Ingrid, 'quite recently, as a matter of fact. A staff nurse in the transplant unit – I've forgotten her name. She started making wild allegations after the death of a patient, poor woman.'

'What sort of allegations?'

'One of the patients in the unit, a young girl who had been very ill for a long time, died after an unsuccessful kidney transplant, one of the few deaths in that unit, I have to say. I think that's maybe the only death they've had.'

Dunbar managed to stop himself pointing out that there had been another.

'I think the nurse had been very attached to the patient. She was very upset and started saying all sorts of ridiculous things, making wild accusations about the negligence of the medical staff and things like that.'

'What happened to her?'

'In the circumstances, Dr Ross and Mr Giordano were very understanding about it. They arranged for her to have professional counselling and lots of time off but she persisted with her claims, and in the end I'm afraid they had to let her go.'

'Poor woman,' said Dunbar, deciding to let the subject drop. 'How about showing me around?'

'What in particular would you like to see?'

'Absolutely everything.'

Dunbar was impressed by what he saw on his guided tour. He wasn't allowed to enter any of the rooms currently occupied, as that would have been regarded as an invasion of patient privacy, but he did see from the empty ones the type of accommodation on offer. The rooms would have done justice to a top hotel, each being equipped with telephone, radio, satellite television and space-age communications systems. Wherever possible, medical equipment was hidden from view, much of it secreted behind sliding wall panels. Cardiac monitoring equipment, oxygen supply points and drip-feed equipment were all within easy reach of the bed but out of sight until required. It was hard to tell that this was a hospital room. Even the air smelled fresh and free from antiseptic odour. Dunbar looked up at the ceiling and saw grilles for air-conditioning.

The X-ray suite was state-of-the-art, as was the physiology lab with its gleaming respiratory function equipment. The operating theatres were fitted with the latest in lighting and table technology. Anaesthetics were available through a colour-coded bank of regulators, each gas with its own gauge and flow monitor and not a cylinder in sight. Endoscopy monitors were mounted on swinging arm platforms that could be adjusted to any height and angle required by the surgeon.

As they waited for a lift to take them up to the transplant unit, Ingrid asked, 'What do you think so far?'

'It's hard to believe I'm in a hospital,' said Dunbar. 'Apart from anything else, it's so quiet. There just don't seem to be any people about. I always associate hospitals with bustle and activity.'

'Company policy,' said Ingrid. 'They don't just hide the equipment, they hide the nurses too! But whenever you need one, one will materialize at your shoulder.'

The lift doors slid back and three people got out, a man in pristine white Arab clothes and two others whom Dunbar recognized as the driver and bodyguard he'd seen getting out the limo earlier. Ingrid smiled and said something to them in Arabic. She sounded fluent.

'I'm impressed,' said Dunbar as they got into the lift and the doors slid shut.

'Omega patients expect no less,' Ingrid replied.

As they stepped out into the reception area for the transplant unit, Ingrid said, 'I'll have to check with Dr Ross first to see if it's all right to show you round.'

Dunbar nodded.

Ingrid leaned over the reception desk and asked the nurse sitting there if she would tell Dr Ross they were here. The woman smiled, nodded and picked up a telephone. Ross appeared in the foyer a few moments later. He acknowledged Ingrid with a nod, then turned to Dunbar, stretching out his hand. 'Big Brother is watching us,' he said with a smile.

'It's not that bad,' smiled Dunbar in reply. 'As long as you're not carrying out operations for nothing.'

'As a matter of fact we will be tomorrow,' said Ross conspiratorially. 'One of my colleagues is carrying out facial reconstruction work on one of the NHS patients we agreed to take on for free as part of the funding agreement.'

'A laudable exception,' said Dunbar. 'Actually, I was rather hoping I might be able to see round your unit? Meet the staff?'

'Of course,' replied Ross. 'That is, the bits that are empty. Ingrid has probably told you that patient privacy is paramount.'

'It's what I keep hearing,' agreed Dunbar.

'The plain truth is that many of our clients don't want anyone even to know they're in hospital, let alone what they're having done. And if they pay the piper . . .'

'They call the tune.'

'You can see the transplant theatres, of course, and one of the intensive-care suites for post-operative use. The individual rooms are pretty standard throughout the hospital.'

'Even for Omega patients?' asked Dunbar.

Ross exchanged an uncertain glance with Ingrid before smiling and saying, 'Perhaps a few more little goodies for them.'

There were smiles all round. Ross said, 'Come and meet the staff.' He led the way to a room where a man dressed in surgical greens was standing in front of a blackboard addressing several medical and nursing colleagues. He paused as the newcomers entered but Ross indicated that he should continue and ushered Dunbar and Ingrid to seats at the side of the room.

'Staff briefing,' he whispered. 'We have one every morning. I'll let John finish.'

Dunbar nodded and listened with interest to the briefing. There were seven patients in the unit. The current condition of each was discussed in turn and staff were asked for any observations they might have. Updates were made to all their charts and all staff were made aware of plans for each patient for the day. Again, Dunbar was impressed. This was a well-run unit.

'Any questions?' asked the man Ross had called John. There were none.

Ross stood up and said, 'Just before you go everyone, I'd like you to meet Dr Steven Dunbar. He's been assigned to the hospital by the Scottish Office to keep an eye on us, but he tells me he's not such a monster once you get to know him.'

There was polite laughter. Dunbar saw that Ross was popular with his staff. He was introduced to each member of staff in turn, starting with the theatre sister, Trudy Sinclair, and ending with John Hatfull, who had been giving the briefing.

'John is my surgical registrar,' explained Ross. 'Also my right-hand man.'

Hatfull was slightly shorter than Ross, brown-haired and hazel-eyed. He had an air of intensity that Dunbar often associated with highly intelligent people. It was as if they radiated energy. It was hard to imagine them relaxing. He shook hands with Hatfull.

'Did I hear James say you were a doctor yourself?' Hatfull asked.

Dunbar nodded.

'What speciality?'

'Field medicine,' Dunbar replied.

Hatfull looked surprised then amused. 'From field medicine to accountancy? Quite a change. I suppose you were looking for more excitement.'

The others laughed. Dunbar smiled dutifully, but offered no explanation. He didn't want anyone thinking too much about the unlikelihood of such a switch.

'Well,' said Ross, 'I'll show you round. Or maybe you'd care to do that, John, if you have the time?'

'My pleasure,' replied Hatfull. 'Anything in particular you'd like to see?'

'Anything and everything,' said Dunbar. 'I just need to get a general feel for the unit. I need to relate its size and facilities to the figures I see on the balance sheets.'

'Of course.'

As they started the tour Dunbar sensed that Hatfull was on his guard. He thought he'd try a little flattery to see if he could soften him up. 'Dr Ross seems to rely on you a lot.'

'He's a very busy man,' replied Hatfull.

'Of course,' said Dunbar. 'He has research interests too. Are you involved at all in that?'

'No, I'm just a work-horse. I leave research to the clever people.'

'As a transplant surgeon in this unit, you're not exactly among the intellectually challenged of the world,' countered Dunbar with a smile.

'One does what one can.'

'The withdrawal of research funding must have been quite a blow to Dr Ross?'

'Must have been.'

Dunbar didn't ask any more. He accepted he wasn't going to get anywhere with Hatfull.

The tour of the transplant unit took about thirty minutes, including the time taken by Hatfull to answer questions as mono-syllabically as possible. Dunbar reverted to asking the kind of questions he thought he should be asking. They related to length of patients' stay in the unit, numbers of staff involved in pre-operative and post-operative care, in fact, anything he thought an accountant might be interested in. He made notes in a small leather-bound book he took from his inside pocket. There was very little to ask about the equipment and accommodation. The facilities were simply the best. When he'd asked everything he thought he should, they were re-joined by Ross, who asked if he'd enjoyed his tour.

'Very interesting,' replied Dunbar. He thought he'd risk trying a different tack and asked, 'What actually happens when you hear that an organ has become available for one of your patients, Doctor?'

'Quite a lot,' smiled Ross. 'And all at the same time! The proce-dure usually starts with a computer alert that a matching organ is available. We first double-check that this is the case and then contact the hospital or clinic holding the organ to establish personal contact and agree terms of transfer. A lot depends on where the donor organ is and how long it's going to take to get here. At the same time, we alert our patient to the possibility of an operation and arrange for him or her to be admitted if they aren't already in hospital. The operating teams are put on stand-by, round the clock if necessary. Time is always of the essence where live tissue is concerned.'

'Of course.'

'Apart from the actual theatre teams, we also need lab support and a supply of blood from the transfusion service available at exactly the right time. A lot of people are involved in a successful transplant. It's a team effort and there are so many things that can go wrong. A flight gets delayed, a traffic jam, a driver takes the wrong turning. So many things, so many links in the chain, and all of them important.'

Dunbar nodded and pushed his luck. 'And do they?' he asked.

'I'm sorry?'

'Do they go wrong?'

'Very rarely,' said Ross with a smile and a touch-wood gesture. 'There have been a few close calls as regards time but we've always managed to get the job done.'

'That's interesting,' said Dunbar. 'I suppose the clock starts ticking as soon as the donor organ is removed?'

'Absolutely. There's only a finite time before it becomes useless for transplant purposes.'

'I suppose the ideal thing would be to keep the donor on a life-support system until everything was ready?'

'In a cold, clinical sense, yes,' agreed Ross. 'But of course the moral implications of such a procedure dictate that hospitals can't actually do this – well, not overtly. There'd be a public outcry.'

'Of course. So with time ticking away, and traffic jams and airline delays all playing their part, you must have to get the organ into your patient almost as soon as it comes through the door?'

'Almost,' agreed Ross. 'The theatre staff are usually prepped and ready.'

'No time for any last-minute checks on the organ itself?' said Dunbar, feeling as if he'd just jumped into water without knowing the depth.

There was a tense pause before Ross said, 'I don't think I'm quite with you. What sort of checks are you referring to?'

'Oh, I don't know,' said Dunbar, trying to appear off-hand and casual. 'The usual things, blood group, tissue-typing, AIDS, Hep.B screening, that sort of thing.' He had slipped his real question in at number two in the list, hoping it would nestle there without arousing suspicion. A glance at Ross as they proceeded along the corridor made him doubt whether he had succeeded: the smile had gone from his face.

'All these things are usually done at the donor hospital,' said Ross.

'Of course. That would make sense,' said Dunbar. 'I just wondered whether, with an international donor network, standards might vary from country to country.'

'All hospitals in the network work to the highest standards,' said Ross.

'I see,' said Dunbar.

'But when we have time to spare, we do carry out our own screening,' said Ross.

'I felt sure you would,' said Dunbar.

'And here we are back where we started,' said Ross as they returned to the unit's foyer. 'Is there anything else we can show you or help you with?'

'Your research labs,' said Dunbar. 'I didn't see them.'

'No, you didn't,' agreed Ross. 'My labs aren't actually in the hospital. As you're not funding them any more, I didn't think they'd come within your remit.'

Dunbar detected resentment in Ross's voice. He decided on a conciliatory response. 'You're absolutely right. I was just personally interested. Did you manage to get alternative funding for your work, Doctor?'

'Enough to keep going for the moment,' replied Ross. 'Médic International have been generous.'

'I'm glad. It was all very unfortunate.'

'Yes,' replied Ross. He seemed wryly amused at Dunbar's choice of word. 'Most unfortunate.'

'How is the research going?'

'Quite well, thank you, but progress is never as fast as one would like.'

'I suppose not.'

Dunbar shook hands with Ross and Hatfull and followed Ingrid into the elevator.

'I wasn't supposed to know about Omega patients, was I?' he asked as they descended.

Ingrid smiled. 'Don't worry about it. Dr Ross was just a bit surprised that you knew about them. We don't get that many, and you've only been here five minutes.'

'Why Omega?'

'The last letter of the Greek alphabet for the last word in care and attention,' said Ingrid. 'Nothing's too good for them. Nothing's too much trouble.'

'At a price,' said Dunbar.

'Of course. They're used to being pampered. Most of our patients are. Do you know what they're really paying for at Médic Ecosse?'

'Tell me.'

'Secrecy,' she said. 'Absolute discretion. People who come here for cosmetic surgery don't want their friends to know they're having it done. People who come here because they're ill don't want their enemies to know about it. Any suggestion of ill health at the top can trigger a coup or wipe millions off share values. Complete confidentiality is probably the most valuable commodity we offer.'

'I'm surprised you told me about Omega patients at all,' said Dunbar.

'I just thought as you're going to be going through the books you were going to find out everything that goes on anyway.'

'True.'

'I promise you, you are going to be sick of the word "confidential" before you're through,' said Ingrid. 'People here think twice before they'll tell you the time. They're not being obstructive. Their job depends on it.'

'I'll bear that in mind,' said Dunbar. 'But I do have the right to request any information I feel I need.'

'I'll bear that in mind,' she mimicked. 'Is there anything else you want to see?'

'Not at the moment. I think I'll make a start on the paperwork and maybe have a wander around later on my own if there's time.'

'Don't forget your ID badge.'

Dunbar nodded.

'So you won't be needing me any more today?'

'I don't think so. I'll make a note of any questions and maybe we can talk again in the morning.'

Ingrid looked at her watch and said, 'It's lunch-time. Would you like to try the staff restaurant or do you have other plans?'

'No other plans,' said Dunbar.

As they walked towards the restaurant he asked, 'Which wing is the Omega patient in?'

'The east wing of Obstetrics.'

'Then she's having a baby?'

'That would be my guess too,' replied Ingrid. 'Here we are.' She pushed open a swing door and ushered Dunbar in first. The staff restaurant at Médic Ecosse was a light, bright self-service facility which, judging by the crowd, was very popular. Dunbar opted for a tuna salad and looked around for a table while Ingrid collected her baked potato. He saw two nurses about to vacate a table by the window and timed his approach to coincide with their leaving. He waved to Ingrid, who had momentarily lost sight of him.

'You've done this before,' she said as she joined him.

'London-trained,' he replied. 'Push or die. Is it always this busy?'

'Most days,' replied Ingrid. 'There aren't too many other places round here. Apart from that the meals are heavily subsidized.'

'I noticed.'

'Oh dear,' said Ingrid.

'The price of a tuna salad isn't going to make much difference to government investment in Médic Ecosse,' he assured her.

'What is?' she asked.

'It's quite simple really. You must either attract more paying patients or charge the patients you're already getting a lot more.'

'I think our prices are pretty well in the top of the range as it is,' said Ingrid.

'That's my impression too,' said Dunbar. 'So it's a case of

developing a marketing strategy that will you bring you more custom, identifying your strengths and capitalizing on them.'

'Our patients seem well satisfied with the treatment they get here,' said Ingrid.

Dunbar smiled ruefully and said, 'The trouble is they can't tell anyone about it. You said yourself that they don't want people to know they've been here. You're selling confidentiality.'

'I hadn't considered the down-side of it,' said Ingrid. 'I suppose we can hardly ask them to tell all their friends!'

'Apart from that, their friends will be pretending there's nothing wrong with them anyway!' said Dunbar with an extravagant shrug that made Ingrid smile.

'Dr Ross mentioned an NHS patient getting plastic surgery here tomorrow?' he went on.

'That's right,' replied Ingrid. 'It's a face reconstruction, a young girl. She was born with a protruding jaw that disfigured her whole appearance. The surgeons are going to fix it so that she can lead a normal life.'

'I take it the hospital has put out a press release?'

'Oh yes,' replied Ingrid. 'I'm told the results will be quite dramatic, so the before and after pictures should be spectacular.'

Dunbar nodded. 'Especially as there's no scarring with that particular operation. They do all the cutting from inside the mouth, even removing portions of jawbone from either side. It should be very good publicity for the hospital.'

Ingrid said quietly, 'I don't think that's the only reason the surgeons are doing it.'

'Of course not,' he conceded. 'I'm sorry if I sounded cynical. The hospital needs as much good publicity as it can get.'

'You seemed very interested in Dr Ross's unit this morning. Is transplant technology a particular interest of yours?'

'Not really,' he said, immediately on his guard.

'You seemed very interested in the logistics of transplants and what happened to the donor organs when they arrived,' she persisted.

Alarm bells rang in Dunbar's head. If Ingrid thought that, the chances were that Ross and Hatfull must have thought the same. Damn it! Had he overplayed his hand on his very first day? 'I was just curious,' he lied.

SIX

Dunbar spent the afternoon looking through the computerized staff and accounting files provided by Leo Giordano's office. He found it all extremely boring but felt obliged to identify some questions to ask in the next few days, in order to make his role in the hospital seem genuine. As for the real purpose of his visit, he was just looking and learning. So far, everything about the hospital, and the transplant unit in particular, seemed impressive. Its record in terms of successful transplants was second to none, it was staffed by people of the highest calibre, the equipment was state-of-the-art, it was led by one of the finest transplant surgeons in the country, if not the world, and the unit was not under pressure – the usual cause of things going wrong in a hospital. If first impressions were anything to go by, Ross's unit was the last place on earth he was going to find evidence of mix-ups or sloppiness.

The thing that still bothered him, of course, was the same thing that had bothered the Sci-Med computer, the fact that the same allegation had been made not once but twice, by two trained nurses, who didn't know each other. At least, he had assumed they didn't know each other. Was it possible that they did? He took the Sci-Med personnel files from his briefcase and checked the dates. Sheila Barnes had left Médic Ecosse almost two years before Lisa Fairfax started work there.

He would have to talk to them, he decided. If he ruled out sloppiness or bad management as possibilities, he would have to consider alternative explanations for the women's allegations. Those would include malice and hysteria. He would have a word with Staff Nurse Fairfax first, find out what made her tick. You could usually tell more from a two-minute conversation with someone than from reading a fifty-page personnel file.

Sci-Med had supplied Lisa Fairfax's address and telephone number. He picked up the phone and then thought again. He stared at the receiver for a moment, wondering if the hospital operated a call-logging system. He wouldn't like anyone to know he was calling a dismissed member of staff, particularly as Ingrid had noted his interest in how donor organs were handled when they arrived. Any suspicion that the authorities were giving credence to a totally un-substantiated allegation against such a prestigious unit as the Médic Ecosse transplant unit, and he really would be asking for trouble. He decided to make the call using his own mobile phone.

Dunbar didn't hold out much hope of Lisa Fairfax being in on a weekday afternoon. He thought she'd be out at work but, as it turned out, she wasn't.

'Hello,' said a well-modulated voice.

'Miss Fairfax? My name is Dr Steven Dunbar. I'm sorry to ring you out of the blue like this but I wonder if we might arrange a meeting? I'd like to talk to you about your time at Médic Ecosse Hospital?'

'Why do you want to see me?'

'I work for a government department. We investigate allegations of irregularity in patient care.'

'Do you now?' said Lisa. 'You're a bit late, aren't you?'

'Well, you know what they say about wheels that grind slowly: they grind exceeding small,' said Dunbar. He immediately regretted it; it sounded flippant. 'I know you must be very busy,' he continued, 'but I really would appreciate it if you'd agree to see me.'

'Busy? I haven't worked since I left Médic Ecosse,' said Lisa.

'I'm sorry. I didn't realize. Could we talk?'

'I don't think so,' she replied. 'I said all I had to say at the time and everyone ignored me. Look where it got me! It lost me my job and probably all chances of getting another, if those people at Médic Ecosse have anything to do with it.'

'I'd like to hear your side of the story,' said Dunbar.

'So you can do what? File it under "Ramblings of a neurotic woman" like they did last time? Offer me sympathy and counselling? Patronizing bastards.' The words were angry but controlled.

'I can't say what I'd do until I hear what you have to say,' replied Dunbar. 'But if I thought there was any substance to your claims, I promise I'd see they were investigated fully.'

Lisa sounded unconvinced. She said, 'I really don't think there's any point in going through the hassle all over again. It must all be in the files and I simply haven't the stomach for it any more.'

'Could that be because you've had a change of heart over the matter, Miss Fairfax?' goaded Dunbar. 'Maybe you decided that you'd been a bit hasty with your allegations at the time? And now that you've had time to think—'

'No, it couldn't,' said Lisa icily. 'I simply don't want to go through it all again. It was unpleasant enough last time. Nothing I can say will bring Amy back. She's dead but I'm alive. I need a job. I need to earn my living.'

'Was Amy Teasdale special to you, Miss Fairfax?'

Lisa sighed. 'Not that old thing again. I was not unduly attached to Amy Teasdale. I liked her; she was a nice kid. I was sad when she died. I was always sad when one of the patients died, but that was as far as it went. I'm a professional nurse. These things happen.'

'Then you worked with children a lot?'

'Yes. Why d'you ask?'

'Nothing. I'd still like to meet you.'

'Look up the files. You'll find everything you need there.'

'I'm not interested in the files. I'm conducting an investigation on my own. No one else up here is involved, and you have my word that everything you say will be kept absolutely confidential.'

'I really don't know,' said Lisa uncertainly.

'Why don't I buy you dinner and we can talk while we eat?'

'No,' she replied quickly. 'You'd have to come here.'

'All right. Where's that?'

She gave him her address and he pretended to write it down.

He didn't want to give away that he already knew where she lived from the Sci-Med file on her. 'When can I come? Tonight?'

'I suppose that would be as good as any other time,' replied Lisa. 'About eight?'

'Very well.'

Lisa Fairfax lived in a sandstone block of flats off the Dumbarton Road, the arterial road that leads out from the heart of Glasgow to the banks of the River Clyde and the great shipyards that once built vessels for the world. The huge cranes were still in evidence but the contracts and the jobs had all but gone.

The street she lived in was quiet, but finding somewhere to park was a problem. Already at that time in the evening, cars were double-parked making negotiation of the area difficult for Dunbar in a car he was not used to and not that familiar with in terms of width when judging the size of gaps it could go through. There was a small piece of waste ground at the end of the second street he inched through. It was actually the frontage of a double lock-up garage with the message NO PARKING, IN CONSTANT USE painted on the doors. The paint was peeling and the padlocks were very rusty, so he took a chance and parked the Rover there. He didn't think he'd be that long.

He walked back to Lisa's street and found the number he was looking for. He pressed the entryphone button.

'Yes?'

'Steven Dunbar. We spoke earlier.'

The electronic lock released with a loud buzz that made Dunbar think of an electric chair and he entered the building. The entrance hall was well lit and had recently been painted. It was lined with terracotta tubs that would hold pot plants in season. At the moment they held nothing but bare earth. He climbed the stairs quickly to the third floor and found one door ajar. There was no name-plate on it but he assumed this to be the one. He knocked. 'Miss Fairfax?'

'Come in. I'll be right with you. The living room's on your right. Find yourself a seat and sit down.'

Dunbar closed the door behind him and walked up to the end of the hall and in through the door to his right. He chose to look out of the window rather than sit. Although it was dark outside, the curtains had not been drawn and he could see the lights on the far side of the Clyde like strings of pearls on black velvet. He thought he heard a movement behind him and turned to greet Lisa Fairfax.

'Hello, Miss . . .' His eyes widened as a woman in her late seventies came towards him with a wild look in her eyes and her arms outstretched.

'Joshua! You've come home,' she exclaimed, and made to embrace him warmly.

Dunbar was taken by surprise. He tried to fend her off, gently because she seemed so frail, but she persisted in her attempts to hug him.

'I think there's been some mistake,' he offered weakly. He retreated and fell backwards over the arm of a couch – he hadn't realized it was so close behind him.

'Oh my God,' exclaimed another woman as she came into the room. 'Mother, stop that! Stop that at once!'

Dunbar did his best to recover his composure and looked up into the distressed face of Lisa Fairfax.

Lisa was in her early thirties, slim, attractive, with shiny jet-black hair tied back and deep, dark eyes that suggested intelligence but at the moment were filled with alarm and embarrassment.

'I'm so sorry,' she said. 'I thought she was still asleep. She suffers from senile dementia.'

Dunbar nodded and let out his breath in a long sigh. 'I'm sorry I'm not Joshua,' he murmured kindly as Lisa put her arms round her mother and led her out of the room, remonstrating with her gently as if she were a small child. She returned alone a few minutes later.

'I'm sorry, I was sure she was asleep, otherwise I'd never have let you come in like that. Can I get you a drink?'

Dunbar smiled at the progression to social normality. 'Gin, if you have it.'

Lisa poured them both a gin and tonic, the slight tremor of her hands still betraying her embarrassment. She handed a tumbler to Dunbar and said, 'Please sit down.'

'Shouldn't she be in hospital?' Dunbar asked.

'She should,' replied Lisa. 'But there's little chance of that these days. Her condition can't be cured so the hospitals won't take her. She's been "returned to the community" after a brief admission for assessment. That's government policy.'

'Surely you must get some kind of help?'

Lisa shook her head. 'I am the "community" as far as the authorities are concerned. She's my mother so it's down to me to care for her. The only way I can get help is if I buy it. I was doing that but I don't have a job any more.'

'Sounds awful.'

'I've known better times,' said Lisa.

She said it matter-of-factly rather than with self-pity. She struck Dunbar as capable woman who was up against it but coping well.

'Tell me about Amy Teasdale.'

Lisa's face relaxed into an extremely attractive, albeit distant, smile. Her eyes said that she was grateful for Dunbar glossing over what had happened. 'Ah yes, Amy,' she said, before pausing for a moment to compose her thoughts.

'Amy was a perfectly ordinary little girl apart from the fact that her kidneys weren't properly functional. Practically from the time she was born she'd been in and out of one hospital after another, so she was well used to them. Because of that she wasn't the uncomplaining little heroine the press likes kids like her to be. In fact, she could be a right little madam at times, if things weren't to her liking. I suppose that was because she'd been spoilt by parents and relatives because of her condition, but in spite of it we all liked her. She was one of ours, and we were delighted when word came through that a suitable kidney'd been found. She'd been waiting for years and within weeks of coming to us a kidney had been located and the word was that the match was good, something around eighty per cent compatible, if I remember rightly. It seemed like a dream come true.'

'So you expected a good result?'

'Of course. It was an excellent match and kidney-transplanting has become practically routine these days. There was no reason to expect anything else. We were looking forward to seeing Amy skipping down the ward and saying good-bye. She could look forward to a normal life.'

'But that didn't happen.'

'No. She rejected the kidney and died soon after the operation.'

'Who carried out the operation?'

'Dr Hatfull, one of Dr Ross's surgical team.'

'What did you think of him?'

Lisa looked shocked at the question. She said, 'It's hardly my place to pass comment on the medical staff.'

'I'd still like to know what you thought of him. This is all confidential, remember. Nothing you say will be repeated outside this room.'

'I thought Dr Hatfull was an excellent surgeon. In that unit they all were. It's a very prestigious place to work, a good career move, as they say. There was always a waiting list for surgical and nursing appointments.'

'But you still think something went wrong?'

'I am convinced Amy was given the wrong kidney. Her reaction was so strong that it must have been due to the presence of radically foreign tissue inside her. The immunosuppressants she was given just couldn't cope. She died in agony, poor mite.'

'Have you any idea how she could possibly have been given the wrong kidney?'

She shook her head. 'I've been thinking about that ever since it happened and I know all the arguments against it. There was only one organ sent from the donor hospital, so how could there be a mix-up? The tissue type was tested both at the donor hospital and at Médic Ecosse and found to check out, but I know what I saw. I've seen rejection problems before and Amy was a classic case of a patient being given incompatible tissue. Nothing will convince me otherwise.'

Dunbar found himself impressed by Lisa Fairfax. She wasn't over-emotional or hysterical. She was a sensible, straightforward, down-to-earth woman with a lot of common sense.

'What did you do about it at the time?'

'I went to the director of nursing staff and told her what I felt. It went down like a cotton-wool sandwich. I was told to pull myself together, that I was emotionally overwrought and that I should think about the damage I could do to the hospital with such "wild allegations".'

'But you weren't put off?'

'No, although in my present circumstances I sometimes wonder if I should have kept my mouth shut,' said Lisa with a strained attempt at a smile. 'But no, I went to Dr Kinscherf and Mr Giordano and asked them to investigate the possibility that Amy had been given the wrong kidney.'

'And got the same reaction?'

'More or less. They said my concern for my patients did me credit but becoming emotionally involved with them could distort my judgement. Amy's rejection of the donor kidney had been just one of those things, an unfortunate roll of the dice. There are still lots of immune responses that the medical profession doesn't fully understand. They suggested I take some time off – in practice they suspended me from duty. They kept paying me but it was conditional on my seeing my GP and some old trout with a frontal lobotomy they called a counsellor. She was supposed to "help me through my trauma" i.e., make me see sense and keep my mouth shut. When I failed to play ball with the trout or take the GP's Prozac highway to inner peace and content-ment, they sacked me. Now here I am with no job, locked up twenty-four hours of the day with a doolally old person who used to be my mother, secure in the knowledge that things can only get worse.' She threw the remains of her drink down her throat.

Dunbar felt uncomfortable. Saying he was sorry seemed inadequate, so he just nodded.

'I'm sorry,' said Lisa. 'I shouldn't be saying these things to a total stranger.'

'Total strangers are often the best people to say these sort of things to,' he replied.

She smiled slightly, as if happy at finding someone else who knew that.

'You've given me a problem,' said Dunbar.

'How so?'

'I came here expecting to find a nurse who had got too involved with her patient and who had made a hysterical allegation born of grief. You're not the type. I find myself believing you, but perhaps you can see my difficulty?'

'I know what I saw.'

Dunbar's look suggested to Lisa that her reply was inadequate. She said, 'Oh, I accept that the right organ was sent and that it arrived safely and checked out, but nothing will convince me that it was transplanted into Amy.'

'Does the name Sheila Barnes mean anything to you?'

Lisa looked blank. 'I don't think so,' she said.

'Sister Sheila Barnes?'

'A nurse? At Médic Ecosse?'

'Yes.'

'Doesn't ring a bell. Should I know her?'

'Not really,' replied Dunbar, getting up out of his chair. 'I just wondered. Thanks for seeing me. It's been a big help. I really hope things get better for you.'

'What's coming for me won't go past me,' said Lisa.

'Pardon?'

'It's a Scottish expression,' said Lisa. 'The equivalent of *que será será.*'

Dunbar pulled up his collar and looked up at the stars as he stepped out into the street. It was nice to see a clear sky but the price for it was a temperature now dropping below zero. He was unsettled. Lisa Fairfax was absolutely sure that Amy Teasdale had been given the wrong organ at her transplant operation. From what he'd seen and heard of Lisa, he could not dismiss her as neurotic, nor as someone who had been too involved with her patient. But how could she be right? Where could this 'wrong organ' have come from? You didn't find drawers marked DONOR ORGANS in hospitals. If the correct organ had been sent and received, surely that was the end of it. The rejection response must have been just one of those inexplicable things that sometimes happened. Fine, but in the case of Médic Ecosse it had been two of those things.

The only thing he was sure of as he pulled out into the traffic on Dumbarton Road was that he was going to see Sheila Barnes at the hospice in Helensburgh. He was beginning to feel more than a little uneasy about the whole business.

Dunbar spent the following morning at his desk in the hospital making notes from the figures on the computer disks and asking Ingrid to provide some more information about certain topics. He had identified a lack of information about catering costs at Médic Ecosse and thought that asking her to prepare a breakdown of meal costs over the past eighteen months should keep her busy while he concentrated on other things. He was relieved not to have stumbled on anything that had been missed from the disks supplied by Giordano's office. The information given to him was on the whole pretty comprehensive.

Halfway through the morning he noticed something else. The patient records had at first seemed satisfactory in terms of listing treatment given and correlating this with itemized costing, enabling him to check billed sums against monies received but, in treating this as an academic exercise to fill in the time, he noticed an anomaly. The records of Omega patients' bills were not itemized. There was no way of checking on their treatment.

He could see why Giordano's office had thought he might well be satisfied with only the final sum – it was many thousands of pounds in all cases – but it was something he could ask Ingrid about. In the meantime, he rang The Beeches Hospice on his mobile phone and asked if he might visit Sheila Barnes that afternoon.

'Are you a relative?' asked the female voice.

Dunbar paused momentarily to reflect on how often that question was asked every day. 'No, just an old friend,' he lied.

'I see. Well, I don't see any problem there. We encourage our patients to live as normal a life as possible up to the very end. Shall we say three o'clock? I have to suggest a time so that we can adjust Mrs Barnes's medication accordingly. It would be a wasted journey if she was asleep when you arrived. On the other hand, we have to keep her as comfortable as possible. It's sometimes a fine line.'

'I understand,' said Dunbar, starting to feel guilty about what he was doing, though not guilty enough to call the whole thing off. 'I'll be there at three.'

Ingrid returned shortly before lunch-time with facts and figures about how much patient meals cost to prepare, what the clients were charged and what the profit margins were. 'I'm sure you'll find we haven't been undercharging.' She spoke pleasantly but managed to convey that she thought she'd been sent on a fool's errand.

'It's as well to have all the figures to hand,' said Dunbar, hoping he sounded like an accountant.

'Is there anything else you'd like me to do?' asked Ingrid.

'As a matter of fact there is. I'm a bit puzzled about the information given to me on the Omega patients.'

Ingrid's expression became serious. 'Really? Why?' she asked.

'Well, basically there isn't any.'

Ingrid looked puzzled. She came over to stand behind Dunbar and peered down at the screen. 'I was sure I saw figures for them when I copied the disk for you.' She leaned over and tapped computer keys until patients' records came up, then kept one elegant finger on the down-key to scroll through them.

'There,' she announced, removing her finger and pointing at the screen. 'There's one. A ten-day stay, netting seventeen thousand pounds. Not bad, eh?'

'But for what?' asked Dunbar.

Ingrid looked at Dunbar in a way he found hard to interpret. She was either puzzled or seeing him as some kind of mental defective. 'Forgive me, Doctor,' she said. 'I thought your interest lay in establishing that we were maximizing our income from clients and getting the best possible return for the investment of taxpayers' money?'

'That's broadly true,' agreed Dunbar.

Ingrid appeared to have difficulty in controlling her impulses which Dunbar, reading her body language, guessed were to throw her hands in the air, shake her head and shout, 'Then why in God's name do you want to know anything as irrelevant as that?' Instead she said, 'I suppose we thought that a profit of seventeen thousand pounds for a ten-day stay would be enough to satisfy you without itemizing the patient's treatment.'

Dunbar mutely agreed that this was the case. He wondered for a moment just how far he should press this point. On the one hand, he wanted to establish that he had the right to ask for any information he wanted. On the other, he didn't want to push his credentials as the village idiot when all he was doing was thinking up things to keep Ingrid busy. 'It doesn't even say what the patient was in here for,' he said.

'I'm sorry,' said Ingrid. 'It's this confidentiality thing we have. I suppose we thought you'd be happy with the final income figures. If it's any help, I can tell you that this particular Omega patient had a baby here. It was feared that there might be complications but in the end everything was fine. In fact, if I remember rightly, all three Omega patients we've had were in for obstetrics care. Very rich men are always anxious that their wives have the best of care during pregnancy when problems are thought possible. Would you still like me to organize an itemized costing of their stay?'

Dunbar shook his head. 'No, I don't think that'll be necessary.'

'Is there anything else I can help with?'

'Not for the moment,' smiled Dunbar. 'I'm going to take the afternoon off, see the delights of Glasgow.'

'Don't hold your breath,' said Ingrid.

Why was a sneer considered by so many to be the basis of sophistication? he wondered idly as he watched the door close.

He set off for Helensburgh just after one o'clock after checking the route in the AA road maps thoughtfully provided with the car. It seemed straightforward enough, just a matter of following the northern shore of the Clyde down to where Helensburgh sat at the foot of the Gare Loch. As he drove along the Clydebank expressway and out along the Dumbarton Road he passed the turn-off to Lisa Fairfax's place. He couldn't help but think of her sitting there in the flat with her demented mother. It made him reflect on how people's lives could be ruined by notions of filial duty.

The sun was shining when he drove into Helensburgh and parked down by the sea front. The matron of The Beeches had told him to follow the signs directing tourists to Charles Rennie Mackintosh's famous Hill House; the hospice was located in Harlaw Road, the street running parallel to and a little behind Hill House, but he had time in hand so he decided to stretch his legs first and also find something to eat. He had given lunch a miss in Glasgow because he hadn't been sure how long the journey down would take him. In the event it had taken under an hour. He watched the waves for a bit until the wind chilled him, then he went in search of a bar or cafe. He found an outlet of the Pierre Victoire chain, where he had a mushroom omelette and a glass of wine. He followed this with two cups of good coffee and a consideration of what he was going to ask Sheila Barnes – if, indeed, she was in any position to answer.

The Beeches was a large, stone-built Victorian villa with ivy clinging to its walls on the two sides Dunbar could see as he approached. In another setting it might have been forbidding but here, above the town and with views over the water, it seemed pleasantly neutral in the pale yellow, wintery afternoon sunshine. Dunbar rang the bell, and was led along to the matron's office by a woman orderly dressed in a pink uniform and thick brown stockings. Her shoulders sloped dramatically from left to right. As he followed her he had to fight a conscious urge to emulate her posture. He was very aware of the warmth of the building and suspected that they must keep the heating full on.

'Dr Dunbar, please come in,' said a pleasant woman in her late forties in response to the orderly's announcement of his arrival. She had prematurely white hair, suggesting that she had been blonde in her youth, and wore the kind of professional half-smile affected by senior nursing staff to put strangers at their ease.

'Mrs Barnes is awake, although I have to say that she couldn't recall you when I told her you were coming.' The smile didn't waver but her eyes asked the question.

Dunbar felt a pang of guilt. 'It's been a very long time, Matron. Many years.'

'Well, I'm sure it'll all come back to her when she sees you, and you can have a nice chat. We like old friends to call, and Sheila doesn't have much longer to go, I'm afraid.'

'Is she comfortable?' asked Dunbar.

'She has her moments of discomfort, but on the whole we've got her pain under control. You may find her a little sleepy. She's on morphine.'

'Someone told me her husband has cancer too,' said Dunbar.

'It's true, I'm afraid. They both contracted it at almost exactly the same time. Very strange. I can't ever recall that happening before. Cyril has the room next door to Sheila. Would you like to see him too?'

Dunbar shook his head and said, 'I never knew Cyril.'

'I'll have Morag take you up now.'

The orderly was summoned back and she led Dunbar along the carpeted corridor and up the stairs to a pleasant bay-windowed room on the first floor.

'Mrs Barnes, your visitor is here,' said the orderly as she entered. Dunbar entered and the orderly backed out and closed the door. He approached the bed, where a painfully thin woman lay. Dunbar knew her to be forty-seven, but she looked twenty years older. Her face was etched with pain lines and her eyes seemed unnaturally large because of the hollowing of her cheeks.

'Mrs Barnes, I'm Steven Dunbar.'

'I don't know you,' said Sheila Barnes in a voice that didn't rise above a whisper.

'No, I'm afraid you don't,' he agreed, 'but I had to ask you about an allegation you made while you were a nursing sister at the Médic Ecosse Hospital.'

Sheila Barnes gave the tiniest snort of derision. 'After all this time?'

'Yes. I'm sorry, but something happened recently that makes these questions necessary. You maintained that a patient had been given the wrong organ in a transplant operation. Is that right?'

'There was no other explanation.'

'Was it a patient you were particularly fond of?' asked Dunbar.

Sheila Barnes shook her head slowly. 'No,' she said. 'He was a little shit, as I remember. Why are you asking me this now?'

Dunbar saw no point in telling her anything but the truth. He said, 'Because another nurse working there has made exactly the same allegation.'

Dunbar imagined he saw a sharpness appear in the big eyes. 'Has she now?' she said thoughtfully.

'A staff nurse in the transplant unit.'

'Did anyone listen to her?'

'She was dismissed.'

Sheila Barnes frowned and said, 'What are they doing in that place?'

'That's what I'm trying to find out,' said Dunbar. 'I'd like you to tell me all you remember about your patient.'

Sheila Barnes rested her head back on the pillow and let out a long sigh. She looked up at the ceiling in silence for a moment, then said, 'I can do better than that. Get my handbag. It's over there on the chest of drawers.'

Dunbar did as he was bid.

'You'll find a set of keys in the front.'

Dunbar found the keys.

'They're the keys to our house in Glasgow. I wrote everything down at the time. You may find that more useful than the suspect memory of a sick woman. Go there. Cyril and I won't be coming home. It's a black notebook. You'll find it in the right-hand dressing-table drawer in our bedroom.' She gave Dunbar the address.

'If that's what you want.'

Sheila Barnes fell back on her pillows again as if exhausted. 'One mix-up is possible, but two . . . ?' she said distantly.

SEVEN

Dunbar looked back at The Beeches as he closed the gate behind him. The meeting had seemed strange but that was often the way with people who were very ill and under heavy analgesia. They had an air of detachment about them which suggested wooziness but they often still retained a clarity of thought that was as sharp as a razor and could take you by surprise. Despite the travails of her illness, Sheila Barnes had struck him as an intelligent, down-to-earth woman and, like Lisa Fairfax, not at all the type given to hysterical outbursts. Another nail in the coffin of the 'neurotic nurse' theory.

But, he wondered as he got back into the car, did that help? As far as he could see, eliminating one possibility left two others. Either both nurses had been mistaken in their conclusions or – the least attractive scenario of all – both were right and if that were the case . . . God knows where that was going to lead him. He decided he would go round to the Barneses' house that evening and pick up Sheila's journal. Maybe that would help him get a better feel for what had really gone on at the time.

Sheila and Cyril Barnes had lived in a neat, tidy, white-painted bungalow in the Glasgow suburb of Bearsden. It was in darkness when Dunbar arrived but a security light clicked on and illuminated the path as he approached the front door, keys in hand. The curtains of the neighbouring house to the left moved and a man looked out. Dunbar ignored him and concentrated on opening the door; it was well secured.

When he stepped cautiously inside, fearing a burglar alarm he had not been warned about, he paused in the darkness for a moment before running his palm down the wall to find the light switch. The place smelt musty, but he supposed it had been empty for some time now and the windows, of course, had been kept closed. Feeling very much like an intruder, he walked slowly through the hall and found the living room. The silence and emptiness were almost tangible as he clicked on the light.

It was a comfortable room with a cottage-style suite covered in light-coloured floral material positioned round a stone fireplace and various small tables handy for receiving cups and saucers. A large television set sat silently gathering dust in an alcove by the window. Photographs occupied most of the flat surfaces and souvenirs from past holidays sat easily with them. From these Dunbar deduced that the Barneses had one son. A wedding photograph of Sheila and her husband took pride of place on the writing bureau, a graduation photograph on the mantelshelf. It was old, so Dunbar assumed the man was Cyril.

He went in search of the main bedroom and found the dressing table where he'd been told he'd find the journal. It looked solid – a family heirloom perhaps. The tall mirrors had a number of chips round their edges, a legacy of many removals, he guessed. The make-up items lying on a coloured glass tray struck him as poignant as he thought of Sheila's gaunt, pain-lined face. He opened the drawer and found the book where she had said it would be.

He had just sat down back in the living room to read it when the doorbell rang. It seemed uncommonly loud in the silence and made him jump. He answered it and found a short man with ginger hair and a moustache standing there. He was wearing a check shirt under a yellow cardigan, and brown flannels pulled well up over his midriff so that the belt nestled just below his chest. On his feet were sheepskin slippers, the kind you bought from craft centres on bus trips, and he was carrying a cardboard box.

'Yes?'

'Good evening. My name's Proudfoot,' said the stranger. 'I live next door.'

'Oh yes.'

'I saw you arrive. I was wondering if there was any news of Cyril and Sheila?'

'They're very ill,' replied Dunbar, suspecting that the man was really checking up on him. 'Sheila asked me to pick something up for her.'

'I see,' said Proudfoot uncertainly. 'Are you a relative, might I ask?'

'No.'

'I see, then that makes things a bit difficult . . .'

'What's on your mind, Mr Proudfoot?' asked Dunbar. The man obviously wanted something more than information.

'Actually, it's my camera,' said Proudfoot with some embarrassment.

'Your camera?'

'I hate being petty at a time like this, but Cyril was using my camera. His own was being repaired but it's back now. In fact, I've got it here. The postman brought it this morning.' He held up the cardboard box. 'I rather hoped I might have mine back.'

'I see,' said Dunbar. 'Why don't you come in? I'm sure Cyril wouldn't mind in the circumstances.'

'Thank you very much,' said Proudfoot, immediately relaxing and stepping inside.

'Do you know where it is?' asked Dunbar.

'Oh yes. Cyril keeps his photographic equipment in this little cupboard here.'

Proudfoot bent down and pulled open a small cupboard door to the left of the hearth. 'Here it is,' he announced, pulling out a leather camera case. 'I'll just put his back, though I don't know what he's going to say when he hears they didn't find anything wrong with it. He's been having problems with spoilt film. Three have come back completely fogged. It's been driving him up the wall.'

'Probably a defective batch.'

'I think he tried more than one,' said Proudfoot.

'You're both keen photographers, then?'

'It's our hobby. Birds mainly, but Cyril liked atmospheric stuff too, you know, derelict cranes in the old shipyards along the river, girders against the sky, twilight of an industry, that sort of thing. Maybe it had something to do with his illness, *sic transit gloria mundi* and all that.'

Dunbar nodded.

'We're planning a trip down the Clyde to Arran in the spring.'

'Sounds nice,' said Dunbar, but somehow he didn't think Cyril would be going.

Dunbar decided to take Sheila Barnes's journal back to the hotel. That way he could photocopy anything he thought relevant, and return the journal later in the week. He stopped on the way and bought a bottle of gin and a litre of tonic water. He had no wish to go out or to spend the remainder of the evening in the shallow fraternity of the hotel bar, but he did need something to take the edge off the day.

After a long shower, he wrapped himself in a dark-blue towelling robe and poured himself a drink. He placed it on the bedside table while he got comfortable on the bed and opened Sheila Barnes's journal. He had assumed that it would be a personal diary in which she mentioned the patient at the centre of her allegations but it proved to be much more comprehensive than that. She had kept notes about the progress of all the transplant patients she had nursed during her career. She had obviously been a dedicated, professional nurse, who cared deeply about the people in her charge, and they had played a major role in her life. There was genuine concern in the pages of her journal and it wasn't specific to any one patient.

When he came to the time when Kenneth Lineham's transplant had gone wrong, he could feel her involvement reach out to him from the page. The sudden rise in temperature leading to fever and delirium, the successive changes of immuno-suppression therapy which had proved ineffectual, the anguish of the boy's parents, the consultations with colleagues and the growing belief that her patient had been given an incompatible organ. Her initial reluctance to voice her fears and then the relief when she finally did. It was there in black and white and there was nothing hysterical about it.

After the boy's death, the journal recorded her bitter disappointment that her observations were not taken seriously and her anger at being considered neurotic. Her gradual disenchantment with the establishment became obvious as it closed ranks against her. There was a record of a subsequent meeting with a local journalist who seemed interested at first in what she had to say but then did not follow up with a story.

Dunbar was struck by the similarity between what Sheila Barnes had written and what Lisa Fairfax had told him the previous evening. It worried him; he couldn't dismiss it as coincidence. It wasn't just the end result that had been the same. The details struck him as being identical. He leaned his head back on the wall for a moment and looked up at the ceiling before continuing to read.

The operation on Kenneth Lineham had been performed by a Doctor Phillip Cunningham, James Ross's senior registrar at the time. According to Sheila Barnes, he had taken the boy's death badly, as had all the staff, and had even agreed with her privately that the severity of the rejection suggested that there was something wrong with the donor organ, but he had been reluctant to voice this openly at the time, preferring instead to accept the official view that it had just been one of those things. After all, the lab reports from both the donor's hospital and Médic Ecosse agreed that the organ was compatible, so there was nothing more to be said. He had a career to consider.

Sheila's journal went on to record her departure from Médic Ecosse, her fall into ill health, the subsequent diagnosis of her cancer and then her husband's and the full hell of radiotherapy and chemotherapeutic treatment. Dunbar felt exhausted when he finished reading. He now knew Sheila Barnes to be a woman worthy of respect and a credit to her profession. Despite her shoddy treatment at the hands of the Médic Ecosse authorities there was surprisingly little anger or bitterness against those who had chosen to ignore her allegations and who had dismissed her as a misguided neurotic. The only time she showed any signs of spleen was when she thought an Omega patient was getting more attention than her dying transplant boy. She wrote of 'mercenary toadies falling over themselves to chase the cheque-book'.

Dunbar closed the book and rubbed his fingers lightly over the cover for a few moments before getting up to pour himself another drink. He wondered what he was going to tell Sci-Med in his first report due at the end of the week. A couple of days ago, before he had met the two nurses, it would have been easy. He'd have reported that the nurses' allegations were probably without foundation. His own inspection of the set-up at Médic Ecosse had shown it to be a centre of medical excellence, well organized, well managed and under no pressure. It was just an unfortunate coincidence that two transplant patients had experienced fatal but non-specific rejection problems.

Now things had changed. He couldn't dismiss the nurses' claims as being neurotic or malicious or even, more kindly, as the result of over-involvement with their patients. His computer search for other such cases, and its failure to come up with any, was also a factor that had come back into play. He wouldn't be returning to London just yet. He would simply have to report that his investigations were continuing.

Ingrid was already in the office when Dunbar got in next morning. 'How was your afternoon?' she asked.

Dunbar looked at her inquiringly, then remembered telling her he was going to see the sights of Glasgow. 'Very interesting,' he replied.

'I'm afraid I couldn't get you an itemized costing for the Omega patients but I did manage to get some more information on what they were in for and when.'

'That was good of you. I'm obliged.' He took the file and slipped it into his briefcase.

'What's the plan for today?'

'I thought we might take a look at the figures for the Radiology Department. I thought the running costs were a bit high in proportion to patient charges.'

'You think patients should be charged more for their X-rays?' asked Ingrid.

'Or overheads should be cut. Maybe you could get a printout of staffing levels in Radiology and their rates of pay?'

'Of course. Anything else?'

'I'd like to take a look at the unit, get a feeling for the place, see what facilities they have. Would you contact the head of department and ask when would be a convenient time?'

'Will do.' She picked up the phone.

'Dr Svensen says any time you like,' she said a few minutes later. 'They've got the service engineers in this morning, so they won't be taking patients until this afternoon. You couldn't have picked a better time.'

'Good,' replied Dunbar.

'Want me to come with you?'

'I don't think so. Why don't you concentrate on getting the figures and I'll have a poke around on my own.'

Dunbar resolved to make the visit to Radiology take up most of the morning. He was running out of ideas to keep Ingrid occupied. There were several areas of the hospital he had not yet been to so he thought he would remedy this by taking a circuitous route to Radiology. He had wondered about a staircase leading down from the ground-floor corridor. There was no signboard nearby. As he walked along the ground-floor corridor on his way to Radiology, he decided to take the opportunity to find out where the stairs led.

Glancing over his shoulder to check that there was no one behind him, he turned off and ran lightly down the steps. He found himself facing double doors. He pushed one gently and it opened. There wasn't much in the way of light down here below ground level, so it took a moment or two to accustom his eyes to the gloom which was only occasionally relieved by overhead bulbs protected by wire cages. Leading off the narrow corridor, which seemed to run the entire length of the building, there were a number of doors. Dunbar tried them in turn.

The first three led to store-rooms, all of similar design and furnished with rows of metal shelving coded with an alpha-numeric system and bearing a variety of spares for medical equipment, along with a variety of consumer items in large cardboard boxes. The fourth door opened into a dark room which immediately struck Dunbar as being cold and damp. He recoiled slightly as he felt cold air brush his cheek. It was the hospital mortuary. There was no outward sign but the plain white walls, the simple wooden cross on one of them and the solid fridge door told Dunbar immediately. The small size puzzled him until he reminded himself that this was a private hospital – selected procedures for selected patients. People weren't supposed to die here. He released the clasp on the fridge door and swung it open. A waft of cold air chilled his face. There were only two body trays inside, a lower and an upper one, both unoccupied.

There was, however, an interesting-looking door to the right of the fridge. It didn't have a handle. He investigated and found a button to the right of the frame. He pressed it and the door slid open to reveal a lift. It was narrow and deep, designed to accommodate a horizontal coffin, he concluded. He checked the buttons inside; the lift went to all floors. He tried to work out in his mind where the mortuary was in relation to the building above, and concluded that it was at the back about two-thirds of the way along. He remembered seeing an anonymous-looking green door in about that position on the ground floor when he'd parked his car round the back.

It made sense. If you were unfortunate enough to die in Médic Ecosse, your body could be taken directly to the mortuary, using the custom elevator, instead of being wheeled along main corridors. You would lie in the fridge until the appointed undertakers came with a coffin for you, and, using the back door, your body could be removed with the minimum of public display.

Dunbar closed the mortuary door and continued along the corridor. More store-rooms, including one for gas cylinders. They stood in rows, secured to the wall by chain-link guards. He tried to remember the colour code for them but couldn't do better than a black body with a white top for oxygen. He supposed the others were anaesthetic gases. He had almost reached the far end of the corridor, hoping to find a way back up to the ground floor, when he came upon a closed set of double doors. He opened one and stepped into a small ante-room leading to an inner scrub room and another set of double doors. A number of plastic aprons were hanging on pegs and white Wellington boots stood in a row below. He pushed open one of the inner doors and found the light switch. Several fluorescent tubes stuttered into life. It was a post-mortem suite, tiled and smelling slightly of formalin and antiseptic.

Dunbar thought the table seemed unusually large. He approached it and ran his fingers along its smooth metallic surface and drainage channels leading down to the large stainless steel sink at the foot. There was a puzzling system of wheels and wires in the ceiling above it, but apart from that everything seemed normal. Trays of instruments sat on a long bench by the wall, gleaming knives and scalpels, saws and drills and a chain-mail glove used by pathologists to wear on their non-cutting hand to avoid accidental injury from the knife they were using. Dunbar shivered although it wasn't cold.

He found he was wrong in his assumption that there would be a way up to the ground floor at the far end of the corridor. There wasn't. He had to return the way he had come. He thought it odd but then supposed that having the PM suite at the far end meant that 'passing traffic' would hardly be welcome. As it was, very few people would have occasion to visit that end of the corridor. Dunbar was thinking about this when a door to his left suddenly opened and startled him. The orderly who emerged from the store-room pushing a trolley was equally surprised.

'Who are you?' stammered the man. 'What are you doing down here?'

'I was curious,' replied Dunbar. He showed the man his ID.

'Oh right, I heard about you. The government busybo – inspector, right?'

'Something like that. And you are?' said Dunbar.

'Name's Johnson. I'm one of the porters. I've been picking up some equipment.'

'Like working here?'

'Money's better than what I was getting. It'll do me.'

Dunbar noticed the symbol on the side of the cardboard boxes on Johnson's trolley. It was a wine glass.

'Wine glasses?' he asked.

'For the PR party tomorrow.'

'What's that all about?'

'The press have been invited to see the little girl they operated on, the one they took on for free.'

'Oh I see.'

'I guess she can't insist on confidentiality like the others,' said Johnson.

'I suppose not,' agreed Dunbar. It was something he hadn't considered. They had come to the parting of the ways. Johnson stopped outside the mortuary door. 'I'm going to use the lift in here,' he said. 'How about you?'

'I'll take the stairs. You and the trolley will just about fill it.'

As soon as the words were out, Dunbar regretted them. He had just admitted to knowing about the lift and its size. That was tantamount to admitting he had been snooping around earlier. He thought he saw a questioning look in Johnson's eyes but that could have been just his imagination. After all, he was known to be an inspector. He was expected to be nosey. The problem might come when people compared notes and wondered what he was doing in the basement when he had told Ingrid he was going to Radiology.

Dunbar paused for a moment at the head of the stairs, wondering whether or not he should go on with his plan to take a look at the second floor or go directly on to Radiology. 'In for a penny,' he decided and walked briskly along to the main stairs. He ran up the steps to the first floor and the signs announcing the transplant unit, then walked up the next flight.

'OBSTETRICS AND GYNAECOLOGY', said the sign at the head of the stairs. Dunbar suddenly had the feeling that this was as far as he was going to get. Two Arab gentlemen sitting on chairs outside the entrance doors rose to their feet and barred the way.

Dunbar showed his ID card and one of them examined it in some detail before handing it back with a shake of the head. Faced with the two unsmiling faces in front of him and the thought of what they might be carrying inside their jackets, he shrugged and retreated downstairs. It was obviously time to visit Radiology.

Erland Svensen was a man who took life seriously, as became painfully apparent to Dunbar over the course of the next hour. The tall, fair-haired, lantern-jawed Dane was completely devoid of anything resembling a sense of humour. When Dunbar attempted to lighten the atmosphere with a joke, he simply looked blank for a few seconds, then continued his monologue on his sole interest in life, radiology. Having been warned that Dunbar would be visiting his department he had assembled facts and figures on all items of equipment in his department and proceded to justify them in comparison with rival systems by subjecting Dunbar to an in-depth technical appraisal of their relative performance figures.

When Svensen finally had to stop for breath, Dunbar quickly interjected, 'That all makes perfect sense to me, Doctor.'

The comment seemed to take the wind out of Svensen's sails. He had obviously expected some kind of cost-cutting argument from Dunbar and was surprised when none materialized.

'It does?'

'Of course. You're obviously a man who knows his job inside out. The patients expect the best and they're getting it. As long as they're being charged enough for your excellent services, I'll be happy.'

'I don't work out the charges,' said Svensen weakly. 'Mr Giordano's office deals with that.'

'I thought that might be the case.'

'Would you like to meet the staff while you're here?'

'I certainly would,' replied Dunbar. Anything would be better than more technical details of X-ray machinery.

'I have two radiographers and a dark-room assistant,' said Svensen, leading the way out of his office.

Dunbar had a bet with himself that the radiographers would be glamorous young women.

'Girls, I'd like you to meet Dr Steven Dunbar,' said Svensen as they entered the main X-ray suite. 'This is Melissa Timpson and Annabel Waters.'

Dunbar stepped forward to shake hands with two glamorous young women. His smile was as much about winning the bet as it was about social nicety. What was it, he wondered, that attracted women who looked as if they belonged on a yacht in the Med to become radiographers? Once before, when he had wondered this aloud, his girlfriend at the time had offered the cynical opinion, 'The plan is to marry a doctor. It's either that or become a trolley-dolly and hit on a pilot.'

Melissa and Annabel had been talking to the service engineer about some problem with one of the machines. Dunbar decided to let them get back to it, rather than do a bad impression of a member of the royal family asking questions for the sake of it. 'What's through here?' he asked Svensen, moving towards an exit route.

'This is my pride and joy,' replied Svensen breaking into a smile that boded ill, thought Dunbar. He was about to get enthusiastic again.

'A small tumour radiation facility,' announced Svensen. 'A brand-new development in the treatment of such tumours.'

'What's special about it?' asked Dunbar with some trepidation.

'I'll show you,' replied Svensen. 'Come, put this on.' He handed Dunbar a protective apron and put one on himself. 'Not that we need it with this machine, but rules have to be obeyed.'

Svensen put an X-ray plate on the table beneath the front lens of the radiation head and then put a radiation-detection meter very close to it. He used a tungsten light source in the head to align the target and then said, 'Do you see how close the light circle is to the meter?'

'Yes.'

'Watch the meter.'

Dunbar looked at the needle but it didn't move when Svensen triggered the radiation source. 'Nothing happened,' he said.

'Exactly,' said Svensen triumphantly. 'This machine is so well focused we can hit the tumour without fear of damaging the surrounding tissue. We can use higher doses than before and there's much less risk to the patient.'

'Oh, I see,' said Dunbar, getting the point of such a negative display.

Svensen walked across the room to where an illuminated sign said, DARK ROOM KEEP OUT. He pressed the button of an intercom on the wall and said into it, 'Run this one through for me, Colin, would you?'

There was a two-way wall safe next to the door. Svensen pulled the handle of the metal door and it opened a few inches at the top. He slipped the X-ray cassette into it and closed it firmly with a metallic clunk. 'Won't be long,' he said to Dunbar.

A buzzer announced the return of the film and Svensen collected it from the wall safe. He held it up in triumph. 'Now then, what d'you think of that?'

Dunbar took the film from him and saw an almost perfectly edged circle where the film had been exposed to the radiation. The area around it was totally unexposed. 'Remarkable,' he said, handing the film back. 'I'm most impressed.'

Svensen held the film up again and marvelled at it. 'Hot damn, this is a good machine,' he enthused. 'Here! Keep it as a souvenir.'

Dunbar accepted the film and smiled at the man's total immersion in his job. He thanked him for showing him around.

'Any time,' smiled Svensen.

* * *

'A good morning?' asked Ingrid when Dunbar returned to his office.

'Dr Svensen's certainly very knowledgeable,' he replied.

She signified her understanding with her superior little smile. 'He's certainly that,' she agreed. 'I've got the figures you asked for.'

'Good.'

'And an invitation too.'

Dunbar raised his eyebrows.

'There's going to be a press conference and photo opportunity followed by a reception for the NHS patient who had the jaw-realignment surgery with us.'

'Before and after pictures,' said Dunbar.

'They're quite dramatic, I believe,' said Ingrid. 'All good publicity for the hospital I think you'll agree.'

'It's certainly that. I only hope she doesn't mind being a circus animal for the afternoon.'

'A small price to pay,' said Ingrid. 'Her whole life will be changed by the work of the surgeons here.'

'You're right,' smiled Dunbar. But he suspected that the patient had been selected because she would provide dramatic publicity in return for some relatively simple surgery, and that she'd taken precedence over more difficult patients who wouldn't have provided the same photo opportunity. He wondered just how much the scheme was going to benefit patients chosen for free referral and had the depressing thought that it might all be just window-dressing. There was no doubt that the specialist skills and equipment of Médic Ecosse could be used on occasion to great effect in the treatment of difficult NHS cases, but would that be how it worked? Or would Médic Ecosse go for the safe option every time? He wondered if there might be a way of investigating precedent and getting an indication from that.

'Who has the final say in selecting patients for the free treatment scheme?' he asked.

'A committee of three. Dr Kinscherf, Mr Giordano and the head of the department concerned,' replied Ingrid. 'Why d'you ask?'

'Just interested. As I understand it, the hospital has taken on a few NHS patients for free in the past. Do you think you could get me a list and information about what treatment they had?'

Ingrid obviously wondered how this could possibly interest someone employed to monitor financial dealings, but she merely said, 'I'll see what I can do.'

Dunbar knew well that he had no business asking for this information. It was plain curiosity on his part and perhaps the thought that even if his other inquiries came to nought he could at least bring the failings of the free referral scheme – if that's what they turned out to be – to someone's attention at the Scottish Office.

EIGHT

Clive Turner was looking forward to coming off duty after a ten-hour shift at the Children's Hospital when he was called to the phone. It was Leo Giordano at Médic Ecosse.

'Dr Turner? I have some good news for you. Dr Kinscherf and Dr Ross have agreed to take on the Chapman girl as a patient.'

'That's not good news; that's wonderful news,' exclaimed Turner. 'I had to tell her parents earlier that neither of them would be suitable as a donor. They were pre-warned, of course, but it's never easy to hear things you don't want to. I honestly didn't think there was much chance of you taking Amanda on.'

'Frankly, I didn't hold out much hope either but your eloquence won the day. I told Ross and Kinscherf what you said about these folks deserving some kind of a break and I guess they agreed with you!'

'I'm absolutely delighted,' said Turner. 'I'm sure her parents will be too. Where do we go from here?'

'Well, there is one obstacle left to clear, I'm afraid.'

'What's that?'

'You may have heard that we were recently subject to a review by government officials.'

'I remember.'

'We got agreement over finances but part of the agreement was that we should have one of their people on site to see that we weren't wasting public money on champagne and caviar as we private hospitals are prone to do.'

Turner chuckled.

'I think we're going to have to clear it with this guy first, or maybe you'd like to approach him yourself to plead your case? Like we said, transplants are expensive so we're talking serious altruism here. This guy's name is Dr Steven Dunbar. I can give you the number of his office here at the hospital if you like. What do you think?'

'I'll do it,' said Turner. He wrote down the number and asked, 'Do you think this will be a real problem?'

'Frankly, I've no idea but you can tell him we've all agreed to it. Maybe that'll help to put some pressure on him.'

'Good idea,' said Turner. 'And if he says yes?'

'We can admit her on Friday. That gives us both time to get the paperwork in order.'

'Sounds good to me.'

'There is one thing,' said Giordano with a note of caution in his voice.

'Yes?'

'We'd be happy if there wasn't any publicity over this one.'

Turner was slightly taken aback. 'But this is a wonderfully generous gesture on your part,' he said. 'I thought you'd be only too happy to get some good press out of it. You deserve it!'

'Thanks, but the truth is this kid is pretty sick by all accounts and it's always in the lap of the gods whether a suitable organ will come along in time. The public like instant success or they get bored, so we'd appreciate it if this particular freebie could be kept among ourselves.'

'Of course, if that's what you'd prefer,' said Turner.

'Good,' said Giordano. 'Don't get me wrong. If a kidney becomes available, then the kid's chances will be as good as any other patient's. It's just that if there should be a long delay and she's stuck with the tissue-degradation problem, then we'd hate to have a really public failure on our hands. That's not going to do any of us any good.'

'Understood,' said Turner.

'I take it she's already on the transplant register?'

'Yes.'

'Then it'll just be a case of changing patient location details. If you can give me her registration number I'll get one of the secretaries to post the update.'

'I can give you that right now,' said Turner, opening the folder that sat by the computer terminal on his desk.

'Shoot.'

Turner read out the number and Giordano read it back to him.

'Good. So it's all down to Dr Dunbar. If he plays ball we'll expect her on Friday, barring any unforeseen complications.'

'On Friday, and thanks again. I'm sure I speak for everyone concerned when I say we're all very grateful.'

'You're welcome.'

Turner put the phone down and looked at the number on the paper in front of him. One more hurdle, just one more. A bloody government official! But at least he was a doctor. He couldn't decide whether that was good or bad. He picked up the phone and dialled the number.

'I'd like to speak to Dr Steven Dunbar, please.'

The call was answered at the first ring.

'Dr Dunbar? My name is Clive Turner. I'm a doctor in the renal unit at Glasgow's Children's Hospital.'

'What can I do for you, Doctor?'

Turner went through Amanda Chapman's case history and how her chances of survival were slim, if she didn't at least become stable on dialysis soon, and perhaps negligible in the long run, if she didn't receive a transplant.

'I see.'

'Dr Ross has agreed to take Amanda on in his unit as a free NHS referral and Dr Kinscherf and Mr Giordano have also agreed, but they referred me to you as the final arbiter.'

'I see,' replied Dunbar. He was totally unprepared for something like this. He'd received no warning but could understand why not. It would be much easier for him to turn down a request from the hospital authorities. Hearing it from Turner was almost as effective as hearing it from the child's parents. He now had a dilemma. If he was who he was supposed to be, he should certainly be objecting on the grounds of cost, but he wasn't. He, as a person, thought the kid should have every chance that was open to her. 'It's all right by me, Dr Turner,' he said.

'You're serious?' Turner spluttered, taken off guard. He had been preparing himself for a long desperate argument.

'I wish her well,' said Dunbar.

'I can't thank you enough. I'll never hear another word against civil servants.'

'Then it's all been worth while,' said Dunbar with a smile and put down the phone.

Turner was delighted. This was wonderful news and couldn't have come at a better time. Amanda Chapman was not doing well. Continual dialysis was taking its toll on her youthful resilience and she was beginning to weaken mentally. Once that started, there was a real chance that she would go into a downward spiral and the end would come quickly.

The patient's mental state was often underrated in serious illness. A strong, positive attitude – the will to live – was often the difference between life and death in Turner's experience. He'd seen kids put up such a fight that it brought tears to his eyes when they eventually lost. He'd also seen children drift away seemingly without so much as a backward glance. Amanda was coming to crisis point. It could go either way.

Her illness had taken its toll on her parents too. He had seen stress and tiredness affect them both more and more over the past few weeks. They had aged visibly. He found their phone number from Amanda's admission card and called it.

A woman's voice said, 'Yes?'

'Kate? It's Clive Turner at Amanda's hospital in Glasgow.'

'Has something happened? What's wrong? It's Amanda, she's—'

'It's nothing awful, Kate, I assure you,' Turner interrupted. 'Far from it. I've just had a call from the Médic Ecosse Hospital. They've agreed to take Amanda on as a patient.'

'They have? Oh my God, that's wonderful! We've been so

worried about her. I was just saying to Sandy last night that she's been getting weaker over the past few days.'

'I think that might well change when Médic Ecosse put her on their dialysis machinery,' said Turner. 'No one can promise anything but it's my guess she's going to do a whole lot better. If they do manage to stabilize her, it will be back to waiting and hoping for a kidney to become available, but at least she'll have more time.'

Turner heard Kate start to sob at the other end of the line. 'I know,' he soothed. 'This kind of worry eats away at you until you are under so much tension that it takes over your entire life and you don't even realize it until you suddenly burst into tears.'

'That's it exactly,' said Kate, regaining her composure. 'I can't thank you enough, Clive. You were the one who thought of this in the first place.'

'It was just by chance I'd seen the circular from the Scottish Office that morning.'

'When will she be moved?'

'Friday, if everyone's agreeable.'

'The sooner the better,' said Kate. 'I can't wait to tell Sandy. He's on duty tonight.'

'I'll let you do just that then,' said Turner. 'Give me a call tomorrow and we can finalize the arrangements.'

Kate put the phone down and sank into a chair. It was as if all strength had left her. She cradled her head in her hands for a few moments, staring down at the floor. Please God, this would be the turning-point in their nightmare. From now on things would start to get better. They'd get back to being the happy family they'd been before all this happened. Laughter would return to their lives. Feeling suddenly more resolute, she picked up the phone again and called Sandy.

The rain on Friday morning could do nothing to dampen the optimism that filled the Chapman home in the wake of Clive Turner's phone call. The silent and preoccupied looking out of the window at breakfast time, which had been the norm for the past few weeks, was now a thing of the past. Smiles and animated conversation were the order of the day. This was the lucky break they had both been praying for. They would still have to wait for a suitable organ to become available for Amanda but for some reason they now both felt sure it would. They had come to a turning-point in the nightmare.

'What time did you say we're supposed to be there?' asked Sandy as he got up from the table to fetch the coffee pot from the hob.

'Clive said if we're there about two we can take her over ourselves. That would be nicer than travelling in an ambulance, don't you think?'

'Absolutely,' agreed Sandy. 'The three of us together again.' He gave Kate's shoulder a squeeze as he returned to his seat and re-filled their cups.

'Shall I make more toast?'

Sandy shook his head. 'Let's stop off on the way up to Glasgow for a pub lunch somewhere. What d'you say?'

'Sounds good,' agreed Kate. 'It's ages since we did anything like that.'

The good mood persisted throughout the journey. The lunch they had at a roadhouse just off the main dual carriageway wasn't wonderful but it was adequate, and the fact that they were doing something socially together seemed more important than the ordinariness of the fare. Apart from that, it gave them the chance to joke about Scottish culinary skills.

They had the usual problem in finding somewhere to park when they reached the hospital, but today it didn't seem important. Sandy didn't seize on it, as he usually did, as an excuse to vent pent-up emotion as anger.

Clive Turner saw them as they entered the ward and gestured to them to come into the office first.

'How is she?' asked Sandy.

'She's fine,' replied Turner. 'She came off dialysis an hour ago so she'll be okay for a wee while yet.'

'Plenty of time to get over to Médic Ecosse?' said Kate.

'Oh, more than that,' replied Turner. 'She'll be stable for several hours. You can take her for a drive around if you like. Spend some time together. Be a family again.'

'Do you think she's up to it?' asked Kate.

'She's tired of course, but I think she'd like to see something other than hospital walls for a while. She's not up to doing anything strenuous but a bit of visual stimulation will do her nothing but good.'

'Won't Médic Ecosse be expecting us?' asked Sandy.

'I spoke to them earlier. They're aware of the situation. Any time before six suits them.'

'That was very kind,' said Kate. 'We owe you a lot.'

'Not at all,' said Turner. 'I only hope it works out well for you. You deserve a bit of luck.'

'Thanks,' said Sandy, shaking Turner's hand. They went through to the ward and found Amanda being dressed by one of the nurses.

'I'll do that,' said Kate, taking over with a smile. 'It's not often I get the chance these days.'

Sandy went off to get the car while Kate finished dressing Amanda. He was parked in one of the ambulance bays when Kate emerged, holding the door open for Clive Turner, who was carrying Amanda. Kate and Amanda got into the back of Esmeralda and they left the hospital with much hand-waving from the back window.

'Dr Turner says you can have an ice cream this afternoon,' said Kate to Amanda as she cuddled her. 'Will that be nice?'

Sandy positioned the rear-view mirror so he could watch Amanda's response. She gave a slight nod and managed a frail smile. Sandy swallowed. She was very weak. 'I know where we can get the best ice cream in the city,' he said.

'Let me guess,' said Kate. 'Danielli's?'

'Give that woman a coconut,' said Sandy. 'We're going to get the biggest cones Mr Danielli can manage.'

Amanda made a brave attempt at eating hers but quickly lost

interest, preferring instead to cuddle against her mother on the back seat. Sandy's eyes asked the question, what next? Kate shrugged and stroked Amanda's hair. 'We could go and see the ducks in the park?'

This idea appealed to Amanda, who nodded with something approaching enthusiasm.

'Right,' said Sandy. 'First we'll buy some bread.'

They stopped at a bakery on the way to the park and Sandy bought half a dozen bread rolls. Amanda and Kate were given the task of tearing them up into beak-sized pieces while Sandy drove them round to the park and parked Esmeralda by the edge of the pond.

Kate and Amanda stayed in the car – they didn't want Amanda to catch a chill – while Sandy got out and drew an audience of ducks with the bread. He started edging backwards, laying a trail that brought the ducks towards the car, Pied Piper-fashion. When they were close enough, Kate opened the window and she and Amanda fed them from the window. Sandy watched from the side. More than anything he wanted to hear Amanda laugh; it had been so long since he'd heard the sound. But it wasn't to be. Amanda dropped breadcrumbs slowly and deliberately and watched the ducks squabble briefly over each offering, but the look in her eyes suggested she was far away.

By four o'clock Amanda was showing signs of sleepiness and Kate said quietly, 'Maybe we should think about taking her over?'

Sandy nodded and started the car. They were at Médic Ecosse within fifteen minutes.

'Did Clive Turner give us any paperwork?' asked Sandy as he parked in the visitors' bay at the hospital.

'I don't think so,' replied Kate. 'I thought all that had been dealt with.'

'Hope you're right,' said Sandy. He was anticipating having to explain to a succession of staff members just who they were and why they were there. He was proved wrong almost as soon as they'd entered.

'Mr and Mrs Chapman?' said the receptionist with a smile. 'And Amanda. We've been expecting you. I'll just call Dr Ross. He'll be down directly. Why don't you make yourselves comfortable over there.'

She indicated a comfortably furnished waiting area.

Kate sat down with Amanda on her knee; Sandy sat opposite. Amanda was sucking her thumb as she always did when she was tired. She looked at the box of toys put there to keep waiting children amused, but displayed no real interest. Her eyes still had the distant look that brought a lump to his throat. Amanda turned to look at her father and he smiled quickly to hide his sadness. 'Dr Ross will be here soon, Princess,' he said. 'He's going to make you all better. I promise.'

Amanda continued sucking her thumb.

James Ross appeared, accompanied by Thomas Kinscherf and two nurses. He came over to the Chapmans and introduced himself. His outgoing friendliness immediately put Sandy and Kate at their ease.

'And this is the little lady who's not been well,' said Ross, going down on one knee to take Amanda's hand and give it a little squeeze. 'Well, we'll see about that, won't we? We've got a surprise for you. Do you like surprises?'

Amanda, thumb still in mouth, nodded.

'Good,' said Ross. He turned to one of the nurses, who handed him a gift-wrapped parcel which he in turn handed to Amanda. 'This is for you. Shall I help you open it?'

Amanda nodded again and Ross tore away the paper to reveal a fluffy toy rabbit. 'This is Albert. What d'you think?' he asked.

Amanda took her thumb from her mouth and smiled broadly as she took the toy. It was infectious. They all smiled.

'That was very kind,' said Kate. Sandy nodded his agreement.

'Not at all,' said Ross. 'We do this for all our young patients.'

Sandy started to remind him that they were not paying customers but Kinscherf stopped him almost immediately. He held up his hand and said, 'As far as we are concerned, Amanda is our patient

114

and will be treated exactly as any other of our patients. All our people deserve and get the best.'

'Thank you,' said Sandy.

'I think we should see about getting this young lady admitted, don't you, Nurse?' said Ross.

One of the nurses stepped forward and took Amanda gently from her mother. There was a moment when it looked as if Amanda was going to protest loudly but Ross said quickly, 'Don't worry. Mummy is coming along too. Shall we move?'

Everyone walked over to the lift, which took them up to the transplant unit. There, Kate and Sandy were ushered out last by the nurse who had been detailed to look after them while her colleague took care of Amanda. She made small-talk about the weather as they followed Ross and Kinscherf along the corridor.

'Here we are,' said Ross. 'This is Amanda's room.'

Kate and Sandy broke into smiles as they entered. The room looked as if it had been specially designed for a little girl of Amanda's age. Characters from *Alice in Wonderland* and *Winnie the Pooh* lined the walls in friendly profusion. A number of dolls and cuddly toys were arranged around the room, making a link between reality and the characters on the walls. A giant doll's house stood in the corner beside the bed.

Ross turned to Amanda and said, 'Mummy and Daddy and I are going to have a little chat next door while Nurse gets you ready for bed. We'll come back in a few minutes, I promise. Will that be all right?'

Amanda nodded and Kate and Sandy smiled at how quickly she had succumbed to Ross's obvious way with children. They followed Ross along to his office and sat on two leather chairs in front of his desk while he opened Amanda's case notes.

'We'll get her on to dialysis this evening and then see how she does before we go any further,' said Ross. 'The important thing will be to try to get her into a stable condition so we can establish a routine for her instead of constantly altering dialysis times and schedules. If we can do that, she'll settle down and her general level

of fitness will improve. There's also the problem of tissue degradation to deal with, but first things first, eh?'

'Absolutely,' said Kate.

'But a word of caution. Our colleagues at the Children's Hospital
didn't manage to succeed and I can't promise anything either,' said
Ross. 'We'll do our best, but a transplant is still Amanda's best
option. It may be her only one but that, as you know, is outside
our control.'

'We understand,' said Sandy.

'Good.'

'About visiting, Doctor,' began Kate.

'Any time you like,' said Ross. 'And any time you feel like staying
over, that's quite all right too. You may stay as our guests.'

'That's good to know,' said Kate.

'I suggest that you don't stay tonight, however. We'd like Amanda
to get used to us. It's important that we gain her trust. Don't worry,
we'll look after her.'

'I'm sure you will,' said Kate. 'Thank you, Doctor. We're most
grateful.'

Kate and Sandy returned to Amanda's room to find her in her
pyjamas, listening to the nurse, who was explaining the ins and
outs of the doll's house to her.

'There's a little switch at the back here that makes the lights go
on. See?'

The windows of the doll's house lit up and Amanda grinned.
She looked up at her mother and father and then back at the
doll's house, as if a little embarrassed at being so outwardly
pleased.

Sandy and Kate exchanged glances and smiled.

'Would you like Daddy to build you one of these for when you
come home?' asked Sandy, although there was little doubt about
the answer. Amanda nodded and cuddled down into her pillow.
Sandy knelt down beside her. 'It's a deal then,' he said. 'You be a
good girl and do what the doctors and nurses tell you and I'll
build you the best doll's house you ever saw.'

'Will it have lights?' asked Amanda.

'In every room,' said Sandy and kissed her lightly on the forehead. Amanda put her thumb in her mouth.

'She's tired,' said Kate, taking Sandy's place beside her and stroking her hair back from her forehead. 'Mummy and Daddy are going to go now, but we'll see you tomorrow. Be good.'

'Don't worry,' said the nurse, seeing the vulnerable look that appeared in Kate's eyes as she got up, 'we'll look after her.'

Outside the door Sandy put his arm round Kate's shoulders. 'Hey, come on,' he said. 'This is the start of better things, remember?'

Kate squeezed his hand. 'You're right,' she said. 'It's just that sometimes she looks so small. She's really just a baby and she's had such a lot to put up with.'

'She'll come through,' said Sandy. 'You'll see.'

'God, I hope so,' said Kate dabbing at her eyes with a crumpled tissue she'd extracted from her handbag. She sniffed deeply, then straightened her shoulders and said, 'Come on, let's go.'

Outside in the car park Sandy stopped abruptly as they neared Esmeralda.

'What's wrong?' asked Kate.

'Do you get the impression that we may be ever so slightly . . . out of place?'

Kate looked puzzled; then she saw what he meant. Esmeralda was flanked by a Mercedes saloon on one side and a BMW coupé on the other. 'Oh dear,' she said. 'I fear you may be right.' A quick glance around showed few of the cars were over two years old and most were top marques.

Sandy held the door open for her and put on his butler's voice. 'If Modom would care to enter?'

'Idiot,' smiled Kate and got in.

Sandy turned the ignition key, but nothing happened save for a clicking sound. 'Shit,' he said.

'You're kidding,' said Kate.

''Fraid not,' said Sandy with a grimace. 'Esy's doing the dirty on us.'

'She knows how to pick her moments,' said Kate glancing over her shoulder. 'Any idea what the problem is?'

'The solenoid's engaging but the starter motor isn't turning. Maybe it's jammed.'

'Can you fix it?'

'Can a bird fly?' Sandy opened his door and got out. Kate waited patiently while he disappeared under the open bonnet. Various swear words told her that work was in progress. The car rocked a little.

'Give it a try, Kate.'

She moved into the driving seat and turned the key. There was a solitary click, followed by a curse from under the bonnet.

'No luck?' asked Kate with slight trepidation.

'The battery's flat. We'll have to bump-start her.'

Kate let off the handbrake and took hold of the steering wheel, while Sandy pushed the car backwards out of its slot. 'Ready?' he asked, going round to the back of the car to begin pushing.

'Ready.'

The car park was flat, so there was no convenient gradient to make use of. Sandy found it hard work getting some momentum into Esmeralda. 'Right!' he said lifting his hands off the boot and straightening up. Kate let up the clutch and the car jerked to a halt, showing no interest in starting.

'Right, we'll try again,' said Sandy.

'Can I help?' said a male voice at Sandy's shoulder.

Sandy turned to find a tall, dark-haired man standing there.

'She seems a bit reluctant,' the stranger went on.

'I don't understand it,' said Sandy. 'She can't be that cold. She's only been parked for half an hour and the battery goes flat.'

The two men gave Esmeralda a good shove and built up more momentum than the time before. 'Right!' yelled Sandy.

Once again Esmeralda jerked, then lurched to a halt in mechanical silence.

'Third time lucky,' said the stranger, resting his hands on the boot again.

Sandy nodded, then suddenly looked up as if he'd had an idea and said, 'Kate?'

'Yes?' came the reply.

'You have got the ignition on, haven't you?'

There was a long pause before a small voice said, 'Sorry.'

Sandy and the stranger smiled at each other and gave Esmeralda another shove. This time her engine came to life when Kate let up the clutch, and Kate drove her round the square while Sandy thanked the stranger for his help.

'Not at all. Been visiting one of the patients?'

'Our daughter's just been admitted to the transplant unit.'

'That'll be Dr Ross's unit.'

'Then you work here?' said Sandy. 'A doctor?'

'Sort of.' The man held out his hand and said, 'Steven Dunbar.'

'Sandy Chapman. That's my wife, Kate, just starting lap two in the green Williams Renault, known to us as Esmeralda.'

Dunbar at once recognized the name 'Chapman' from his conversation with Clive Turner, and smiled.

Esmeralda came slowly past with Kate looking anxiously out of the window. 'When can I stop?' she asked.

Both men laughed at the look of mock anguish on her face.

'Any time,' replied Sandy. 'Just don't stall the engine.'

She brought Esmeralda to a halt and listened to the idle speed for a moment. Satisfied that it was steady enough, she got out and joined Sandy.

'Kate, this is Dr Dunbar.'

'Hello,' said Dunbar. 'I'm not really a doctor here – more of a civil servant. I look after the government's financial involvement in the hospital.'

'Sounds interesting,' said Kate politely.

'Then you wouldn't have been too keen on taking our Amanda on for free?' suggested Sandy.

'On the contrary, I'm delighted we have,' said Dunbar.

'Thanks for the push,' said Sandy.

'Don't mention it,' said Dunbar.

He watched as Kate and Sandy got into Esmeralda and drove off, waving to them as they disappeared out of the gate. He was glad he had okayed their daughter's admission. He must have misjudged Médic Ecosse's referral policy when he suspected that they were taking only straightforward 'show-business' cases to use for self-promotion.

There was one strange thing though. He'd just come from the press reception for the jaw-operation patient, and at it there had been no mention of the hospital taking on a free NHS transplant case. Why not? Why miss the opportunity to gain some good publicity?

The reception hadn't been as bad as he'd feared. The patient was an ordinary girl from the local area, who hadn't suspected for a moment that she was being exploited. She seemed to enjoy being the centre of attention, turning this way and that at the request of the photographers, posing with the staff and with the local councillor for the area, who had seized on the occasion to make political capital. Dunbar remembered him. He was the Labour councillor who had taken every opportunity to express his opposition to private medicine at the meeting between the Scottish Office and the hospital. Now here he was, smiling into the cameras with his arm round the star patient, doing his best to create the impression that he had been the prime mover in the whole affair.

None of this made Dunbar angry because, as Ingrid had said, the bottom line was sound enough and the bottom line was that the girl had been given a new and better life because of the operation. The hospital was going to get some positive publicity that would do no one any harm and if a local politician grabbed the chance to promote his own interests, what the hell? That's what politicians did. That was the way the world worked. Nature abhorred a missed opportunity in the world of self-interest.

That was why it was so surprising that there had been no mention of the Chapman girl. A transplant was a much bigger deal than the relatively minor jaw surgery they had just been celebrating. He'd ask Ingrid about it after the weekend. In the meantime, he was going to drive over to Bearsden to return Sheila Barnes's journal.

He was almost halfway there when he started to have doubts. Was there any point in returning the journal to the house, when it seemed certain that neither Sheila nor her husband would ever return there? On the other hand, he would feel guilty about hanging on to it. It was far more than just a diary of events; it said so much about the woman herself. He decided that he'd return it to Sheila in person. He'd take it down to Helensburgh at the weekend and tell her how useful it had been.

As he headed back to town, he found himself thinking about Lisa Fairfax. He really should have told her about Sheila Barnes – who she was and what she'd claimed. But he was so used to telling people nothing more than they needed to know that he'd kept quiet. But the knowledge that someone else had made the same allegation as she had about Médic Ecosse would have been a comfort, and if anyone deserved to feel better Lisa did. She didn't have much of a life with no job and being at the constant beck and call of a deranged mother. On impulse, he drove over to her flat and pushed the entryphone button.

'Yes?'

'It's Steven Dunbar. Can I come up?'

'I suppose so,' answered Lisa a little uncertainly.

The door lock was released and Dunbar climbed quickly to the third floor.

'I didn't expect to see you again,' said Lisa, ushering him inside.

Dunbar looked to right and left as he entered the hall.

'She's asleep,' said Lisa.

'I was passing,' he lied. 'There's something I didn't tell you the other day that I think I should have. Something about Sheila Barnes.'

'Sheila Barnes?' repeated Lisa. 'She's the nursing sister you asked me about. You wondered if I knew her.'

'That's right. She left well before you started at Médic Ecosse, but what I didn't tell you was that she had a very similar experience to yours. She said much the same thing about a patient who died in the transplant unit in her time.'

Lisa looked at him as if trying to decide whether or not she should be annoyed at not having heard this before. 'You mean I wasn't the only one?'

'No, you weren't,' confessed Dunbar. 'That's really why I was sent up here to Scotland. There were two of you who maintained that patients had been given the wrong organ in transplant operations.'

'Did they treat her like an idiot too?'

'No one took her seriously either,' agreed Dunbar. 'Unfortunately, both she and her husband are suffering from cancer. She's dying. I went to see her in the hospice she's in, down in Helensburgh.' He explained about the journal. 'She wanted me to see the entries she made at the time of the incident.'

'Did you learn much?'

'They were very detailed. In the end I was struck by how similar her version of events was to yours.'

'So you might even believe us?'

'I'm finding it difficult not to.'

'Good. Did you say Sheila's husband had cancer too?'

'He's in the same hospice.'

'How strange, and what rotten luck. I hope they're able to comfort each other.'

Dunbar silently acknowledged a nice thought.

Lisa got up and turned down the heat on the electric fire. 'Don't you ever miss being a practising doctor?' she asked.

'Not a bit. I didn't really like it, I had no feel for it, I gave it up. Simple as that.'

She smiled. 'What a remarkably honest thing to do. I've known lots of doctors who have no feel for it but giving it up is the last thing on their minds. They'll be hanging in there till it's carriage-clock time with a vote of thanks from the poor sods who managed to survive their ministrations.'

'It's hard to escape once you've started,' said Dunbar.

'Maybe,' agreed Lisa. 'Would you like a drink?'

He nodded. 'I would. It's been a long day.'

Lisa poured them both gin and tonic, handed one to Dunbar, then sat down again.

'Why did you really come here?' she asked with sudden directness.

The question took him aback. 'To tell you about Sheila Barnes. I thought you had a right to know.'

'But I don't have a right,' said Lisa. 'You were under no obligation at all to tell me, so why did you?'

'I thought you should know anyway,' said Dunbar. It sounded weak, even to him.

'Was it pity? Pity for my situation?'

'I . . .'

'I don't like people visiting me out of pity. I don't need it.'

'It had absolutely nothing to do with pity, I promise,' he said quietly. 'I simply enjoyed your company last time and since I know no one else up here, I looked for an excuse to come back.'

'That's better,' she said after a slight pause to consider.

'Lisa!' came a cry from the bedroom. 'Where's my breakfast? I want my breakfast!'

'Coming, Mum,' replied Lisa without taking her eyes off Dunbar.

Dunbar automatically looked at his watch. It was 10 p.m. He got up and said, 'It's time I was going anyway. Would it be all right if I popped back again? Sometime soon?

She looked at him doubtfully for a few moments before saying, 'Providing you don't bring pity with you.'

'I'll bring gin,' said Dunbar.

NINE

Dunbar watched *Newsnight* on the television in his room, then switched it off. The silence was broken by the sound of rain on the window, at first a gentle, irregular patter but then quickly becoming a harsh rattle that made him go over to the window to look out briefly before closing the blinds. He decided on an early night.

As he lay in bed, he looked back on the evening. He was glad to have re-established contact with Lisa. He liked her a lot, not least because of her obvious care and concern for other people. Like Sheila Barnes she was a born nurse. It wasn't something you could instil in people through qualification and training. It had to be there at the start. He had particularly liked her hope that Sheila and her husband could give comfort to each other in their dying days.

It was an aspect of the situation he himself hadn't considered, although there was something about it that had been niggling away at him. Lisa was right; it was strange that both Sheila and her husband had contracted cancer at the same time; the matron at The Beeches had also remarked on it. Neither of the Barneses had ever smoked, yet both had developed a particularly virulent form of lung cancer at almost exactly the same time. It was as if they had been simultaneously exposed to some sort of trigger mechanism, although in the leafy suburb of Bearsden that possibility seemed remote. The area did not exactly abound with chemical factories pumping out toxic fumes. They didn't live next door to a nuclear power station, and he couldn't imagine the rafters of Bearsden bungalows dripping with blue asbestos.

On the other hand . . . He remembered the nosey neighbour,

Proudfoot, and the problem with Cyril Barnes's camera . . . only there wasn't a problem with Cyril's camera. The repair company had reported nothing wrong with it, despite the fact that films kept coming out ruined as if they had been exposed to light . . . or maybe something else. Dunbar sat up in bed, now fully alert. Light wasn't the only thing that could ruin photographic film. Exposure to radiation would damage it in exactly the same way . . . and prolonged exposure to radiation would almost certainly cause cancer in a human being . . . or two human beings if they were exposed to it together.

Was it possible? Was it conceivable that Sheila and her husband had been exposed to a radiation source in their own home? Questions queued up in his mind. What could it be? Where was it and how had it got there?

Dunbar tried convincing himself that such a possibility could not be real. Surely it was a flight of fancy on his part, an academic exercise, a tribute to his powers of imagination but too bizarre to be real . . . wasn't it? He found he couldn't stop thinking about it. The seed had planted itself in his mind and insisted on growing. Sleep was now out of the question. He had to know. He had to find out for himself. But how? He would need specialist equipment for this kind of investigation.

Although he could get practically anything he wanted in the way of specialist equipment and expert advice from Sci-Med, it would take a little time and he couldn't wait. He had to know right now, even if it was just to eliminate the notion from his head. What he needed most was a radiation detector, a Geiger counter or something along those lines.

He looked at his watch. It was just after eleven thirty. Unless there was some kind of emergency at Médic Ecosse there was every likelihood that the Radiology Department would be empty and unmanned at this time of night. A radiographer would be on call but probably not on the premises. He could get hold of a radiation monitor there. He threw back the covers and swung his legs out of the bed.

Rather than sneak into Médic Ecosse unobserved, he decided he would drive quite openly into the car park and tell Reception he had come back to check some figures for a report he was working on. He didn't think that would arouse too much suspicion and might even chalk up some brownie points for the civil service. A stay of about fifteen minutes would seem about right. That should give him enough time to get down the back stairs and along the corridor to Radiology. His cover story would account for his carrying a briefcase – it should be big enough to hold the monitor and some protective gear. What if the department was locked for the night? He couldn't risk a break-in, he decided. If it was locked he'd abort the plan and make his request through Sci-Med in the morning.

As he walked from the car park up to the main door of the hospital he wondered if there was any chance that there'd be no one at the Reception desk. Of course not: the desk was run like everything else in Médic Ecosse, very well. Not only was there a smiling receptionist on duty, but there were two uniformed security men in the hall, silver-haired but fit-looking and alert. Despite the fact that the receptionist recognized Dunbar and greeted him by name, one of the guards still asked to see his ID.

'I won't be long. I just came back to check on some figures,' said Dunbar to the receptionist.

'And I thought you people drank tea all the time,' she smiled.

'A cruel myth,' said Dunbar with a backward glance and a half-smile as he headed for the double doors leading to the main corridor.

He climbed the stairs to his office and became aware that his palms were sweating. It was some time since he'd done anything like this and he was nervous. He switched on the light in his office and put his briefcase on the desk. His heart was thumping. Did he really want to do this? Maybe he'd lost his nerve. There was, however, no doubt in his mind that he still had a yen for an occasional walk on the wild side, if only to ask questions of himself.

With his pulse rate still rising, he opened his office door and looked out into the corridor. It was deserted. He stepped out and went quickly and quietly along it until he reached the head of the back stairs. Another pause to listen for any signs of activity but there was still nothing. Médic Ecosse was sleeping.

He was halfway down the stairs when suddenly he heard voices; they were getting louder. His first fear was that whoever it was might turn into the stairwell and find him there. He was debating whether to run back upstairs, when the sound of trolley wheels registered. They couldn't bring a trolley up the stairs. Reassured, he continued down to the bottom landing and shrank into the shadows in a corner from where he could see through the round glass window in the door.

The trolley party comprised four people. All wore blue cotton surgical garb with masks obscuring their lower faces. Dunbar could tell only that two were male and two female. Lying on the trolley was a young girl of five or six. Her eyes were closed and a drip-feed into her arm was being held up by one of the nurses as they waited for a lift at the door opposite the stairwell. The child seemed peacefully asleep but, in view of the lateness of the hour and the surgical dress, he supposed it more likely that she had been prepped for surgery. 'Good luck,' he whispered as the lift arrived and the doors slid open to spill light on to her pale little face. The doors closed. Dunbar watched until the indicator told him the party had stopped on the second floor, then edged out into the corridor and went quickly on down to Radiology.

The wide blue doors, which had earlier been propped open to permit the easy passage of trolleys, were closed, and Dunbar prepared himself for the worst. It would be in keeping with everything else about Médic Ecosse if the department had been responsibly and securely locked for the night. He looked to both sides before trying the handle; it moved all the way down. He pushed gently and the door opened. Swallowing hard, he slipped inside and closed it behind him.

He was in complete darkness with only the sound of his own breathing for company. He remembered that there were no outside windows in Radiology, so switching on the lights would not be a give-away. The light would show around the edges of the door, of course, but there was little reason for anyone to come here at this time of night. It was a chance he would have to take. He ran the palm of his hand up the wall, found the panel and clicked on all four switches.

For some reason the room's equipment looked threatening. The X-ray guns were waiting for him to make a move before turning on him. The immobilizing straps on the scanner bed were only pretending to hang lifeless. They were snakes, ready to ensnare him should he stray too close, waiting to secure his limbs and forehead like steel bands before feeding his body into the dark maw of the scanner, a black hole leading to . . .

Get a grip! thought Dunbar, raising his eyes to the ceiling. He really was out of practice at this sort of thing. He tried to remember where he had seen the radiation monitoring equipment. In a cupboard somewhere – Svensen had brought it out to demonstrate his new toy. But in which room? He walked around slowly, hoping for inspiration, and found it when he looked into Svensen's office. He remembered the radiologist opening the cupboard to the left of his desk and taking out a monitor.

Dunbar opened the cupboard and found three monitors. Two were mini-monitors for the routine checking of surfaces. The third was more sophisticated, with accurate metering capacity for measuring dosage. One of the mini-monitors would suit his purpose admirably. It comprised a rectangular metal box about eight inches by four with what looked like a microphone clipped to its top surface; this was the probe. It was attached to the main unit by about three feet of spring-coiled cable. There was a single control knob on the side to alter sensitivity settings and to provide a battery check. Dunbar turned it to this position and the needle swung upwards, well past the red line on the meter; the battery was in good condition. He unclipped the probe and moved it around. Random intermittent clicks from normal background radiation indicated that the monitor was in working order.

He turned his attention to the idea of protective clothing. If a small thing like a monitor was missing, people would assume someone else was using it or that it had been left in another room. It would be a while before anyone realized it wasn't in the department. The same applied to protective gloves. He would take just one. He debated taking one of the heavy aprons worn by the radiographers, but decided it was too bulky and would be too easily missed by the staff. The last thing he wanted was for them to come in in the morning and see that there'd been a break-in. He'd make do with the monitor and the glove.

He took a last look round to make sure that everything was as he'd found it, before clicking out the lights and listening for a moment at the door. Everything was quiet. He slipped out into the corridor and made his way back to his office. He let his breath out in a long sigh as he put the things he'd taken into his briefcase and secured the catch. So far so good. There was no denying that he'd got quite a buzz from the whole thing. He walked confidently past the reception desk and said good night with a friendly smile. The adrenalin was coursing through his veins.

As he neared the Barneses' street, Dunbar checked that he had the keys ready in his pocket. It was the third time he'd done it; they were still there. He frowned as he remembered the security light outside the house; it would come on when he walked up the path. Despite the lateness of the hour, this might alert the neighbours. People would not come out to ask questions at this time of night; they would phone the police.

That was the last thing he needed. He tried to remember the angle the light was set at. It had come on almost as soon as he opened the garden gate, so the detector beam must be set high. He should be able to slip under it if he made his approach from the side of the house along the wall.

He parked the car well away from the bungalow and outside a house whose high conifer hedge meant that the residents wouldn't be able to see it. He didn't want it reported as a suspiciously parked vehicle. He walked briskly and purposefully along the street, a man with a briefcase, not the kind of figure to arouse suspicion. There would be no lingering outside the Barneses' house, no furtive looks to right and left and no hesitation.

With only one backward glance to check that no one was coming, he scissored his legs over the corner of the Barneses' fence and dropped to a crouch in the shrubbery. He remained motionless for almost a minute, just looking and listening. No lights had come on in any of the nearby houses. There was no sound of voices.

Mr Proudfoot's house was in darkness. Hopefully everyone was asleep. Dunbar moved silently up to the corner of the building and pressed himself to the wall. He stared at the intruder detector above the door as he edged closer. Some of these things had heat sensors as well, he reminded himself, but it was now or never. With the keys ready in his hand he moved directly under it and opened the door as quickly as he could. He was inside and the light still hadn't come on.

He closed the curtains of the living room. They were reassuringly heavy and he made sure there were no cracks before switching on his torch. As a further precaution he kept his body between the torch beam and the window area as he opened his briefcase and took out the radiation monitor. He set it to its most sensitive setting and held the probe in front of him as he moved round the room.

Click . . . click . . . click click . . . Nothing to worry about, just background levels. He moved towards the cupboard by the fireplace where Cyril kept his camera gear. Click, click, clickety, clickety, clickety. The frequency of the clicks started to rise and the signal was markedly stronger. The blood was pounding in his ears as he homed in on the source. It was a white plastic telephone junction box fixed to the wall.

He moved away from the box and put the probe down on the floor, where it sat giving occasional clicks as it returned to background levels. He brought out the protective glove from his briefcase, along with a screwdriver to remove the cover of the box. With the heavy glove on his right hand making dexterity a lot more difficult, he undid the two starpoint screws retaining the cover and removed it. There was nothing inside.

He frowned and brought the monitor up to the front of the box again. Once more the clicks increased in frequency and the needle swung round on the meter. There was only one explanation; the box did not contain a source of radioactivity at the moment . . . but it had done recently.

The monitor Dunbar was using was a simple one. There was no way he could tell anything about the radiation source from it save for its current level and range. Holding the probe in front of him, he backed away until he was about eight feet from the junction box and the slowing clicks indicated he was out of range. He had to think what to do now. He hadn't counted on this situation arising at all. He shone the torch around the junction box area and then followed the thin telephone cable leading to it. The cable ran straight through without interruption. There was no need for a junction box at all; it was a fake; it was unnecessary.

The sole purpose of the box had been to house the radiation source. Someone had deliberately installed it there in order to expose Sheila Barnes and her husband to the effects of radiation damage. Or had Sheila alone been the real target? Because surely this was Médic Ecosse's doing. They just had to be the number-one suspect. Radiation sources weren't exactly freely available over the counter but they were common enough in hospitals, where a wide range of isotopes was used for tracing and treatment purposes.

He looked again at the empty box. The source – and therefore the evidence – had been removed, presumably when it had done its job and Sheila and her husband had been taken into hospital. Was that it? Were they now going to get away with it? Was there nothing he could do to prevent that? He reminded himself that the monitor was still registering so there must still be traces of the substance in the box. Maybe that would be enough to identify the isotope and trace its origins.

As he wondered how he could take some sort of sample from the inside of the box he remembered Sheila's make-up tray in the bedroom. Among the things she kept there was a series of little brushes. One of those would be ideal. He went and selected one, then turned his attention to finding a suitable container. His first thought was a plastic 35mm film container from Cyril's camera cupboard but plastic would not contain the radiation too well. He would need better shielding. His next thought was to try some kitchen foil. He brought some through from the kitchen.

Very carefully, to avoid dust rising into the air and him inhaling it, he brushed out what little debris there was inside the junction box and collected it on a square of foil. He folded it over into a little packet and checked the outside with the monitor. The reading was still high. The foil was too thin to block the radiation even when folded into several thicknesses; he needed better shielding.

He was facing the depressing thought that he might have to wait until Sci-Med sent up a suitable container before it would be safe to transport the sample, when he remembered that the bungalow was quite old. Although it was unlikely still to have any original lead piping in it after all the health scares of a few years ago, it might have remnants of these days. It was worth looking. He took the torch through into the kitchen and examined the piping under the sinks. It was modern. Copper, steel and plastic. The same applied to the bathroom.

There was one last possibility: the cistern in the loft. Did the Barneses have a loft ladder? They did. Dunbar found the short pole with the hook on the end and used it to open the hatch cover and swing down the ladder. He climbed up the metal treads, torch in hand, and swung the beam around the dark recesses of the roof space. He saw a grey plastic cistern and modern piping, mostly wrapped in plastic lagging.

It was plain that the plumbing in the house had been entirely re-done in the not too distant past. He was about to close the hatch when he saw, below the red plastic tank used to back up the central-heating water supply, something lying between the rafters. He picked it up. It had once been part of an overflow pipe from the old cistern. It was about eight inches long and, more importantly, it was made of lead.

He closed up the loft and brought the pipe down into the living room. He slipped the little foil packet inside it and, using the handle of the screwdriver, flattened the ends of the pipe to seal the packet inside. He ran the probe over the outside and was pleased to hear that the radiation was now in check. He could hear only background clicks. He screwed the plastic cover back on the junction box and stood up. He had a sick, hollow feeling in his stomach as if he had been going up too fast in a lift. It was one thing being afraid of what you were up against, but when you didn't know what that was it made you doubly fearful. He looked back at the junction box and wondered who had installed it. It must have been so easy. Someone posing as a telephone engineer perhaps? Supposedly checking a fault in the line? He could see how it could have been done without arousing any suspicion.

He put his things back into his briefcase along with the lead-shielded sample of debris and shone the torch around the floor area to make sure he hadn't left anything behind. He composed himself for a few moments before preparing to run the gauntlet of the security light once more.

This time he wasn't so lucky. He had only taken one sideways step with his back pressed against the wall when the light clicked on, illuminating him and the garden. He felt as if he had just come on stage at the London Palladium. Instinctively he sprinted to the corner of the house and threw himself flat in the shrubbery. As he did so a light came on in the Proudfoots' upstairs bedroom and a face appeared at the window; a hand started clearing a patch in the condensation on the glass in order to see out.

Dunbar wasn't at all sure about his cover so he was reluctant to move a muscle lest movement attract attention. He couldn't even afford to turn his head to look up at the bedroom window. His peripheral vision suggested that there was someone still there.

At that moment a cat chose to saunter across the garden path, sniffing the night air and haughtily ignoring the human being at the window above him. The cat sensed Dunbar's presence and stopped in its tracks to stare at him. Dunbar closed his eyes and prayed. This could go either way. Either the neighbour would think that the cat had triggered the light and go back to bed or he would notice that the cat had found something and get suspicious himself.

After what seemed like an eternity, the bedroom light went off and all was quiet again. The cat moved off to more interesting things and Dunbar lay stock still for a further three minutes until the security light had reset itself. Moving slowly backwards and out of range, he quickly glanced both ways in the street before jumping over the fence and walking briskly back to his car. The night air and the icy cold did nothing to help his state of mind. He was filled with apprehension. He had become involved in something that was much bigger than he could ever have imagined at the outset. Sheila Barnes and her husband getting cancer had been no accident.

Thinking about Sheila made him wonder about Lisa. If they – whoever they were – had set out to murder Sheila Barnes, might they not try to do the same to Lisa? Dunbar's foot flew to the brake pedal and the tyres squealed in protest. He executed a three-point turn with more noise than elegance and started racing through the streets to her flat.

'Who is it?' asked a sleepy-voiced Lisa.

'Steven Dunbar. I have to talk to you!' said Dunbar into the entryphone.

'Do you know what time it is?' she protested.

'I have to see you. It's important.'

'It had better be,' said Lisa, releasing the lock.

Dunbar sprinted up the stairs, carrying his briefcase under his right arm. Lisa was waiting for him at her front door, wearing dressing gown and slippers. Her arms were crossed over her body in deference to the cold. She quickly ushered him inside.

'This had better be good.'

'I think you're in danger.'

'What? What are you talking about?'

The sleep had gone from Lisa. She was now wide awake and alert. She watched as Dunbar, ignoring her, brought out the radiation monitor from his briefcase and unclipped the probe. He went directly to the telephone and started tracing the cable back along the wall. There was no sign of any new junction box.

'Have you had any visits from a telephone engineer in the past few weeks?' he asked, starting to move the probe to other areas of the room.

'Telephone engineer? Will you please tell me what's going on?'

'Have you?'

'No.'

'Are you sure?'

'Of course I'm sure.'

'Any other workmen calling unexpectedly?'

'No, no one.'

Dunbar began to relax.

'Will you please tell me what all this is about?' said Lisa.

'I'd better just check your bedroom.'

Lisa said, 'Dunbar, I've heard some crummy lines in my time, but this takes the prize.'

Dunbar didn't smile. He said, 'It looks as if Sheila Barnes and her husband didn't get cancer through some quirk of fate. I think someone may have planted a radiation source in their house.'

Lisa's eyes went as round as saucers. 'A radiation source? You mean it could be murder?'

Dunbar nodded. 'Could be.'

'But why? I mean who?'

'Only one name comes to mind,' said Dunbar.

'You mean Médic Ecosse?' exclaimed Lisa.

Dunbar shrugged. 'You can't buy radioactive isotopes at the corner shop. Who else would have access?'

Lisa sank into a chair and held her hands to her face.

Dunbar said, 'I had the awful thought they might be doing the same to you.'

Lisa shook her head slowly. The confidence had gone from her eyes. She looked like a little girl who had suddenly become very afraid.

He put down the probe and wrapped his arms round her for a few moments. 'There doesn't seem to be anything here,' he assured her. 'But I'd better check the other rooms.'

She nodded and led the way. The flat was clean.

'Are you all right?' Dunbar inquired gently when they returned to the living room.

Lisa looked up and shrugged. 'I don't know. Where do we go from here?' she asked.

'Until I know for sure, I have to assume that they did this to Sheila to shut her up about the child who died, although the method is positively bizarre. We could call in the police right now but that might stop us finding out what's behind it all.'

'Then you do believe there's something in what Sheila Barnes and I have been staying?' asked Lisa.

'I think I did even before this.'

'Supposing you don't call the police. What's the alternative?'

'Sci-Med can continue the investigation in secret.'

'I want to know why Amy died,' said Lisa. 'I want someone to pay for it.'

Dunbar nodded.

'On the other hand, I'm scared,' she confessed.

Dunbar did not offer false reassurance.

'What about the radiation source you mentioned? What's going to happen to it?'

'It had already been removed but I found traces of it. They'd concealed it in a telephone junction box on the wall – that's why I was checking your phone line. I collected some debris from the box. I'm going to ask the Sci-Med people if they can identify the isotope and find out where it came from. There aren't many establishments that supply radioactive materials in the UK, and they're all obliged to keep strict records.'

'So they'll be able to tell if it was ordered through Médic Ecosse?'

'That's my hope,' said Dunbar. 'If we can show that Sheila was murdered, and link her death to Médic Ecosse, all the stops will be pulled out in a search for the motive. If we call in the police right now and then find that we can't link the two, the whole thing will be blown.'

'Who else would want to kill Sheila Barnes?'

'Agreed,' said Dunbar, but there was hesitation in his voice.

'Something's troubling you?'

'I can't help thinking it was a very odd way to shut someone up. You'd think they'd want to do it as quickly as possible, not let nature take its course.'

'Thanks,' said Lisa flatly. 'Very reassuring.'

'Sorry, I didn't mean to alarm you. I was just thinking out loud. Obviously they must think time's on their side. What do you think?'

'Let's see what your people come up with before we call in the police,' said Lisa.

'If you're sure?' said Dunbar.

She nodded uncertainly, as if she was using up every ounce of bravery she could muster in the gesture.

'Good girl. In the meantime don't open the door to any tradesmen unless they've got proper identification and credentials. Even at that, I'm going to arrange for surveillance outside.'

Lisa nodded again.

As soon as he got back to the hotel, Dunbar established a modem link with the Sci-Med office in London, using his notebook computer, and sent a two-word message, GLASGOW RED. Sci-Med would now know they had a criminal case on their hands, and any request made by Dunbar would be given priority. At some point in the next few days he would have to justify his action. If at all possible he would have to do it in person in London but, as he was the man on the ground right now, the decision was his.

After a few moments his computer bleeped, and Sci-Med's reply came up on the screen: GLASGOW GREEN. His message had been received. There followed an instruction to adopt one of three encrypting procedures available on Sci-Med computers. From now on, to ensure complete security, all his messages would be encoded automatically before travelling down the phone lines, as would the return messages from Sci-Med. Dunbar did as instructed and was asked if he had any immediate requests. He asked for discreet, low-level surveillance at Lisa's address. He didn't believe she was in any immediate danger, but it was as well to think ahead. He was assured that this would be done. Asked if there was anything else, he replied that there was nothing that couldn't wait until daybreak. He needed some sleep; it was two thirty in the morning.

Despite the lateness of the hour, sleep did not come easily. The events of the day went round in his head like scenes on a fairground carousel. The more he searched for answers, the bigger the questions seemed to get. Even niggling little worries demanded his attention. He was thinking about how he would return the equipment he'd borrowed from Radiology when a thought struck him. At the hospital, when he'd seen the surgical team get into the lift with the child, they'd taken her up to the second floor. He'd thought nothing of it at the time but now he realized that that would have taken them up to the east wing of Obstetrics, the one being used for the Omega patient. Why were they taking the child up there?

TEN

Dunbar was up early in the morning. The first thing he did was check his coded computer mail file. It had already been updated with a list of phone numbers, which he noted down in the small notebook he always carried. They were special numbers for the police and other authorities in the area, and would get him whatever assistance he needed, at priority level. There were also two bank account numbers he could use to obtain emergency funding. There was a Sci-Med telephone number to be used at any time of the day or night in making special requests and, finally, a directive that he should make personal contact at his earliest convenience. It was the standard package for Sci-Med investigators in the field when they asked for full operational status.

For the moment, everything depended on establishing the origins of the radioactive source. He asked Sci-Med to get the radioactive sample couriered to London and to arrange laboratory analysis of it. The evidence, he warned them, was little more than radioactive dirt. Would they do their best to identify the unknown isotope and its source?

As usual, he was impressed at the way Sci-Med didn't question his requests. They simply accepted them and asked if he had any more or if there was anything else they could do to assist. This is the way an administration should work, he thought. They smoothed the way for the real function of the organization. In many government institutions administration had become an end in itself. In the worst cases, roles were reversed. Front-line workers existed only as administration fodder, to be administered, to provide information, data and statistics for administrators. Their true function had been totally undermined.

From what he'd heard from friends and colleagues, the NHS was well on the way to this state already. More and more medical and nursing time was taken up with the filling in of forms, the answering of questionnaires and complying with audit and monitoring procedures – generally being subject to the whims of an administration seeking to justify and multiply its own existence.

Dunbar scrounged some cardboard and adhesive tape from Reception and used it to make a small parcel of the lead pipe containing the debris. He checked the outside thoroughly with the radiation monitor before taking the package downstairs to await collection. He brought some black coffee back up with him and thought about what he was going to do next. He was going to drive down to Helensburgh to see Sheila Barnes, ostensibly to return her journal to her. He had planned to do so anyway, but now his number-one priority was to ask her if she could remember who had installed the phone junction box on her living-room wall and when. Maybe she could come up with a description or even a name.

After much heart-searching, he had decided not to tell her about the radiation source. She was dying and had accepted her fate with good grace. Telling her of his suspicions would only bring bitterness to her last days. It might also oblige him to inform the police, he acknowledged. Was that the real reason he wasn't going to tell her? Sometimes it was all too easy to fool oneself about true motivation. He hoped it really was for Sheila's sake, but he couldn't be sure.

He had not yet left the hotel when a courier arrived to pick up the parcel containing the isotope. The man was surprised at how much the small package weighed. 'What you got in here then?' he joked. 'Lead?'

Dunbar took his time driving down to Helensburgh. Driving at moderate speed meant that he didn't have to concentrate too hard on the road ahead. There was time to think of other things and he definitely needed time to get his thoughts in order. The question was where to begin. There seemed to be no logical starting-point. He had never felt so much at sea in an investigation. The only real crime to come to grips with was the planting of the isotope in Sheila Barnes's house, but surely that had been done to keep her quiet about something that had gone before, the death of a child. So what were the real circumstances surrounding the child's death – and presumably Amy Teasdale's too – that warranted murder to conceal the truth?

The room was being kept shaded but Dunbar could see that Sheila was close to death. Her emaciated body was so fragile that it seemed that the slightest breeze coming in the window might turn her to dust. He watched her sleep for a few moments after the care assistant had gone, wondering whether it might not be better if he just left. If she was sleeping she wasn't in pain and that was probably the most important consideration . . . but he needed to ask her about the junction box. A moral dilemma.

'Sheila?' he said quietly.

There was no response.

He tried once more, then turned on his heel to leave. He had almost reached the door when he heard Sheila stir behind him. 'Peter? Is that you?'

Dunbar turned round. Her eyes were still closed. He was about to announce himself when Sheila continued.

'I knew you'd come. I'm so glad you did. I know we didn't part on the best of terms last time, dear, but I knew you'd come to say good-bye to your poor old mother. Everything I said was for your own good you know. You do realize that, don't you?'

Dunbar found himself saying, 'Yes, of course.'

'I was just thinking about that holiday we went on when you were about eight. D'you remember? You and your father went out in that small boat and caught three fish and I cooked them for tea. The look on your face . . . you were so proud . . .'

'I remember,' whispered Dunbar. He retreated into deep shadow in case she should open her eyes.

'I'm so happy you came, my dear. I do love you, you know.'

'I know, Mother, and I love you,' murmured Dunbar. 'Get some rest now. We can talk later.'

'That would be nice, dear,' said Sheila distantly, and she drifted back into sleep.

Dunbar tiptoed out of the room and decided to have a word with matron about the exchange before he left. He explained what had happened and how he'd played along. 'I hope I did the right thing, Matron.'

'I think that was exactly the right thing to do under the circumstances. Sheila's very near to death.'

'I take it her son hasn't come to see her or his father?' asked Dunbar.

Matron shook her head. 'I understand Peter is a bit of a black sheep. There was a serious family falling-out over money. Peter wanted funding for some new business venture but it was something he'd done before. Sheila and Cyril said no. These things happen I'm afraid.'

'Indeed,' agreed Dunbar. He thanked the matron for her reassurance and left the hospice knowing that he would have no reason to return.

On the way back to Glasgow, he decided to fly down to London on the following day and report to Sci-Med. He'd go into the hospital this evening and leave a note for Ingrid. He'd leave it until late. He didn't want to talk to anyone there.

All Sandy and Kate's new-found optimism disappeared in one awful moment when a nurse showed them into Amanda's room and they found her looking like a starving refugee from a Third World country. Her skin was deathly white and her eyes seemed huge. She was awake but she simply stared up at the ceiling. The white rabbit the hospital had given her lay beside her on the pillow, its colour not dissimilar to Amanda's.

Sandy turned to the nurse, while Kate tried to make contact with Amanda. 'What's happened?' he asked hoarsely.

'It's not as bad as it looks,' replied the nurse. 'Amanda was kept off dialysis yesterday while Dr Ross ran some tests on her.'

'What tests?' asked Sandy.

'There were a number,' replied the nurse vaguely. 'Would you like me to find a member of the medical staff? They're actually a bit busy at the moment but I'm sure I . . .'

Sandy shook his head. He felt confused. He didn't want to make a fuss.

'Dr Ross says she'll feel much better tomorrow,' said the nurse. 'It's mainly just a reaction to some of the procedures.'

Sandy again wanted to ask what procedures. He didn't understand what tests were so vital that dialysis had to be suspended, but on the other hand he didn't want to make trouble. The hospital had been good to them. He didn't want to seem ungrateful. He knelt down at Amanda's bedside, struggling to keep the tears from his eyes at his daughter's pathetic appearance.

'How's my princess?' he asked, gently taking her hand as if he were afraid it would break.

Amanda gave a wan smile. 'It's sore, Daddy,' she said.

'What's sore, Princess?' he asked. 'Have you got a pain in your tummy?'

Amanda put her hand to her chest and Sandy ran his hand over it. Despite the gentleness of his touch, he saw her wince. He could feel a surgical dressing under her nightie and worried at its position over her breast bone. He frowned.

'Nurse?' he asked. 'Did Amanda have a marrow puncture yesterday?'

'I believe she did,' replied the nurse.

This time Sandy couldn't stop himself. 'Why?' he asked.

'It's not unusual for transplant patients to have a marrow puncture for immunology typing,' said the nurse.

'But Amanda's already had these tests done,' said Sandy. 'She had them done ages ago at the Children's Hospital. She's already on the transplant register. It must be in her notes. Her immunology profile is known.'

'I'm sure Dr Ross had his reasons,' said the nurse.

Sandy bit his tongue. 'Of course,' he said and went back to trying for some response from Amanda.

'Would you like me to see if I can find Dr Ross for you?' asked the nurse. Her tone had changed slightly. It was more of a challenge than a question, the response of a professional to what she considered unwarranted lay questioning.

'No, that won't be necessary,' he replied.

'Oh God,' sighed Sandy as he and Kate walked to the car. His limbs felt like lead. 'Maybe we were expecting too much,' he said. 'We were looking for magic in a world that doesn't have any. Like all desperate people, we've been fooling ourselves. We wanted to believe in fairies and Santa Claus.'

'The nurse said Amanda will feel better tomorrow,' said Kate. 'It's probably just the aftermath of the tests she's been having. She'll pick up. You'll see.'

Sandy gave Kate a half-smile and put his arms round her, hugging her to him.

'That's better,' she said.

'Good on you, kid,' he said softly. 'God knows what will happen if we both hit a downer at the same time.'

Dunbar left it until after ten before going into Médic Ecosse and checking his desk. Ingrid had left him the information he'd asked for about patients treated free of charge since the hospital's opening. It was not a detailed account but it gave him the basics he wanted: the number of patients taken on, the type of treatment or operation they'd received and the notional cost to the hospital to be set off against tax as charitable acts. While most of them were relatively low-risk, high-profile procedures that would have attracted a deal of good publicity, the hospital had in fact taken on three transplant patients. The list was not specific; there were no names, but he knew that Amanda

Chapman was the third. Three? This was a big surprise. The hospital apparently had been more than generous with its resources. He stopped short of thinking they had perhaps been too generous, considering the state of their finances. People were more important than money. He put the list away in his desk drawer and penned a note to Ingrid saying that he would be going to London in the morning.

As Dunbar was about to start his car in the front car park, an unmarked black Bedford van came in through the gates and made its way slowly round to the car park at the rear. The driver was dressed in what looked like hospital whites, as was the man sitting beside him. Dunbar's curiosity got the better of him. He got out of his car and walked quickly round to the back of the building, courting the shadow of the walls.

The van had stopped opposite the green doors that led to the hospital's basement corridor. The two men had opened up the back doors of the van and were now joined by two other men who came out of the building. All four removed what appeared to be a very heavy patient on a stretcher. It required one man at each corner.

Despite the fact that he had moved closer, using the cover of what few parked cars there were at that time of night, Dunbar could not make out much more than that. The lighting was poor and the patient was draped with a dark top cover.

'What on earth?' he murmured as the green doors closed and the van drove off. Why would any patient be brought to the back door under cover of darkness? Then he remembered that the mortuary was located in the basement corridor. It wasn't a patient they had brought in, it was a corpse.

This new thought was no more understandable than the first. He couldn't think of a good reason for delivering a body to Médic Ecosse any more than he could a patient to the basement. If he couldn't work it out in his head he would have to find out for himself, he decided. He returned to his office and considered for a moment before deciding on a direct approach. He would go down to the mortuary and find out who the body belonged to.

He waited ten minutes, which he hoped would be long enough for the attendants to have put the body into the mortuary fridge, and left. He paused to listen at the top of the stairs leading to the basement. All was quiet. He tiptoed down and moved silently along to the mortuary door. He paused again, putting his ear to it. Again, there was no sound. He opened the door and slipped inside, feeling safer when the door had closed behind him. He let out his breath, which he hadn't realized he'd been holding, then froze again when the refrigeration plant sprang into life and startled him. The sooner this was over the better.

He pulled back the heavy metal clasp securing the door and it swung back revealing, to his surprise, two occupants, both hidden under white sheets. He had expected to find only one. He removed the head cloth from the body in the upper tray and saw the parchment skin of a woman. She'd been in her late sixties, judging by her hair and teeth. He slid out the tray on its runners until he could reach the name tag tied to her toe: Angela Carter-Smythe.

He slid the tray back in and covered the dead woman's face before shifting his attention to the occupant of the bottom tray. The size told him that this was the corpse he'd seen being carried in from the van. Unusually, the covering over the body was not a traditional shroud, which tended to follow body shape, but appeared to comprise several layers of waterproof material with white top sheets wrapped round it. Maybe this was because the corpse was so large, thought Dunbar. He gripped a loose corner of the material near the head, but couldn't pull it back because of the sheer weight of the body; he couldn't support the head with the palm of one hand.

Expecting to find the body of a very heavy, thickset man, he worked with both hands to free the head-sheet and recoiled when he looked down at the snout of a fully grown pig. The smell of it, freed from the waterproof sheeting, assaulted his nostrils. Its dead eyes looked through him.

When he'd recovered his composure, Dunbar searched for rational answers. The kitchen cold store had broken down or run out of storage space? Unlikely and highly unethical. Apart from that, the pig, as far as he could tell on cursory examination, was complete, not the sort of cleaned carcass a slaughterhouse or butcher would supply. This was seriously strange.

Dunbar slid his hand down under the sheeting covering the pig and felt its belly. He kept his hand there for a few moments so that surface cold and dampness from its short time in the fridge would not obscure what he was looking for. He felt his palm become slightly warm. The pig had not been dead long. He was more than a little bemused. He couldn't make up his mind whether or not his discovery contravened any criminal laws or ethical rules. Why was the animal there? Why had a recently killed pig been brought to Médic Ecosse under cover of darkness?

After a few moments it occurred to him that it might not be any old pig, it might be some kind of experimental animal. James Ross's research would almost certainly involve the use of animals. All transplant research did. The animal might be a laboratory pig. In the early days of transplant research, when research work had been largely concerned with technique, dogs and monkeys had played major roles; they had been used by surgeons to practise on. In more modern times the emphasis had swung away from technique, which had largely been mastered. Pigs had taken over in the research laboratory as eventual possible donors of organs to humans, once the immunology problems had been sorted out.

As a leading researcher in the field, Ross would almost certainly have a Home Office licence for animal work. That being the case, Dunbar started to view his discovery as bizarre rather than sinister. But why had the animal been brought here to the hospital? Surely Ross's research labs must have their own animal autopsy and dissection facilities – unless, of course, the cuts in his budget had forced him to seek alternatives. Was that it? Dunbar was considering this when he heard voices in the corridor. He mustn't be discovered in the mortuary. That would call for explanations he didn't have.

He looked about him for somewhere to hide but there was nowhere. The only furniture was a simple table, which was too narrow to hide

him from view if he got under it. That left the mortuary fridge . . .
He opened the fridge door and looked at the inside of the clasp. It
had a standard through-bolt release pin, which meant it could be
opened from the inside in emergencies; not that emergencies would
be common inside a mortuary fridge.

The voices were getting louder. There was no time for hesitation. He gripped the beam along the top of the interior frame and
swung his legs up on to the top tray beside Angela Carter-Smythe.
He wriggled round on to his stomach in the confined space and
stretched down to ease the door shut. It clunked softly on to its
clasp and he was suddenly in complete, suffocating darkness.

He squirmed down the tray, trying to get as far from the door
as possible, but he was still vulnerable to a casual upward glance
from below. To combat this he manoeuvred himself into the tiny
gap between the top of Angela's body and the ceiling of the fridge
and lay still on top of the dead woman, as if locked in some hellish
embrace.

As the minutes passed and there was no sound from outside, he
started to have doubts. Was it silent because of the heavy insulation
on the fridge doors and walls, or was there really no one out there?
After all, the voices needn't have been those of people on their way
to the mortuary.

The fridge door suddenly opened and light flooded in. Dunbar
froze. He saw that the head cloth had fallen away from Angela's
face. Please God no one had come for her! He held his breath.

With unutterable relief, he heard the lower tray being slid out.
The pig was removed, to the accompaniment of much grunting
and groaning from its bearers.

The fridge door slammed shut again, causing a sudden rise in
internal air pressure that hurt Dunbar's ears. When the buzzing
stopped, he found himself in deep, dark silence again. He was
surprised at how quickly the air inside the fridge was used up.
Although it was cold, he was soon aware of a film of sweat forming
on his forehead and of starting to feel generally uncomfortable.
Time to leave.

He started to wriggle his way up to the front again, inevitably becoming less and less reverential towards Angela as he manoeuvred awkwardly in the confined space. He finally reached the bulkhead over the door and stretched down his right arm to grip the release pin on the clasp. There was just enough room for his arm if he kept it in one orientation, but when he tried to turn it to grip the pin properly he couldn't do so and was forced to bend his wrist round at an unnatural angle. To his horror, the pin came clean away and fell with a clang on to the empty tray below.

Fear gripped him like a vice. His throat tightened and his head filled with nightmare thoughts. He was trapped. There wasn't room for him to get down between the top tray and the wall of the fridge. The pin must be at least two feet below the limit of his reach, not that he could see it in the dark, anyway. Panic welled up in his throat but throwing in the towel and yelling for help would be of no use. The insulation on the fridge would reduce any sound to a murmur, and in any case there was no one out there to hear it. He'd be yelling his way into eternity and using up the limited air supply even faster.

He rolled on to his back and tried to get his wits back. He ran through his surroundings in his head, the framework, the dimensions of the trays, the gaps between the trays and the walls, the gap between his body and the ceiling. There was only one chance, he concluded. If he could dislodge the top tray and tip it up so that it fell down through the frame, giving him access to the lower tray, there was a chance he could get out of this mess. The trouble was, both he and Angela were lying on it.

There wasn't room to dislodge it sideways, he reckoned. It would have to be dislodged front to back and then twisted so that it fell diagonally through the frame. The chance of achieving this seemed so slim that he didn't want to think about it. He simply started trying. He felt that the bones in his fingers must snap as he applied more and more pressure to the metal tray in an attempt to lever it and the combined weight of two bodies over the end of the frame. At the third attempt he managed it, sweat running down his forehead and stinging his eyes despite the cold. Fear was triumphing over temperature.

The next thing was to edge the tray forward. This time his arms had to take the strain as he took as much of his own weight as possible off the tray by pressing his hands against the side walls. He hooked his feet over the back edge of the tray and inched it slowly forwards so that as much of it as possible rode up on the front lip of the frame until it was stopped by the door.

Dunbar took a breather. He was literally poised between life and death. His right foot was going to decide the outcome of his predicament. If, when he thumped it down hard on the bottom edge of the tray, the tray didn't twist and go crashing down through the gap, complete with Angela and himself, he could forget any other plan. There wouldn't be any.

He took a moment to focus all his attention on the toe of his shoe. There could be no drawing back in deference to pain. Every ounce of strength he possessed had to go into the kick. He slowly raised his foot until his heel was stopped by the ceiling – a pitifully small length of travel. He brought his foot down with all the force that fear and focus could muster. The tray twisted and went down through the gap, bottom first. Dunbar and Angela finished up in a semi-erect embrace, leaning against the door.

Dunbar eased the tray slowly out of the way and tried to prop Angela up in the corner so that he could feel for the pin. After a few seconds, the searching palm of his right hand made contact with the pin. He felt his way up the back of the door until he found the hole for the pin, keeping his left index finger in it until he had the pin in place. He inserted the pin and gave it an almost despairing thump with the heel of his right hand. The clasp released and the door swung slowly and mockingly back. Dunbar put his hands down on the floor outside and dragged himself free. He lay on the floor for a few moments, breathing deeply and looking back at the maw of the fridge that had so nearly become his tomb.

His relief at being alive gave way to considerations of his present predicament. He had to put things back in order in the fridge and return Angela to her upper berth. He got somewhat unsteadily to his feet and pulled her fully out of the fridge. It took only a moment for him to restore the fallen tray to the top runners and slide it in. When he was satisfied it was running true, he slid it half out again, lifted her up and fed her slowly on to it. He closed her eyes with his finger tips and replaced her head cloth. 'Requiescat in pace, Angela,' he said. He slid the tray home and closed the door.

As he recovered from his ordeal, Dunbar turned his attention to the question of the pig and what had happened to it. He was almost certain that it had been taken to the post-mortem suite along the corridor. The chains above the operating table, he now knew, must be animal hoists. The question was, could he find out what exactly they were doing to it there without being discovered?

The affair in the mortuary fridge had taken a lot out of him; he had no heart for more heroics, but he did think he could get into the ante-room outside the PM room without being seen. Once in there, he might be able to see something of what was going on inside.

Dunbar went through his usual routine of listening at the door before opening it and then cautiously looking up and down the corridor. Luck was still with him. He ran along to the door to the PM suite and listened for voices again. He couldn't hear anything but this was a bit of a gamble. If there was someone in the suite he'd better have his story ready. Nothing too elaborate, he decided. Better to play the bumbling English civil servant just having a look around the hospital. He opened the door; there was no one there. He entered quietly and looked through the glass panel in the door leading to the scrub room. Three jackets were hanging on pegs on the wall. Taking a deep breath, he moved through the scrub room and sidled up to the glass panel in the door leading to the PM room itself.

He saw what he supposed he had expected: an autopsy being carried out on the pig. Three gowned and masked figures were working on the carcass, which was secured to the table by leather straps. Its insides were exposed through a sweeping incision from its throat to its genitals. The huge operating light above the table illuminated the scene with a brilliance that made the scarlet hellish bright.

Dunbar was puzzled. Why should the three people at the table be fully gowned, gloved and masked for an animal autopsy? Such precautions were more appropriate for work on a living patient, when aseptic technique was paramount in avoiding subsequent infection. They seemed to be removing certain of the pig's internal organs and transferring them to plastic wrapping and then to stainless steel containers. Dunbar presumed this was for histological work later in the lab, but then a sudden awful doubt crept into his mind. That *was* why they were removing them, wasn't it? Surely they didn't intend using the animal's organs for anything else?

He tried to make out who the masked figures were but it proved impossible. He gave up and slipped out of the scrub room, through the ante-room and out into the corridor. As soon as he got back to his office he phoned Lisa.

'I know it's late, but can I come over?'

'Of course.'

'A pig?' exclaimed Lisa.

'They were dissecting it with full aseptic precautions.'

'But why?'

'I think it's reasonable to assume that it must have had something to do with Ross's research programme.'

'He'd be using pigs?'

'Almost certainly. The pig stands in line to become man's best friend in that department. The immunology journals are full of experimental work on them. Their organs are the right size for us if the rejection problems can be dealt with, and there's a lot of work going on into that.'

'But at night and in the Médic Ecosse Hospital?' protested Lisa.

'That worries me too,' agreed Dunbar. 'That's why I wanted to talk to you. They were treating the pig as if it were a human patient. Gowns, masks, the whole bit. It just made me wonder.'

'Good God you don't think they were planning to use . . . ?'

Dunbar's mind too rebelled against the thought, but he couldn't dismiss the notion that what he had seen might explain why two patients appeared to have been given the wrong organ.

'But surely you need all sorts of permission and sanctioning for anything like that?' said Lisa.

'I'm sure you do. Unless you just go ahead and do it anyway.'

'Do you think that's what they did to Amy? Gave her a pig's kidney?'

'It's something we have to consider.'

'What are you going to do?'

'Call London. But first I have to check on something back at the hotel. I'll ring you later.'

Dunbar thought hard as he drove to his hotel. He had a clear idea of what he wanted to do next, should it be possible, but felt compelled to consider the consequences. There were people's sensitivities to consider. He could end up causing great distress. Was it absolutely necessary? Was there a way around it? By the time he reached his room back at the hotel he had concluded not. The only thing left to discover now was if it was possible.

The files Sci-Med had given him at the outset contained the information he needed. Kenneth Lineham, the boy who had died in Sheila Barnes's care, had been cremated but Amy Teasdale had been buried. She lay in a churchyard in Lanarkshire. What he was going to request was therefore possible, but he still hesitated before picking up the phone and dialling Sci-Med's number.

'I want her exhumed.'

'Have you thought this through, Dunbar?' asked Frobisher, the number two man at Sci-Med who was on call for any important decisions to be made during the night. 'This is a major undertaking. If we get an official order and exhume the child and you turn out to be wrong, there'll be merry hell to pay. The backlash could seriously damage Sci-Med. I'm not sure we can take that kind of chance at this stage. All you have to go on is the fact you saw a pig autopsy in the hospital.'

'I've thought it through and I think the sooner we exhume her the better,' said Dunbar. 'Does it have to be official?'

'Now we're really getting into dangerous territory,' said Frobisher. 'We're not M15, you know. We can't go around digging up people willy-nilly.'

'I wouldn't have asked if I didn't believe it to be important,' said Dunbar.

Frobisher let his breath out slowly between his teeth. 'There's nothing we can do until morning, anyway,' he said. 'I'll relay your request to Mr Macmillan when he comes in. He won't be any happier about it than I am but maybe together we'll think of some way we can do this without a brass band playing. There's nothing the television people like better than a bloody exhumation.'

Dunbar was about to hang up when Frobisher said, 'Hang on, there's a lab report here for you. Do you want it now?'

'Absolutely,' said Dunbar.

'It's an analysis of some radioactive debris you sent in. The lab say the source was an industrial isotope used in the testing of radiation shielding.'

'Industrial?' exclaimed Dunbar. 'Not medical?'

'Apparently not. They've narrowed it down to four possible companies that use this sort of thing, apart, of course, from the Amersham company which makes the stuff.'

'Any of them in Glasgow?'

'Afraid not. None in Scotland at all. The nearest to you would be Baxters on Tyneside.'

'Shit,' said Dunbar.

ELEVEN

'Something's troubling you,' said Kate as she watched Sandy play with the food on his plate. He'd just turned over the same forkful of mashed potato for the third time.

'Mmmm,' he replied.

'Well, out with it then,' demanded Kate.

'I suppose it was Amanda being so low yesterday. It really got to me. I felt sure she'd be better not worse. To see her like that was just so—'

'But she was much better today,' interrupted Kate. 'Just like the nurse said she would be, and she'll probably be even better tomorrow. You'll see. They're very pleased with her. Yesterday was just because of the tests they had to do.'

'But they didn't have to do them. That's just the point. She'd already had all her immuno-typing done. It must be in her notes. Why did they put her through all that pain all over again?'

Kate shook her head as if it were an unreasonable question. 'You know much more about these things than I do,' she said. 'But the nurse said they were just routine procedures to check her immunology . . . something or other.'

'Immunology pattern. Yes, I know, but that's all been done before. Her blood group, her tissue type, everything has already been done. It all had to be done before they entered her on the transplant register. Why put her through the misery of a marrow puncture?'

Kate shrugged and said, 'Well, I suppose I'm happy to assume that the hospital knows best.'

'Hospitals depend on that,' said Sandy sourly.

'Who's being cynical, then?' said Kate with a cajoling smile.

He relaxed a little and said, 'All right, maybe I am worrying unnecessarily but I work in hospitals, remember. I know they're not infallible. Mix-ups happen, mistakes are made, wrong tests are ordered, overdoses are given. In many ways they're the most dangerous places on earth. Reservoirs of infection posing as havens of hygiene and sterility.'

Kate had heard it all before. 'Look, if you're really upset about this test thing, why don't you make an appointment to see one of the doctors and ask them outright about it? I'm sure they'd be happy to tell you.'

'I suppose because I don't want to be seen as a troublemaker. They're treating our daughter for free and they're the best chance she's got. In fact, they're probably the only one. It would look like ingratitude and, believe me, I'm not ungrateful.'

'I still think it would be all right if you asked politely. After all, you're in the business, so to speak.'

'Hospitals hate that worse than anything,' said Sandy. 'They prefer complete ignorance in their patients and relatives, followed by unquestioning acceptance of anything they care to tell you.'

'Well, if you don't want to ask them, why not ask Clive Turner? Maybe he knows why they did the tests again. He's always been very nice to us and you wouldn't question anything he's done.'

'Now that's a good idea,' he agreed, brightening. 'I might just do that. In fact,' – he looked at his watch – 'I'll try to catch him right now.'

'Paging Dr Turner for you,' said the hospital voice.

'Dr Turner.'

'Clive, it's Sandy Chapman here.'

'Hello there. I was just thinking about you folks this morning. How's Amanda doing?'

'That's really why I'm calling. She was quite ill when we went to see her yesterday and a nurse told me that she'd had her dialysis withheld while they did some tests on her, including a marrow puncture.'

'A marrow puncture?'

'That's what I thought,' said Sandy, acknowledging the surprise in Turner's voice. 'The nurse there said it wasn't unusual for transplant patients. I pointed out that Amanda has already had all these tests done, but I don't think I got through to her. I didn't like to request a meeting with the doctors over it because I didn't want to make a fuss but, on the other hand, I'd still like to know why they put her through that. I thought you might have some idea?'

'I'm embarrassed to say that I haven't,' replied Turner. 'Amanda's immunological data is all known and recorded on the register.'

'That's what I thought.'

'I can't imagine why they'd want to repeat it all, although I suppose there must have been a reason . . . I'm trying to think if there's any way I could find out for you without stepping on sensitive toes.'

'I don't want to make waves, but it's something that's been niggling away at me.'

'I can understand that,' said Turner. 'There's a chap I know over there called Steven Dunbar. He's a doctor but he's not actually on the medical staff so he won't be inclined to take offence. Maybe I'll ask him if he can find out for us discreetly. I know him through the negotiations to have Amanda admitted there.'

'I think I know him too,' said Sandy, recognizing the name. 'He helped me push-start the car one night when it played up. He's some kind of government official, isn't he?'

'That's right. Truth to tell, you have him to thank for Amanda's referral to Médic Ecosse being successful. He had the final say over it and didn't question it at all. Simply gave it his seal of approval. He seemed like a good bloke.'

'I didn't know that,' exclaimed Sandy. 'He never said. I owe him one.'

'An unusual civil servant,' said Turner. 'Anyway, I'll see if he can shed any light on Amanda's marrow puncture.'

'I'm obliged to you again,' said Sandy.

* * *

Turner called Dunbar the following morning. They exchanged pleasantries, then Turner said, 'I know this is not strictly up your street but I wonder if you can help me out with something?'

'Not another free transplant, I hope,' joked Dunbar.

'Nothing like that,' laughed Turner. 'I do realize your resources are finite. I have a question I hoped you might be able to answer for me . . . discreetly.'

'Try me.'

'I've had Amanda Chapman's father on the phone. He was a bit worried about why his daughter had to go through the unpleasantness of a marrow puncture when all her immunological data is already known. He didn't want to make a fuss and appear ungrateful up there, so he asked me and, frankly, I couldn't think of a reason either. I thought I'd try to find out quietly. That's what made me think of you.'

'I see,' said Dunbar. 'You don't want to ruffle any professional feathers in this neck of the woods.'

'Exactly. I thought you might conceivably have access to relevant files and might take a little look for me?'

Dunbar smiled to himself and said, 'I can't promise anything but I'll see what I can do. If I come up with anything I'll get back to you.'

Dunbar put down the phone and thought. He waited until Ingrid had left the room before requesting a current-costs listing for Amanda Chapman from the computer. It was hospital policy that reasons had to be given for all tests and procedures carried out, to avoid possible later accusations of performing unnecessary ones just to inflate the bill. Although Amanda's parents were not paying, the computerized listing procedure was routine and would therefore apply in her case too. It would be too much trouble to change it all for an individual patient.

But the listing that came up on the screen made no mention of any marrow puncture having been carried out on Amanda Chapman. None at all. He checked the date on the file. It had last been updated that morning. Dialysis charges and standard daily fees were given, but there was nothing about any special tests or minor surgical procedures.

Dunbar sucked the end of his pen and considered. It could simply be that the staff had been tardy in keeping Amanda's file up to date, knowing that in the end there would be no bill to settle, but that seemed unlikely in a hospital that ran like clockwork. The only alternative was that someone had taken a conscious decision not to enter the marrow puncture in the notes. Why? Because they didn't want a record of it? Maybe that was being too melodramatic. A marrow puncture was not that uncommon a procedure. It was simply the fact that all her immunology stats were already known that made it seem questionable.

Some kind of mistake? Unnecessary duplication? Had one of the more junior staff, through ignorance of Amanda's case, written her up for a procedure she didn't need? It seemed plausible. Dunbar wondered how he could check. He supposed there must be a record of the test somewhere, even if it hadn't been entered in the patient's notes. He would call up the record of theatre usage for the past few days and find out where the marrow puncture had taken place and who had carried it out. He didn't want to make a big thing out of it; he just wanted to know.

The computer obediently showed the schedules for each theatre in turn. There was no record of Amanda being treated in any of them. There was, of course, a theatre in the Obstetrics wing being used by the Omega patient. No information was available on its use, in keeping with the total confidentiality rule for these patients, but that didn't seem a very likely choice . . . or did it? Dunbar suddenly remembered the little girl being taken into the lift leading to the Omega wing on the night he'd raided the Radiology Department. Now it made sense. The girl must have been Amanda Chapman.

Ingrid returned and said, 'I've done the costings you asked for on transplant patients.'

'Well done.'

'I think you're in for a bit of a shock,' she said, putting the file in front of him.

Dunbar looked at the final figure and let out his breath in a low whistle. 'That much!' he exclaimed.

'I'm afraid so,' said Ingrid. 'It's an expensive business.'

Dunbar nodded and she smiled. 'You'll be regretting having agreed to the free NHS referral case,' she joked.

'Money isn't everything,' he replied.

'I don't think the Scottish Office would be too keen on hearing you say that,' said Ingrid.

'Perhaps not. But maybe a good part of the cost will be offset by the money coming in from the Omega patient?'

'I'm sorry, I don't think I understand.'

'I just thought that Omega patient fees might subsidize the hospital's generosity when it came to free transplant cases.'

'Oh I see,' said Ingrid.

'Amanda Chapman isn't the first transplant patient the hospital has taken on for nothing,' said Dunbar. 'I noticed there were two others in the past. They were on the list of free referrals you prepared for me. I just wondered if the cost of their operations had been offset against Omega patients too?'

'I'm not sure.' She sounded a little uncertain, but soon recovered and said, 'I suppose you may be right.'

Dunbar was puzzled. There was so much money involved that he felt sure Ingrid ought to know how the free transplant referrals had been financed. In fact, he was surprised that more had not been made of the hospital's generosity, in terms of publicity. After all, the news of Médic Ecosse using large fees to finance expensive charity cases would have reflected very well on the hospital and particularly, as most of the costs would have been borne by the transplant unit, on James Ross and his staff. It would, of course, be at odds with a unit callously conducting animal experiments on some of their patients . . .

Dunbar thought he could see a way of asking Ingrid about the tests on Amanda Chapman without arousing suspicion. He looked down her list of transplant costs, then said jokingly, 'It looks like you folks are short-changing Amanda Chapman.'

'What do you mean?'

'According to her costing file, she hasn't had any of these tests you put on the list for transplant admissions.'

Ingrid came over to stand behind him and look at the screen. Dunbar brought up Amanda's file. 'See?'

Her face relaxed into a smile and she said, 'Oh, I know why not. Amanda didn't have these tests because she came here from the Children's Hospital. She had all her immunology stats done over there. She didn't need them. She's already on the register.'

'Of course,' said Dunbar. 'I should have thought of that.'

But her words raised new questions. Just what the hell had Médic Ecosse been doing, giving Amanda-Chapman a marrow puncture at night in the Omega patient's wing? If Ingrid Landes, a secretary, realized that Amanda didn't need further immunology testing, then so without doubt did the nursing and medical staff. Come to think of it, how did Ingrid know about immunology testing? She worked for Giordano in administration; she wasn't even a medical secretary. It made him curious. The next time she was out of the room he would pull her personnel file.

In the meantime, he resigned himself to working his way through the accounts for the last financial year, while he waited for the answer to his request for the exhumation of Amy Teasdale. To offset some of the boredom, and check up on things that it might be useful to know in the long run, he'd try to find out something about the money allocated to Ross's research.

Until the Scottish Office had pulled the plug on the previous arrangement, he recalled, Ross's funding had been a proportion of transplant unit profits. As that was the case, the hospital accounts might hold itemized costings for the research. Dunbar wanted to know what the money was being spent on. He also thought he might find out where Ross's research funding was currently coming from.

At first, the accounts seemed to have no reference at all to money being allocated to a research budget. Dunbar couldn't understand it. It wasn't as if it was secret. Ross was a widely acclaimed researcher.

Everyone knew about his research programme. If the item he was looking for was not listed as research money, it must be listed under something else. He checked the file-names again, and his eye was caught by something called 'Vane Farm Account.' What was that?

He clicked it open and found what he was looking for. Ross's research labs were located at a place called Vane Farm. Dunbar supposed it made sense if a lot of the work was concerned with experimental animals. Everything connected with Ross's research seemed to be itemized in the Vane Farm account, from technicians' salaries to rent for the property, from laboratory equipment to security expenditure. He also noted the purchase of pigs.

There was, however, nothing about alternative sources of funding in the current year. Dunbar had expected to find an increase in core funding from Médic International, which would have been the simplest explanation for Ross having stayed on after the withdrawal of unit-linked funding. But there was no sign of such an increase. He supposed, however, that this could still be the case. There would be no requirement to channel such funding through the hospital accounts, particularly as Ross's research facilities were located elsewhere. That must be the explanation, unless Ross was funding his own research; and for that he would have to be awfully rich.

Dunbar knew what Ross earned. His salary was listed in the Sci-Med files. It certainly wasn't enough to facilitate private research. On the other hand, Ross did have consultancy work in Geneva. Sci-Med hadn't given details, merely noting that he had it. Was this because they didn't know any more? He'd ask them when they finally got back to him about his earlier request. Why were they taking so long?

Ingrid went to lunch. Dunbar said he'd go later, in keeping with his policy of keeping his relationship with Ingrid on a strictly business footing. He still wasn't sure about her. The possibility that she had been assigned to keep an eye on him was always in his mind, so the safest course of action was to keep her at arm's length. While she was away, he pulled out her file.

Ingrid Landes was a fully qualified nurse, he discovered. Besides that she was a graduate in nursing studies from the University of Edinburgh. She had worked in several private clinics before joining Médic Ecosse on the administrative staff. Her last nursing position had been at the St Pierre Clinic in Geneva.

Well, well, well, thought Dunbar. It's a small world. Had Ross been responsible for bringing Ingrid to Médic Ecosse?

His mobile phone rang and broke his train of thought. Thinking it must be Sci-Med with news about the exhumation, Dunbar snatched up the handset.

'Steven? I'm sorry to bother you,' said Lisa's voice, 'but I thought I'd better tell you where I am in case you tried my number and started to worry when there was no reply.'

'What's wrong? Has something happened?' asked Dunbar.

'It's Mum. She took ill during the night. The doctor thinks it's pneumonia. They're taking her into the Western Infirmary. I'm going with her.'

'I'm sorry,' said Dunbar. 'Actually I was going to call you,' he began uneasily.

'Oh yes?'

'It's about Amy . . .'

'What about her?'

'I've requested her exhumation. I didn't tell you sooner because I wasn't sure how you'd take it.'

There was a long pause.

'Are you still there?'

'Yes,' said Lisa. 'It just took me by surprise. It shouldn't have. I suppose it was the obvious thing to do.'

'There's no other way of finding out,' said Dunbar gently.

'I suppose not,' said Lisa distantly. 'Her poor parents. After all they've been through . . . They're going to blame me for this.'

'Why?'

Lisa broke off. 'I'll have to go,' she said. 'They're waiting for me. I'll talk to you later.'

'Lisa—' Dunbar heard the phone go dead. 'Damn,' he muttered.

He sat for a few minutes, then decided to drive over to the Western Infirmary.

He parked in a side street at least a quarter of a mile away from the entrance, thinking that this would be easier than trying to find a parking space any nearer. If he tried, he'd probably fail and spend the next ten minutes kerb-crawling around adjacent streets before ending up where he already was. He walked briskly up to the hospital and followed the signs to the medical admissions ward. He found Lisa sitting on the edge of a plastic chair in the corridor outside, knees clamped together with her clasped hands caught between them. She was staring at the floor as if deeply unhappy.

'Lisa?'

Lisa looked up and he could see that her eyes were red.

'What are you doing here?' she asked, although she did not seem disappointed.

'You're upset. I thought I might run you home.'

She smiled wanly. 'A kind thought.'

'So what's upsetting you most? Your mother or Amy.'

'Both I suppose, in their own ways.'

A plump nurse with flat feet in the 'ten to two' position, and holding a clipboard in one hand and a pencil in the other, appeared in the doorway. She asked, 'Miss Fairfax?'

Lisa stepped forward. 'Yes?'

'Dr Campbell will see you now.' Lisa turned to Dunbar.

'Go ahead. I'll wait here,' said Dunbar.

Lisa was gone for about five minutes. When she returned Dunbar stood up. 'What's the news?'

'She's tucked up in bed. They've started her on a course of antibiotics. That's about it for the moment.'

As they sat at traffic lights on the way back to Lisa's flat, Dunbar said quietly. 'I got the lab report on the isotope from Sheila Barnes's house. There's nothing to link it to Médic Ecosse.'

'You're kidding!' exclaimed Lisa. 'But it must have been them. Who else would have wanted to harm her?'

'My feelings too,' agreed Dunbar. 'But the lab says it was an industrial isotope not used by anyone in Scotland as far as they know.'

'So they covered their tracks,' said Lisa.

'Looks like it.'

They started moving again. Dunbar asked, 'What did you mean when you said that Amy's parents would blame you?'

Lisa sighed at a painful recollection. She said, 'At the time of Amy's death, Médic Ecosse managed to convince her parents that I was some kind of unbalanced trouble-maker because of what I was saying. I suppose to them that's exactly what I must have seemed. I intruded on their grief, and it wasn't a nice feeling, I assure you.'

'I can imagine,' said Dunbar. 'But you did what you thought was right. That's not always easy.'

'And here I am about to do it all over again,' said Lisa, her voice heavy with doubt.

'It's out of your hands, Lisa.'

'Mmm,' she said, unconvinced.

They had arrived at Lisa's place. In the middle of the day there was plenty of room to park. Dunbar drew up outside the entrance to the block.

'Will you come up for a minute?'

He nodded and got out.

'Coffee?' asked Lisa as they entered the flat.

'I'll make it. You go bathe your eyes,' said Dunbar.

The comment made her self-conscious. Her hand flew to her face. 'Oh God, I must look a sight. I didn't think.'

She went off to the bathroom and Dunbar put the kettle on. While it boiled, he looked out of the window.

Lisa returned some minutes later, smoothing her hair and smelling of perfume. She'd put on light make-up. 'That's better,' she said with a smile. 'I feel human again.'

Dunbar smiled too, and responded to her attempts at small-talk as she tried to get back on an even keel. When she fell silent he turned to look at her and saw that her eyes were closed.

'Are you all right?' he asked gently.

'There was something I didn't tell you,' she said.

'What?' Dunbar took her in his arms as the tears started to flow.

'I went to Amy's funeral . . . just to say good-bye to her properly. I tried to keep in the background but her mother saw me there . . . No one ever looked at me the way she did . . . There was such hatred in her eyes.'

'You mustn't dwell on it,' soothed Dunbar. 'She must have been confused and very upset at the time. You said what you believed to be true; that was the right thing to do and when we come up with the evidence of what really happened to Amy, you'll be completely vindicated.' He relaxed his hold a little and Lisa looked up at him.

'Thank you,' she said.

'For what?'

'For being here.'

'Sssh.'

Lisa's face was very close to Dunbar's. He looked down into her soft dark eyes and found himself realizing just how much she had got under his skin in the past few days. Images of her had been subtly invading his mind. He saw her lips quiver and part slightly as she sensed his arousal. She didn't draw back. He brushed an unruly tendril of hair from her face and tucked it gently behind her ear, his fingers tracing on down the curve of her cheek to tilt her face upwards. He brushed a kiss across her lips, still a little uncertain.

Lisa sensed his hesitation and reached up to tangle her fingers in his hair and draw his lips back down to hers. Their kiss, soft at first, deepened as each felt the other respond.

Any reservations Dunbar might have had about Lisa's vulnerability ceased to matter. He was aware only of the closeness of her body and the little darting movements of her tongue inside his mouth. His hands slid down her back and over the neat curve of her buttocks to pull her into him until their hips and thighs met and she could feel him harden.

She drew back slightly. She drew in a ragged breath. 'Come,' she said, leading him by the hand through to the bedroom.

'You're sure?' breathed Dunbar as he took hold of her again.

'Very sure,' replied Lisa, slipping her hands round his waist and easing his shirt free of his trousers. Pushing the fabric from his body, she smoothed her palms across the contours of his chest. Her eyes never left his as she moved her hands down to undo his belt and free him from his trousers.

Mimicking her actions, Dunbar pulled her blouse from the band of her skirt, slipped his hand underneath and ran it across the smooth plane of her stomach. He reached round to unhook her bra before capturing her breasts in his hands, making her groan with pleasure as he sought her nipples. She tilted her head back to expose her neck to his lips and allowed him to lay her down on the bed.

Dunbar trailed a line of kisses down her throat, opening her blouse in front of each kiss. His mouth encircled each nipple in turn, sucking and teasing, while his hand sought the bare skin of her thighs to peel off her panties. He straddled her and held himself poised above her to kiss her long and slow before easing into her and glorying in the depth of her arousal as she lifted her hips and took him in.

Lisa moaned and he shifted slightly to bring his hand between them, touching her softly and skilfully, capturing her cries with his mouth as he drove into her again and again until a shudder went through him and her body convulsed around him.

Passion spent, they relaxed together in a contented tangle. Dunbar was the first to move. He rolled over, kissed Lisa lightly on the forehead and cradled her in his arms.

'God, it's been such a long time,' she murmured. 'I hadn't realized.'

'There's no one special?'

'I was engaged for a while until he realized that Mother was going to be part of the deal. He disappeared like snow in July. It's been over two years now. And you? I suppose this is where you tell me there's a Mrs Dunbar and the twins will be three on Sunday?'

Dunbar smiled. 'No Mrs Dunbar,' he said. He had his arm round her and was gently stroking her forehead.

'You know, that's what I miss most,' said Lisa.

'What?'

'Being touched. It's so nice just to be touched like that. With affection. Sex can be great but feeling someone touch your arm or run their fingers through your hair, or even just pat your bum because they feel nice things for you, that's really good. Does that sound daft?'

Dunbar kissed her hair softly. 'No.'

There was a distant bleeping sound.

'What's that?' she asked.

'My phone,' replied Dunbar, feeling silly.

'You didn't switch it off?'

'I didn't think,' said Dunbar. 'I didn't imagine I'd . . .'

'You'd better answer it.'

Dunbar got up and went in search of his phone. He took the call in the living room. He returned a few moments later and said, 'It was Sci-Med. They've agreed to the exhumation.'

TWELVE

On the day of the exhumation, Dunbar was on tenterhooks. Sci-Med had enlisted the aid of Special Branch in carrying out an unofficial disinterment of the body, rather than taking the gamble of going to the courts for a high-profile official order, with all the subsequent upset that might cause. Dunbar was happy with that but was well aware that covert operations carried risks of their own should anything go wrong. One person in the wrong place at the wrong time and the fall-out could be spectacular.

Amy's parents were out of the country on holiday – her mother was still suffering from depression some five months after Amy's death and her father had thought some winter sunshine might help her. They had been in Tenerife for the last three days and would be away for another ten. It was this fact that had swung Sci-Med in favour of a secret operation. If everything went smoothly, Amy's parents need never know anything about it.

The plan was to exhume Amy in the early hours of the morning, take her to a Glasgow mortuary and have a Scottish Office patholo-gist, appointed by Neil Bannon, carry out an autopsy under special instructions. When he was finished, he would phone his report to Dunbar. Amy would be returned to her grave before the day was over.

Everything was out of Dunbar's hands now, but he still felt like an athlete pacing the area behind the start-line before a big race. The phone rang and he snatched it from its rest.

'Yes?'

'Steven, it's Lisa. Any news?'

'Nothing yet. They seem to be taking a hell of a time.'

'I'll get off the line in case they're trying to get through.'

'I'll call you as soon as I hear.'

Dunbar went back to fidgeting and pacing the room. He began to wonder if there had been a breakdown in communications. Tension could make you imagine all sorts of things, especially when your perceived timescale of things was being stretched. Perhaps the result of the PM had been given directly to Sci-Med in London, the police had already been informed and they would arrive at the hospital at any moment, everyone having forgotten to tell the man on the ground what was going on. He was nursing this paranoia when the phone rang again.

'Dr Dunbar, please.'

'Speaking.'

'Your authorization code, please.'

Dunbar gave it.

'Sorry for the melodrama, but I was told to go exactly by the book on this one.'

'That's OK.'

'My name's McVay. I've been instructed by the Scottish Office to carry out a post-mortem on the exhumed body of one Amy Teasdale at the behest of the Sci-Med Inspectorate.'

'Yes. I've been waiting for your call.'

'Sorry it took so long, but there was a fair bit of lab work to do on this one.'

'I understand. What did you find?'

'Well, no one provided me with too much background on the case. They didn't think to tell me that the child had already undergone extensive PM examination.'

'I suppose that's entirely possible,' said Dunbar. 'She died after a kidney transplant went wrong. A PM would probably be necessary in the circumstances.'

'I just thought I'd mention it. Her kidneys and heart had already been removed for examination and then replaced. I even found a couple of swabs they'd used at the time. I hate it when pathologists are too damn lazy to clean up their mess and use the cadaver as a rubbish bin. Lazy sods!'

Dunbar bit his lip to stop himself betraying his impatience. 'What exactly did you find, Doctor?' he asked slowly and deliberately.

'My specific brief was to concentrate on the transplanted right kidney and carry out immunological testing with a view to compatibility. I was asked to pay particular attention to tissue type and to . . . species.'

'Yes.'

'The transplanted organ was a human kidney; it was also perfectly compatible with the patient's tissue type. We came up with a rating of eighty-one per cent homology.'

Dunbar felt the bottom drop out of his world. 'Human and eighty-one per cent compatible,' he echoed. 'Are you sure?'

It was a stupid question and the snapped answer told him that McVay thought so too. 'Of course. Plus or minus five per cent.'

'Thank you, Doctor,' said Dunbar, now on autopilot. 'You didn't happen to notice anything at all out of the ordinary, did you?'

'Apart from the cadaver having been autopsied before, no. It seemed an unnecessary shame to have dug her up, if you ask me.'

'Quite so,' said Dunbar, and he put the phone down.

He stared at the wall for a few minutes; he didn't know which emotion to address first. He felt disappointed, dejected, foolish and totally bemused. He'd made a fool of himself and it hurt. He knew he should call Lisa, but right now he even felt angry with her – and with Sheila Barnes, for that matter. Between them they had convinced him the children really had been given the wrong organs during their operations. It was this that had made him read so much into what he'd seen in the post-mortem suite at Médic Ecosse.

Now it seemed that Amy Teasdale had, in fact, been given the correct donor kidney and what he'd seen in the basement was probably just an experimental dissection, bizarre to the outside observer but legal and licensed.

Now the only thing against it all having been some huge mistake was the fact that someone had set out to kill Sheila Barnes. But why? If everything to do with the transplant had been above-board and Sheila was mistaken, why set out to kill her? It didn't make sense. But then none of this did. He picked up the phone and called Lisa.

'Well?' she asked anxiously.

'There was nothing wrong with the kidney Amy was given. It was human and eighty-one per cent compatible.'

There was a pause before Lisa said, 'But that's impossible. Her reaction was so strong, it just couldn't have been compatible.'

'I'm sorry, Lisa,' said Dunbar. 'But those are the findings of the pathologist commissioned by the Scottish Office. We have to accept what he says.'

'I just don't understand. There's no way a reaction like that could have been caused by . . .' Her voice tailed off.

'I'm sorry,' said Dunbar.

'Then why try to kill Sheila Barnes?' asked Lisa, clutching at the same straw as he'd found.

'You're right,' he agreed. 'That doesn't fit at all. We thought it did, even if it was a strange way to do it, but not any more.'

'What happens now?'

'I expect to be recalled to London to explain myself. I can't see beyond that at the moment.'

'I'm sorry. I feel responsible,' said Lisa.

'No one's to blame,' said Dunbar. 'With a bit of luck no one will find out about the disinterment, so in the end no great harm will have been done.'

'God, I don't think I could bear it if Amy's parents found out,' said Lisa. 'An exhumation for no good reason, after all the pain I caused them the first time around. It doesn't bear thinking about. I was so sure they were going to find that Amy had been given an animal kidney.'

'Me too.'

'You don't think her parents will find out, do you?' She asked anxiously.

'As far as I know, there were no hitches, so it should be okay. Fingers crossed.'

Lisa sighed deeply, then said, 'You know what? In spite of everything you've told me – and I know I have to accept it – I still know I was right. I don't know how or why, I just do.'

Dunbar didn't know what to say. 'I wish there was some way you could be,' he began.

'It's all right,' she reassured him. 'I don't expect you to fly in the face of the facts as they stand. I just don't understand it, that's all. I really don't. But then I don't think I understand anything any more. The rejections of perfectly compatible organs, Sheila's cancer, the pig experiments in the hospital, and now it seems that everything's fine and above-board in that place?'

'For what it's worth, my gut feeling says there's something terribly wrong too. It's just that I have to have evidence before I do anything and there isn't any.'

'London weren't too keen on the exhumation in the first place, were they?' said Lisa.

'You can say that again,' said Dunbar wryly.

'Are you going to get into trouble?'

'I'm expecting a call at any minute, inviting me to London to face the music.'

'You don't think you'll lose your job over this, do you?' asked Lisa.

Dunbar grimaced and said, 'I think in the circumstances I might feel obliged to offer my resignation.'

'Don't.'

'Sorry?'

'You didn't make a mistake. You acted in good faith. You had the courage of your convictions. Ring a bell?'

Dunbar smiled to himself. 'But the fact of the matter is that the exhumation was a mistake,' he said.

'Only in hindsight,' she insisted. 'No one starts off with hindsight. Don't resign. If they fire you there's not much you can do about it, but don't make it easy for them. You're the one on the ground, not them. You did nothing wrong. Stand up to them.'

'We'll see,' said Dunbar with a shrug, but he appreciated her support.

Dunbar received the expected call just after 4 p.m. He was told to report to Sci-Med in London the following day. The director would see him at eleven. He called Lisa to tell her.

'Come round later,' she said. 'The condemned man deserves a fond farewell.'

Dunbar took the tube into central London from Heathrow. It was raining heavily and the carriage began to smell of wet clothes. There were no smiles among the morning commuters. They were apparently looking forward to the day as much as he was. He passed the time trying to predict what each of his immediate travelling companions did for a living. Unfortunately he couldn't ask them if he was right.

He was glad of the fresh air when he finally got off the train and climbed the stairs to the outside. It didn't matter that it was raining. He started looking for a cab to take him up to the Home Office. Because of the weather it took some time to find one, but he didn't mind the wait. Turkeys didn't long for Christmas.

'Nice to see you again, Dr Dunbar,' said the director's secretary, Miss Roberts, with a welcoming smile. 'Mr Macmillan won't keep you waiting long.'

'I'm in no great hurry,' replied Dunbar with heavy irony.

She smiled but said nothing. A buzzer sounded on her desk and she nodded to Dunbar. 'Good luck,' she whispered as he passed.

'Ah, Dunbar. Come in, sit down,' said Macmillan. Tall and silver-haired, in any other environment he would have stood out as being extremely distinguished-looking, but here in Whitehall he was one among many. The upper echelons of the Civil Service seemed to attract such people. Dunbar often wondered if the job did it to the man or vice versa. On reflection he supposed that there was a type of person for most jobs. There were exceptions, of course, but the Hollywood stereotype for most professions often wasn't far from the truth.

Macmillan closed the file he had been working on and put an end to Dunbar's philosophizing. 'You've dropped us in it, Dunbar,' he said.

'I'm sorry,' said Dunbar. 'I was sure I was right.'

'Do you realize how much it cost us to mount an unofficial exhumation?'

Dunbar had no idea but felt sure he was about to be told. The director told him. Dunbar looked suitably shocked.

'Not to mention the calling in of favours and the fact that we are now beholden to Special Branch, of all people.'

'Everything pointed to the dead child having been given the wrong organ – an incompatible animal organ,' said Dunbar.

'You mean a hysterical woman pointed to the dead child having been given the wrong organ. And you jumped to conclusions.'

'Neither of the women involved can in any way be described as hysterical,' argued Dunbar. 'I've interviewed both of them and made up my mind about that. There's also the fact that one of them, Sheila Barnes, has been the subject of what I believe to be a deliberate murder attempt, one that's going to be successful very soon.'

'Ah yes, the isotope in the wall,' said Macmillan. 'But I must remind you that the lab found nothing that linked the source to the Médic Ecosse hospital.'

'That doesn't mean they weren't involved,' said Dunbar.

Macmillan conceded the point with a doubtful shrug. He stroked his moustache thoughtfully, then said, 'My feeling is that we should hand the Barnes case over to the police. There's little doubt that a crime has been committed so they can take it from there and we can, with a bit of luck, extract ourselves from this mess you've landed us in.'

'Despite your man's findings I still think there was something odd about the two children's deaths,' said Dunbar. 'I did a computer search for deaths under similar circumstances; there were none. Yet Médic Ecosse has had two. I believe we should hang on to the investigation. We're the best qualified people to look into this sort of thing. That's why we exist.'

'Don't try to tell me why we exist, Dunbar!' snapped Macmillan.

'No, sir. I just feel that handing everything over to the police at this stage is a bit of a cop-out. They'll mount an investigation but they won't get anywhere. As for us, we seem to be more interested in keeping our noses clean than in seeing this affair through to a conclusion.'

For a moment Dunbar thought he had gone too far. His P45 form floated before his eyes like a kite in a mocking breeze, but the anger died out of the director's eyes.

'You think that, do you?'

'Yes, sir, I do.'

'I'll tell you what. If you can come up with an explanation of how these two damned women could still be right, in spite of the fact – fact, mind you – that Amy Teasdale's body contains the right organ, then we'll keep hold of the investigation.'

'How long have I got?' asked Dunbar.

'Three days.'

Dunbar left the Home Office with mixed feelings. It could have been worse, he supposed. They could have fired him then and there. Instead they'd given him three days to come up with an explanation he'd been up most of the night searching for already. He walked along the Embankment hoping for inspiration, but all he got was wet. London was his favourite city but today he found himself totally impervious to its charms. In the rain, it could have been East Berlin. He returned to the airport to catch the shuttle back to Glasgow.

On the plane, he succumbed to the lure of a large gin and tonic offered by the stewardess. He was feeling low and his mood was not helped by the arrival of a plump northern businessman in the seat next to him. From the opening of 'D'you go to Scotland a lot, then?' he knew he was in trouble. Monosyllabic responses were no deterrent to Arthur Shelby, who was in hydraulic systems and was determined to fill this particular gap in Dunbar's education during the following fifty-five minutes. There was barely time for

Shelby to get round to 'What line are you in yourself, then?' before the plane landed and Dunbar was free at last. He called Lisa from the airport.

'Well?'

'They didn't fire me. They gave me three days to come up with an idea.'

'Is that good or bad?'

'Depends if I do or not.'

'Are you going to come over?'

'I've got a better idea. Why don't we go out to dinner this evening?'

'We might be seen by someone who works at Médic Ecosse,' replied Lisa.

'We can drive to some place out of town.'

'If you're sure you want to take the risk.'

'Let's do it. Pick you up at seven?'

'I'll be waiting.'

Dunbar arrived at Lisa's place on time and found her ready, She had dressed up for the occasion. He smiled and said, 'You look wonderful.'

'Well, thank you. All this new-found freedom is making me feel dangerously like a human being.'

'How is your mother, by the way?' asked Dunbar, remembering the key to Lisa's freedom.

'She's holding her own.'

'I'm going to have to rely on you to suggest where we go this evening.'

'I thought we might drive up to the Lake of Menteith. It's not that far and there's a nice hotel there. It's right down on the shores of the lake.'

'Sounds good. Do you think we'll get in?'

'I took the liberty of booking after you rang,' Lisa confessed.

The drive up to the Lake of Menteith was straightforward and uneventful, and Dunbar was glad to see there were only four other cars in the car park as they drew to a halt. He wanted a quiet evening with time to talk. They both sipped gin and tonic while deciding what to eat. It wasn't until they had ordered and the waiter had left that Lisa said, 'So, what sort of an idea do you have to come up with?'

'One that explains how you and Sheila Barnes could still be right in spite of everything.'

'It sounds as if you took our part in London.'

Dunbar nodded.

'Well, you were right to,' she said.

Dunbar looked at her in silence for a moment, then said, 'It's a comfort to hear you sound so sure. You haven't wavered once, have you?'

'I came pretty close when you told me of the pathologist's findings,' she confessed. 'But I know what I saw, and it was not the result of the transplant of a compatible organ.'

'So our starting-point must be that Amy was definitely given the wrong kidney.'

'Yes,' said Lisa flatly.

Dunbar paused as their first course arrived. Then he said, 'So if the correct donor kidney was found inside Amy after the exhumation . . . it must have got there some time after her operation. In fact, if she died of rejection problems, it must have been put there sometime after her death . . . At the first post mortem, of course!' he exclaimed as things slipped into place. 'As simple as that. Amy *was* given the wrong organ but it was switched to the right one after she died.'

Lisa's eyes were sparkling with excitement. 'You're right,' she said. 'That's exactly what must have happened. But why?'

'Let's see. A donor organ becomes available; Médic Ecosse obtains it from the source hospital . . . but instead of giving it to the patient, they use him or her for one of their animal experiments.'

'And if it goes wrong, they cover their tracks by substituting the correct one at post-mortem!' said Lisa.

'But how do we go about proving it?'

There was a long silence.

'Let's eat first,' said Dunbar, picking up his knife and fork. 'We're doing okay.'

They didn't talk much as they ate, largely because they were both deep in thought. They reached the coffee stage still without coming up with any good idea as to how to prove their theory. It was, however, early days and both of them were pleased about having solved the first bit of the puzzle.

As they left the hotel and wandered down to the jetty to take a look at the lake in the frosty moonlight, Dunbar said, 'Medical researchers are trained scientists, meticulous people, precise in all things. Facts and figures are of paramount importance to them.'

'What are you getting at?'

'I don't think I've ever come across a researcher who didn't keep notes.'

'So?' said Lisa.

'It's a basic requirement of the job that you keep accurate records of everything you do in order to write up your results for the journals. You also have to be in a position to show data to back up your claims, should the scientific community request it. All your work is subject to peer review.'

'I still don't see what you're getting at,' said Lisa, snuggling down deeper into her coat.

'They must have records somewhere.'

'Secret notebooks, you mean?'

'More likely to be computer files these days,' said Dunbar.

'So if you could get your hands on them you might find all the evidence you needed?'

'That's what I'm thinking,' he agreed. 'They must have kept records of all the experiments they've done, what went right, what went wrong, what their conclusions were, what they're going to do next.'

'Makes sense. But how on earth are you going to get your hands on something like that?'

'Presumably the records are kept somewhere in Ross's research lab. I'd have to get in there somehow, but nothing has happened to spook the people in the transplant unit. They've no reason to be on their guard. I'm sure I can think of a way and once inside I think I'll be able to lay hands on what I need. If I could hand the police records of experiments involving the kids, I think we could nail them.'

Lisa looked dubious. 'I don't think you should rush into this. It could be dangerous. You don't really know what you're up against.'

'They're not professional criminals,' said Dunbar. 'I think we're talking about a few ambitious bastards who've been cutting corners to speed up their research.'

'But they've killed two children and we think they're also killing a nursing sister and her husband. Don't you think that's an unusually high price for even the most ambitious of researchers to contemplate?'

Dunbar had to agree. 'You think I'm missing something?'

'I think it's possible, and I wouldn't like it to kill you,' said Lisa.

'I'll bear that in mind.'

'You haven't had any more thoughts about the isotope, have you?'

Dunbar shook his head. 'I suppose Médic Ecosse were just too clever and careful to use one that could be traced back to them. They seem to think of everything – including switching the organs in corpses in case anyone should dig them up and examine them.'

'You'll get a break soon,' said Lisa, slipping her arm into his as they turned back to the car park. 'I can feel it.'

Dunbar phoned Sci-Med first thing in the morning and spoke to Macmillan. 'Sir, you asked me to reconcile the nurses' allegations with the pathologist's findings. I think I can.'

'Amaze me,' said Macmillan drily.

'They switched the organs after death, probably during the post-mortem.'

'After death?'

'It's still possible they've been carrying out experiments on children, using animal organs. They wait until a compatible donor organ becomes available for their patient and then obtain it. But they don't use it; they just keep it as insurance. If their experiment fails, they replace the animal organ with the human one before releasing the body for burial.'

Macmillan said, 'Good God, what an awful thought. It's possible, I suppose, but damn nearly impossible to prove I'd have thought.'

'I'd like to try but I need more time.'

'But even supposing you're right, Dunbar, don't you think they'd have stopped after the first death?'

'I'm sorry?'

'Why didn't they abandon the whole thing after the first patient died? Why would they continue, knowing the experiment was a failure?'

'Perhaps they believed they'd solved the problem,' ventured Dunbar.

'Mmmm,' said Macmillan, unconvinced.

Dunbar offered no further argument. Lisa had suggested there was more to it than he thought. Macmillan was doing the same. It was just possible they were right.

THIRTEEN

Dunbar went out for a late-night walk. The earlier rain had stopped, leaving the streets wet but the air cold, dry and mercifully still. He pulled up the collar of his overcoat and set out for nowhere in particular. He just needed to think. Darkness and quiet streets were going to help.

Lisa and Macmillan had given him the uneasy feeling that something was wrong with his whole train of thought. It was the feeling you got when, believing yourself to be on the right road to somewhere, you kept on picking up little clues that said you weren't. At first, you were reluctant to acknowledge them because you wanted to believe nothing was wrong. You could even convince yourself that you were seeing the landmarks you were supposed to see. You simply altered or modified your expectation to suit. Even as evidence to the contrary mounted, you continued to hope against hope that everything was going to work out, because the alternative meant admitting that you were absolutely lost.

He was afraid the same might apply to his thinking about the use of animal organs for transplant at Médic Ecosse. He had come up with a get-out-of-jail card over that one by mooting a switch of organs after death so, in theory, he could still be right. But now, as he thought it through rationally and without emotion, he started to worry. The little clues were there. He had to steel himself to look at them dispassionately.

Lisa had stuck to her guns so tenaciously because Amy Teasdale's reaction to her transplant had been so strong. As an experienced transplant nurse, she just couldn't believe that Amy had been given the right organ. The same was true of Sheila Barnes and her patient,

Kenneth Lineham – another strong reaction. What he had found it convenient to ignore until now was the inference that not only had the organs been unsuitable, but they had not even been close in terms of compatibility.

This was a major puzzle and one he'd have to face up to. Ross wasn't some Mickey Mouse researcher who'd transplant any old organ into a patient to see what happened. He was an acclaimed expert in the field of transplant immunology. He'd know beforehand, through extensive lab work, exactly what the chances of success were. In fact, it seemed entirely reasonable to assume that he wouldn't even contemplate carrying out experimental surgery unless he was pretty damned sure of success. Yet there had been two spectacular failures. Why?

This in turn begged the question of how many experiments there had been. Were the two failures exceptions to the rule? Had there been lots of successful animal transplants that hadn't come to light? There was no way of knowing without access to Ross's research records. There was, of course, the nagging possibility that he was completely and utterly mistaken about the whole thing. Ross had done nothing wrong. There had been no animal transplant experiments. The two kids had suffered from some unknown, non-specific form of tissue rejection, however unlikely the coincidence, and the whole damned investigation had been a mistake from the start.

Dunbar knew he'd have to decide soon which seemed the likelier; the decision about a break-in at Vane Farm was going to be his. He'd be putting himself and Sci-Med at risk, and he needed to feel easier in his mind about the justification for doing so. He sought some resolution of the problem in thinking about the other odd things that had happened at Médic Ecosse.

Going back to the very beginning, he still thought it peculiar and out of character that Ross had accepted the Scottish Office cuts in research funding without much more than a whimper of protest. He'd assumed at the time that Ross must have been promised alternative funding, but if that were so where was it coming from? The fact that he hadn't been able to find any trace of it didn't necessarily mean it didn't exist, but if it didn't – and even if it did – it was possible that Ross had some other reason for staying on.

Pursuing that line of thought, he wondered whether Ross had allowed himself to be humiliated in public because he had something going on at Médic Ecosse, something he didn't want interrupted, something so important to him that he was prepared to lose any amount of face. Could research glory be that important to the man? Perhaps. But Ross already enjoyed an international reputation as a researcher. He didn't need the extra kudos. He wasn't some young, ambitious buck out to make a name for himself, who'd cut corners if need be.

The more he thought about it, the more unlikely it seemed that Ross would have risked his career and reputation, and killed two children into the bargain, for the sake of stealing a march on the opposition over the issue of animal organs for human transplant. Apart from that, he couldn't publish the results of his work anyway without advertising his guilt. The best he could do would be to learn from them and start out on a legal programme of research, helped by facts he already knew. Seen in that light, the price seemed unfeasibly high – something Lisa had pointed out. So, if it wasn't research glory that Ross was after, what could it be?

The obvious answer was money. There certainly seemed to be no limit to what people, at any level in society, would do if the price was right. This was a fact of life. But if money satisfied the question of motive, it obscured the crime. He couldn't see how anything connected with animal organs for transplant could attract enough money for a man like Ross to risk everything. There was also the problem that Ross didn't appear to be particularly wealthy. His lifestyle seemed to be roughly in keeping with his eighty-odd thousand a year salary, but of course that could be contrived. Ross was an extremely clever man. He wouldn't do anything as crass as live beyond his means if he really was involved in something sinister.

Thinking about Ross's earnings reminded Dunbar that he'd forgotten to ask Sci-Med for more information about Ross's work in Geneva. It probably wasn't relevant, but they hadn't supplied details at the outset. He'd remind them the next time he was in contact. It was untypical of them to have left that unresolved.

Dunbar realized that if he were to implicate Ross in something steeped in self-interest he'd have to explain away Ross's philanthropic record over transplants for NHS patients at Médic Ecosse. He'd taken on three such patients in three years when he'd been under no pressure at all to do so. The gesture would have significantly reduced profits for his unit and therefore his share of the payout under the old agreement. No one would have quibbled at Médic Ecosse drawing the line at free transplants, especially when they hadn't been doing well financially, yet they'd taken on three.

Ingrid's apparent ignorance about the funding of transplants for such patients was another puzzle. He'd thought she'd have been only too keen to confirm that the costs were set off against profits from Omega patients, but, although she'd finally agreed that this was probably the case, she'd behaved as if it were a novel suggestion. It would be worth investigating the funding of these patients further.

Dunbar reminded himself that he hadn't yet got back to Clive Turner at the Children's Hospital about the marrow puncture on Amanda Chapman. It wasn't that he'd forgotten; he simply did not know what to tell him. Officially it had never happened. It was just another strange happening at Médic Ecosse, not terribly important in itself but, again, out of character in an organization that prided itself on efficiency. It would be silly to pretend that people did not make mistakes there, but it would be fair to say they made fewer than most.

The question he had to face up to now was the big one. Did he believe that there was enough reason to warrant a break-in at Vane Farm, with all its attendant risks? He could think of no other way of getting more information about Ross's research work. The answer, he decided, was yes.

As he crossed one of the bridges over the Clyde, Dunbar paused to lean on the parapet and look down at the dark water swirling below. He was looking for inspiration. Would he attempt the break-in himself or would he call for assistance? He was still pondering this when he became aware of a car slowing down. He half turned and saw that it was a police Panda car; its two occupants were watching him. He returned to looking down at the water, hoping the car would move off. It didn't. Dunbar heard the window being wound down as the car inched towards him. A Glasgow voice asked, 'Not thinking of doing anything stupid, are we?'

Dunbar smiled at the irony of the question before turning. He said, 'Nothing like that, Officer. Just getting some air.'

The answer seemed to satisfy the law. The car moved off.

Definitely not something stupid, thought Dunbar. He had enough egg on his face already over this assignment. He'd ask Sci-Med to arrange expert assistance. Macmillan had said he could stay on the case 'a bit longer'. He wasn't too clear what that meant.

Dunbar made his request for help to Sci-Med first thing in the morning. He also asked for information about Ross's consul-tancy in Geneva. The reply simply acknowledged the requests and told him they would be dealt with as soon as possible. He should stand by.

When he got to the hospital, Dunbar told Ingrid he wouldn't be needing her. He didn't want her around while he investigated how the free transplant referrals had been funded. Confidentiality about the Omega patients was strict, but Ingrid, when pressed, had come up with the information that there had been three; she had also given net profit figures for their stays. Dunbar couldn't remember whether or not she had included dates for them. He wanted to see if he could correlate these dates with the acceptance of free-transplant patients.

He found the information on Omega patients she had given him. The dates of their stays at Médic Ecosse were included. He then got out the list of free NHS referrals and checked one list against the other. He found exactly what he was looking for. The admission of each Omega patient coincided with the acceptance of a free transplant patient. This confirmed that it was possible that the Omega patients had provided cash for the transplants, but it did not tell him why Ingrid had been unsure about the correlation. She had always been fiercely protective of Médic Ecosse, so should have jumped at the chance to point out how philanthropic they had been in spending Omega cash on charity patients. It was out of character. He was missing something.

His mobile phone rang. It was the matron at The Beeches in Helensburgh.

'Dr Dunbar, I thought that, being a friend, you'd like to be told that Mrs Barnes died peacefully at three o'clock this morning. I'm sorry.'

'Thank you for telling me,' sighed Dunbar. 'I appreciate it, and thank you for all you did for her. Did her son manage to come and see her before she died?'

'No, he stayed away. Perhaps you'd like details of the funeral arrangements?'

Dunbar said he would. He wrote them down.

Ingrid came in after lunch to check if he had any work for her. When he said no, she smiled her superior little smile and said, 'You know, I don't think you're an accountant at all.' She sat on a corner of the desk and rested both hands on one knee.

Dunbar felt himself go cold. He tried to appear calm as he asked, 'What do you imagine I am, then?'

'Oh, I don't know. Some kind of detective perhaps?'

'What makes you think that?'

'You pulled my personnel file.'

Dunbar was painfully aware that she was watching his reaction. 'Did I?' he said.

'All personnel files record date and time of last access. It's a data-protection measure. The last request for access to my file came from the computer in this office.'

'I think it's you who are the detective,' said Dunbar with a smile that he hoped looked relaxed. 'You're quite right. I did access your file. I wanted to know a bit more about you.'

'Why?'

'When I asked you about some clinical tests on a transplant patient, you seemed to know all about them. I was curious. Having a computer beside me made it possible to satisfy my curiosity.'

'And what did you discover?'

'That you're really a trained nurse,' replied Dunbar. It was a gamble. He had simply told the truth.

'I was,' agreed Ingrid.

'Then we're two of a kind,' said Dunbar. 'I'm a doctor who doesn't work as a doctor, and you're a nurse who doesn't work as a nurse.'

'I hadn't thought of it like that,' said Ingrid. 'Quite a coincidence, really.'

She left the room and Dunbar let out his breath in uneasy relief. It was short-lived. Almost immediately, he started to wonder how many of the other files he'd accessed had some kind of tag on them. He thought back. He'd been careful not to make any inquiries about either Lisa or Sheila Barnes on the hospital computer system, so that was all right. He'd certainly never tried to access anything at all about the dead children; that really would have been a giveaway. A lot of the information he'd used was on the disks originally supplied; there had been no need to access the mainframe so, again, no one would have been able to follow what he was doing unless . . . How did Ingrid know he'd pulled her file? To check the access record on it, she'd have had to examine her own file. Why had she done that? Or was there some other way she could have found out?

He was aware of the blood pounding in his ears as he started to check the back of the computer monitor. Please God, he was wrong but . . . There were a power-supply cable, a networking cable for connection to the mainframe and for access to printers – and a third cable. He stared at this third cable and felt his pulse rate rise. He couldn't be sure, but a good guess said that this thin grey cable was supplying an auxiliary monitor. Someone was watching everything he brought up on screen.

The thought of it made him feel vulnerable until he thought it through calmly and came to the conclusion that he was still relatively safe. He'd played the role of a nosy accountant quite conscientiously, particularly at the beginning when he had constantly sought facts and figures to compile seemingly endless tables of income and expenditure. He had, of course, asked Ingrid to get him bits of information from time to time: estimated costs of transplants, a list of free referrals from the NHS, and more recently about the funding link with Omega patients.

So why had she let the cat out of the bag about his pulling her file? Had she been instructed to do it to see what his reaction would be? Had someone else been upset by something he'd asked about? He had the uncomfortable feeling that that might be the case. He suspected he'd come a little too close to something he wasn't supposed to know about. It was all the more uncomfortable because he didn't know what it was.

'How is she, Doctor?' Sandy asked as he and Kate were shown into Ross's office for an update on Amanda's condition.

'All is not gloom,' said Ross with a smile. 'We're now making considerable progress with Amanda.'

'How so?'

'I could give you the technical details but I suggest that you go up and see for yourselves,' said Ross conspiratorially.

'All right, we will,' said Sandy, and without further ado a nurse took them up to Amanda's room.

Amanda was sitting up in bed when they entered. She seemed alert and clear-eyed, and her smile when they walked in all but wiped out the despondency of the last few days and did more to raise their spirits than anything else that had happened in a long time. Sandy felt a lump come to his throat as he watched Kate hug Amanda and look up at him over the child's shoulder.

'You're looking wonderful,' she said to Amanda, holding her tightly. 'You must be feeling better. Are you?'

'I'm fed up,' complained Amanda, but she said it in such a normal voice – so different from the tired whimper they had been used to in the past weeks – that Kate and Sandy burst out laughing.

'Fed up?' asked Kate, seeing the puzzled look that came to Amanda's eyes and not wanting to hurt her feelings.

'They won't let me out of bed to play with the doll's house,' said Amanda.

'Maybe tomorrow,' said the nurse.

'That's what grown-ups always say,' complained Amanda, to more laughter.

'I can't believe it,' Sandy said to the nurse. 'She's looking so well today.'

'The doctors have been making progress with the tissue-degradation problem and now they seem to have got the dialysis just right,' she replied. 'Much better than anyone dared hope. Everyone is very pleased with her. She's quite a star.'

Sandy took over from Kate and hugged his daughter. 'It's just so good to see my little princess looking and feeling like her old self.'

The nurse went out and the three of them continued to chat happily about anything and everything. Amanda demanded to know how Sandy was getting on with the doll's house he'd promised her. He assured her that plans for it had been drawn up and construction was under way.

'With lights,' she reminded him.

'In every room,' said Sandy.

As time went by, Kate noticed that Sandy had gone quiet. He seemed lost in thought.

'What's the matter?' she asked as Amanda leafed her way through a colouring-book to find an elephant she wanted to show them.

He shrugged and said, 'I don't know. I suppose I'd started to think this might not happen. I was on the verge of giving up hope and now . . .'

'Let's not analyse anything too deeply. Let's just be thankful,' said Kate softly.

He nodded and put his hand on hers.

'What are you two whispering about?' demanded Amanda.

'Nothing,' said Kate.

'Didn't look like nothing to me,' said Amanda.

'Oh really, young lady,' said Kate. 'In that case we were discussing which one of us was going to tickle your tummy first!' She made a mock attack on Amanda, who broke into a fit of giggles. Sandy grinned broadly at the sound. No symphony could have sounded sweeter.

Later, as she and Sandy walked to the car, Kate asked, 'What do you think?'

'Same as you. Bloody marvellous.'

'You don't think it's just one of these remissions you hear about, when patients suddenly seem to get better but it's only a temporary thing?'

Sandy shook his head. 'No. Cancer patients get those. Amanda doesn't have cancer. I really think it must be the improved dialysis set-up they have here. Now that they've got it right, it must have cleaned her blood better than the other machines, got rid of more toxins. That's what's making her more alert and energetic.'

'She was just like she used to be,' said Kate.

He agreed, adding, 'Better dialysis means more time between sessions; that'll give them more time to work on stabilizing her. They won't be struggling to keep her alive all the time and then, if they succeed in stabilizing her, there'll be more time for a kidney to become available.'

He put his arm round Kate's shoulders and gave her a hug. 'A good day,' he said. 'Let's eat out this evening?'

Kate nodded and returned the hug.

When he got back to his hotel, Dunbar found a message from Sci-Med waiting for him. He was instructed to meet a man named James Douglas in a pub called the Crane in Salamander

Street at eight o'clock. There was also an apology for the lack of information about James Ross's interests in Geneva. They'd had difficulties in obtaining it at the outset and, having assumed that it wouldn't be relevant to the Glasgow inquiry, they hadn't pursued it further. They'd try again.

Dunbar decided to leave the car in the hotel car park and take a taxi to the Crane. That way he wouldn't have problems with parking and he wouldn't have to bother finding out where Salamander Street was. As he climbed into the cab, he gave the name of the pub to the driver and asked, 'Do you know it?'

'Aye. Do you?'

'What's that supposed to mean?' asked Dunbar.

'If you turn up at the Crane in a taxi you're gonna stick out like a sair thumb. They'll figure you as a DHS snooper. You're no', are you?'

'Nothing like that.'

'It's nane o' ma business like, but if you want some advice, pal, you'll get oot the motor a couple o' streets away and walk the rest.'

'Thanks for the warning.'

'Nae problem. Shame aboot the accent. Still, there's nothin' you can do aboot that.'

'True.'

'Mind you—'

'I know,' interrupted Dunbar. 'I could keep my mouth shut.'

'An oldie but a goldie,' laughed the driver.

The cab stopped in an area where street lights seemed an alien concept.

'Place is dyin',' said the driver. 'Bulldozers will be comin' in at the end o' the year.'

Dunbar thanked him, gave him the six pounds for the fare and added four more.

'Cheers. Your place is along there on the left. You canny miss it.'

The cab did an about-turns and clattered off, leaving Dunbar to think how quiet it was. He was in a street with high tenement buildings on either side and yet he could have heard a pin drop. No voices, no radio or television sounds, no dogs barking, no cooking smells, only the smell of diesel exhaust left on the air by the cab. There were no lights in the buildings, either. They were empty black stone monuments, harbouring nothing but the ghosts of families past. Something flitted across the pavement in front of him and disappeared into the dark mouth of one of the closes. He wanted to believe it was a cat but knew otherwise. He quickened his pace.

He was beginning to have doubts about a pub existing in this area at all when he saw light spill out on to the road a hundred yards ahead. As he drew nearer, he could hear male laughter. The Crane was the only inhabited property in the street. Its unimposing exterior suggested it had not always been a pub. It had the flat frontage of a double-windowed shop with clear glass windows. Behind the glass, thick darkgreen curtains, heavy with years of accumulated grime, hung from two round brass rails three-quarters of the way up. Above the curtain line Dunbar could see only the ceiling, which seemed to have been varnished with nicotine.

He had to stoop to get through the door and was surprised to find that there were three steps down to the floor of the bar. He paused at the top for a moment to look around the room. Several customers turned to look at him. Not knowing how to recognize and make contact with Douglas, he thought he'd better just wait, so went to the bar and ordered a pint of lager. The barman complied without comment and placed the glass in front of him. He took the fiver and brought the change.

'Before you ask, I don't know.'

'Don't know what?' asked Dunbar.

The barman leaned one elbow on the counter and said, 'Listen, pal, there's mair chance o' the Queen Mother comin' in here than me pickin' up passing trade. You have a reason for comin' here and it's no' that piss yer drinkin'. You're after information. I'm just tellin' you in advance, ye'll no be gettin' it frae me. Straight?'

'Straight,' agreed Dunbar.

'That's no way to speak to a pal o' mine, Harry,' said a local voice behind Dunbar. He turned and saw a slim, wiry man dressed in black jeans, a dark polo-neck sweater and soft leather jacket. He had close-cropped ginger hair and looked as if he might have been a useful lightweight boxer.

'How you doin', Steve?' the man asked Dunbar.

'Just fine . . . Jimmy,' replied Dunbar.

'Sorry aboot that, Jimmy,' said the barman. 'Nae offence, pal,' he said to Dunbar.

'None taken.'

'Fancy a seat?' asked Douglas.

He led the way to a bench seat with the stuffing protruding in several places. They put down their drinks on a table that was awash with beer slops.

'Why here?' asked Dunbar as an adjacent door opened and the smell of urine wafted out.

'I had to be sure you weren't followed. You weren't.'

'I came by cab.'

'I know. You gave the driver a generous tip.'

Dunbar didn't inquire how he knew. 'Why all the precautions?' he asked.

'I don't know who you are or what you're into. The people who employ me don't tell me things like that. They figure I don't need to know. It's all done through intermediaries so the customers can pretend they know nothing at all about it if things go wrong. I have to treat everyone the same. You could be the most wanted man in Europe, for all I know.'

'What *do* you know?' asked Dunbar.

'You'd like to gain access to a place where the door might be locked. I've to get you inside and then out again.'

'It's a research lab. They work on animals. It's at a place called Vane Farm, three miles north of the city on the Lomond Road.'

Douglas had brought out a notebook and was jotting information down. 'What are you after?'

'Information about what they're doing. I think it'll be in computer files in the building.'

'University or private?'

'Private.'

'A pity. Probably means they've got proper security. Know anything about that?'

Dunbar told him what he'd learned from last year's research budget records.

'How about internal lay-out?'

'Nothing.'

'How much time have we got?'

'Time enough. It's more important that no one knows I've been there,' said Dunbar.

Douglas pursed his lips and said, 'In and out with no trace? That could be a bit more difficult.'

'It's important.'

'I'll take a look at the place and get back to you.'

'When?'

'I'll do a full recce, day and night. Come here again the day after tomorrow. Same time.'

Dunbar left the Crane and found his way back to a main road, from where he took a cab to Lisa's place. She looked more relaxed than he'd ever seen her.

'How was your day?' he asked.

'Excellent.'

'Do anything in particular?'

'I walked for miles,' said Lisa, 'in any direction I fancied. I just walked and walked because I didn't need to be here. I was free to do as I pleased, and it felt wonderful.'

'Good,' said Dunbar.

'And you?'

Dunbar told her about his plans to get into Vane Farm and take a look at Ross's research findings.

'You're going for it then?'

'It could put an end to all the speculation,' said Dunbar. 'Any evidence of animal parts being put into patients at Médic Ecosse and the police can act immediately.'

'When?' asked Lisa.

'In a few days. I'm not going to do it alone.'

'You will be careful, won't you?' she said softly.

'Of course.'

'What are you thinking about?' asked Lisa as Dunbar fell silent.

'Tomorrow.'

'What happens tomorrow?'

'A funeral.'

The following morning Dunbar set off for the Clyde-coast town of Irvine where Sheila Barnes had been brought up. She had asked to be buried there in the graveyard of St Andrew's Church where she and her husband Cyril had been married twenty-six years before. That was the one saving grace about being told you'd got a terminal illness, thought Dunbar. It gave you time to put your affairs in order and make arrangements, something most people put off until it was too late.

There was nothing pretty about St Andrew's. It had a cold, austere look with iron railings surrounding it instead of low walls or hedging. Even the churchyard seemed unnecessarily bleak, lacking as it did trees and shrubbery to break up the lines of tombstones which stretched for more than two hundred yards behind the building. But it had obviously meant something special to Sheila, and that was all that mattered. As he'd heard some churchman say recently on the radio, 'Churches aren't about buildings, they're about people.'

As he entered the building, Dunbar noted that the sky was darkening ominously. He hoped the rain would hold off until after the interment. Earth turning to mud did little to enhance a burial ceremony. Not wishing to intrude on family and friends, he sat down near the back of the section to the right of the main aisle. He noted with some pleasure that the church was nearly three-quarters full. He had liked Sheila Barnes; even in the debilitated state in which he'd known her, she'd struck him as a woman of fine character. It seemed fitting that she be mourned by many.

Cyril wasn't present but that was no surprise; he must be close to death himself.

The service was conducted by a Church of Scotland minister who had clearly known Sheila personally. His voice was deep and resonant and reached all corners of the church without difficulty. The result was an informative and affectionate biography of the woman and her work, so different, thought Dunbar, from the hastily cobbled together bits and pieces gleaned from relatives at the last moment that was usually the case in modern times. He learned that Sheila had spent long periods overseas in the early days of her nursing career, working in Third World countries. Her long, happy marriage to Cyril was held up as an example of the power of love. Her son, Peter, was mentioned but Dunbar got the distinct impression that the minister was back-pedalling on that issue. Like the matron at The Beeches, he was obviously aware of the family rift.

Dunbar could see in the front pew a man whom he took to be Peter Barnes. He stood slightly apart from the other main mourners, who might be Sheila's brothers and sisters, judging by their age. It gave the impression that the rift went deeper than immediate family. Peter Barnes was tall and dark and, when he turned to look at the congregation, wore a slight smile as if amused at some private joke. Dunbar noted that his tie was not black but purple, as was the handkerchief in his top pocket. Although the colour was muted, it seemed strangely disrespectful.

Dunbar, who had kept well out of the way of close family and friends at the graveside, was almost the last to join the slow procession back along the gravel path leading to the churchyard gates. What appeared to be a general shunning of Peter Barnes meant that he too was on his own. Dunbar joined him and offered his condolences.

'Thank you,' replied Peter.

'You didn't manage to see your mother at The Beeches before she died, then?'

'Unfortunately not,' replied Peter. 'My work takes me away a lot. It was a bit difficult to get up to Helensburgh.'

'I see,' replied Dunbar. He hesitated before saying, 'I know it's not really any of my business, but if it's any comfort your mother mistook me for you on my last visit. I let her think I was you. She was very pleased. She died believing you two had made it up.'

Peter smiled and said, 'Thank you for telling me that, Mr . . . ?'

'Dunbar. Steven Dunbar.'

'That gives me a great deal of comfort. Can I ask what your business was with my mother?'

'I had to ask her a few things about her time at the Médic Ecosse Hospital, just to complete some paperwork I was doing.'

'Ah, paperwork,' said Peter Barnes in a way that suggested a sneer to Dunbar. He could understand why people didn't take to the man. What is it you do, Mr Barnes?' he asked.

'I work on the design of warships.'

'That sounds interesting. All aspects or one in particular?'

'Radiation containment.'

Dunbar swallowed hard. He felt the, hairs on the back of his neck start to prickle. 'Really?' he said then cleared his throat against the tightness that had crept in. 'Might I ask what company you work for?'

'Baxters, on Tyneside.'

As soon as he got back to his hotel, Dunbar called Macmillan in London and told him what he now knew.

'I agree, it goes beyond the realms of coincidence,' said Macmillan. 'This Barnes character could have plotted the deaths of his own parents so he could inherit. He must have thought he was going to get away with it, too. It was damn nearly foolproof. Would you like me to arrange for all the information to be handed over to the Glasgow police?'

'I'd be grateful,' replied Dunbar. 'I've no heart for it. The case has nothing to do with what I'm interested in any more.'

'Don't get too down about it,' said Macmillan. 'You've just solved a double murder, and an unusual one at that.'

'But not the double murder I'm interested in,' said Dunbar.

* * *

'You're telling me that Sheila wasn't murdered to keep her quiet after all?' said Lisa.

'Afraid not,' he said. 'In retrospect, I suppose it was wrong from the outset. If you want to kill someone to keep them quiet, you don't choose a slow death. That's more the style of someone who wants to make the death seem natural, the perfect crime committed by someone who can afford to wait a little.'

'Like her own son,' said Lisa with disgust.

'Take a look at life again soon,' said Dunbar.

'So now you have nothing at all to go on against Médic Ecosse,' said Lisa.

Dunbar shrugged and said, 'Nothing except the word of two nurses and one of them's now dead.'

'The remaining one knows what she's talking about,' said Lisa firmly.

FOURTEEN

Dunbar decided to look at some of Ross's published research before going out to Vane Farm; it might help him understand what he found there. Sci-Med had supplied him with reprints of Ross's most recent papers, but he'd put them to one side until now. There were four, three on animal work and a fourth on something called 'Immuno-preparation', which he left in the file while he concentrated on what he thought the more relevant stuff.

He suspected he might find it hard going but Ross had a good writing style and presented his data in straightforward fashion. What really helped was the fact that one of the papers was a review article about current work in the field. Like all scientific reviews, it was aimed at scientists but not confined to those working in the same field. Technical detail was therefore kept to a minimum.

Ross's papers made it clear that he believed the use of animal organs – pigs' in particular – for human transplant was the way ahead. It would eliminate the awful uncertainty of patients having to wait for a human organ to become available, with the attendant moral dilemma of wishing misfortune on someone else. It would also obviate the continual struggle to convince an unwilling public that carrying donor cards was a good idea when their gut instinct told them otherwise. It was seen as tempting fate; courting disaster.

Whenever the medical profession made any headway in that direction, it seemed, a story would break about the recovery of some coma patient who had been declared brain-dead by the experts. This awakened fears akin to the age-old dread of being buried alive. Only now people imagined their organs being removed while they were still conscious but unable to communicate.

A further advantage of using animal organs, according to Ross, was that the donor animal could be kept alive until the very moment the organ was needed. It would therefore be well oxygenated and 'fresh'. There would be no more rushing to and fro across the globe with tissue decaying in transit with each passing hour. There would be no more hoping against hope that unforeseen delays would not render vital organs useless. An added bonus was that the social and moral problems associated with hospitals 'delaying' the death of putative donors by keeping them on life-support machines, solely to keep their organs in good condition, would become a thing of the past.

The main focus of the research was the immunological problem associated with the introduction of foreign tissue. Like tissues from any other source, animal organs had to be made compatible with the patient's own immune system, otherwise they would quickly be rejected as alien material, causing the transplant to fail and the patient to die. Ross's experimental work had shown that it was possible to breed pigs with the immune system of a human patient in addition to their own. This scenario would ensure that the pig's organs would be perfectly acceptable to the patient whose immune system the pig had been given. This was all experimental, of course, qualitative work performed to establish the validity of theory. The idea of preparing a pig donor for each and every human being in case they should need a transplant at some time in their life was beyond practicality. The morality of it was another issue.

Dunbar wondered if it could possibly have been attempted for selected individuals at Médic Ecosse, but concluded not. The timescale would have been all wrong for cases like Amy Teasdale or Kenneth Lineham. These patients had come to Médic Ecosse already very ill and needing transplants quickly.

The more he read, the more depressed he felt. Unless Ross had made some great secret leap forward in technology there would have been no point in attempting to transplant pig organs into human patients. Rejection would have been almost guaranteed. Had Ross made such a breakthrough? He hoped to find out at Vane Farm.

Douglas was already in the Crane when Dunbar arrived at five to eight. They shook hands and sat down on the same seats as last time.

'How'd you get on?' Dunbar asked.

'It looks possible. The staff are all gone by ten o'clock. That just leaves two security men in the gate-house. They're supposed to patrol the grounds every half-hour but they were a bit lax after midnight. They probably rely on the electric fence doing its job.'

'Electric fence?' exclaimed Dunbar.

'Nothing too desperate,' said Douglas. 'It's more of an alarm than a line of defence. Low voltage. We can bridge it easily.'

'How about the building itself?'

'That's our biggest problem. We can't use a window – there aren't any – and the door has an electronic lock.'

'But you said it was possible.'

'I think it's possible,' said Douglas. 'It's going to depend on this.' He took from his pocket a small piece of plastic the size of a credit card. It was unmarked save for a strip of magnetic tape across it.

'A key?'

'We'll call it that if it works.'

'Did you make it?'

'Let's say an acquaintance did. I persuaded him to take time off from giving the Bank of Scotland a hard time to manufacture it for me.'

'Won't there be a code number attached to the lock as well?' asked Dunbar.

Douglas nodded. 'The code is entered on tone buttons. I recorded the tones when one of the guards went into the building. I know the number.'

'And if the key doesn't work?'

'Then it's up to you. We could take out the guards and use their passkey.'

'No violence,' said Dunbar.

'Please yourself.'

'When?'

'Tonight, if you're up for it.'

Dunbar nodded. 'All right,' he said. 'When and where?'

Douglas looked at him thoughtfully. 'Have you done anything like this before?' he asked.

'Yes, I have,' replied Dunbar. He didn't volunteer anything else and Douglas didn't ask. He simply nodded and gave directions on how to get to the yard of a disused suburban railway station on the north side of the city. He could leave his car there and they would go on to Vane Farm in Douglas's Land-Rover.

'Just in case we have to rough it across country later,' said Douglas. 'Do you need clothing?'

'I've got dark stuff,' replied Dunbar. 'I could use a balaclava, though.'

'No problem. Gloves?'

'I've got gloves.'

'One o'clock, then.'

Dunbar returned to his hotel room and turned on the television while he looked out the clothing he was going to wear later and laid it on the bed. He needed some noise as a distraction from thinking about the repercussions if something should go wrong. Scottish Television was showing an episode of *Taggart*. A body was being pulled from the Clyde to the accompaniment of glum faces and bad jokes. This was not the sort of distraction he needed; he switched off the television and turned the radio on instead, tuning it to Classic FM. Mozart's *Horn Concerto* would do.

At half-past midnight Dunbar checked his pockets for the last time, then left his room and walked quietly along to the lift. Adrenalin was starting to flow. He handed his key to the night clerk, who acknowledged it with a nod before returning to his paperback. Dunbar was pleased at his lack of interest.

The directions Douglas had given him were excellent; concise and to the point. He had no difficulty in finding the station yard; it was seven minutes to one when he turned into it. The traffic at that time of night had been negligible. He drove slowly round the yard, his lights illuminating the undergrowth that was encroaching on the pot-holed tarmac. He backed into a secluded corner where he could watch the entrance, and turned out his lights.

The moon slid out from behind a thin cloud curtain to light up the ribbon of road leading uphill from the car park and out into the country. It was nearly full tonight. The last time he'd watched the moon like this had been in the Iraqi desert. He and the others had been waiting for it to disappear before moving off. He was trying to recall the names of his companions that night when he heard the sound of a car approaching. At first he thought the vehicle was going to pass by, but at the last moment it slowed and turned into the car park. Dunbar was momentarily blinded by its headlights as it swung round, then turned slightly to the side. He switched on his own lights and saw that it was a dark-green Land-Rover. He got out, locked his car and hurried over to join Douglas.

'Found it all right, then?' asked Douglas.

'No problem.'

They drove in silence until Douglas said, 'That's it coming up on our left. We'll drive past. There's a farm turn-off about three hundred yards ahead. We'll leave the Land-Rover there.'

Dunbar saw the headlights pick out the sign 'Vane Farm Animal Welfare Institute' as they passed. He smiled wryly.

'That is the place?' asked Douglas, sounding a little worried.

'Oh yes, that's the place. I was just taken with the name, that's all.'

'They're all doing it these days,' said Douglas, catching on. 'I suppose it would be asking for trouble to call it Vivisection House or the Institute for Cutting up Wee Furry Things for No Good Reason.'

'Quite so.'

'What do they work on there?'

'Pigs.'

'Not quite as appealing as bunny rabbits in the emotional stakes, but I guess it doesn't matter too much to the nutters.'

'Has there been much trouble with animal activists up here?' asked Dunbar.

'A fair bit. They burned down a lab over in Edinburgh a few months ago and a couple of researchers got parcel bombs sent to them. They're going to kill somebody soon.'

Douglas turned the Land-Rover off the road and parked it a little way down the farm track. He turned out the lights and said, 'Time to go to work.' He reached behind him and lifted over a small rucksack and two black balaclavas. He handed one to Dunbar and both men put them on.

'We'll go back by the field, hugging the hedgerow until we reach the farm perimeter, then head north along the wire to the north-east corner and go through the wire there. Okay?'

'Understood.'

Douglas handed Dunbar a pair of wire-cutters and said, 'I'll bridge the circuit. You cut the wire.'

They locked the vehicle and slipped quickly off the track down a slight embankment and into the field, where they courted the shadow of the roadside hedge as they made their way back to Vane Farm. Douglas, who led the way, held up his hand and both men dropped to their knees. Dunbar could see the farm gate-house. Through the large, well-lit windows he could see two men. They appeared to be reading.

Douglas gestured to his right and Dunbar followed him as they made their way to the furthest corner of the fence. When they reached the corner-post Douglas removed his rucksack and took out a pair of cables, each with a large crocodile clip on either end. He connected them both in the form of big loops to the fence and Dunbar cut the wire at two places inside the loops so that the electrical circuit was not broken. They separated the severed wires and crawled through the gap, Douglas first, followed by

Dunbar after he had re-packed the wire-cutters and passed Douglas's rucksack through to him.

Douglas signed that they crawl on their bellies from here on. Dunbar felt this was being a bit over-cautious but he was happy to have a companion who was inclined this way rather than the other. He complied without comment. They crawled side by side up to the main building, using their elbows to propel them over the rough ground.

From their position just short of the main door they could see the gate-house. One of the guards was sitting reading a newspaper, facing in their direction. If he looked up while they were unlocking the door, he would see them. Douglas looked at his watch and whispered, 'Let's wait a bit. See if he moves.'

Minutes passed and the guard showed no sign of becoming bored with his paper. Douglas and Dunbar exchanged grimaces but steeled themselves to continue the wait. Another ten minutes had gone by before the guard made a play of folding up his paper and picking up a kettle. He got up from his chair and disappeared from view.

'Let's do it!' said Douglas, getting to his feet and running up to the door to insert his card. He punched in the number code while Dunbar looked anxiously towards the gate-house, fearing the imminent return of the guard. The lock stayed shut.

'C'mon, c'mon!' muttered Douglas as he re-inserted the card and tried again. Still nothing happened.

'We're running out of time!' hissed Dunbar through his teeth.

Douglas tried once more with the same result just as Dunbar said, 'He's back!'

Both men dived headlong to the ground and looked towards the gate-house to see if they had been spotted. The guard opened his paper and sat down.

'What do we do now?' whispered Dunbar.

Douglas looked towards the gate-house and said, 'We could take them?'

Dunbar shook his head. 'Let's take a look round the building. There might be another way in.'

'No windows, no other doors,' said Douglas. 'I reccied it, remember?'

'Humour me,' said Dunbar. He led the way round to the back of the building, where they were out of sight of the gate-house. They crawled along the back wall, which was featureless apart from a large, square pipe about halfway along.

'What do you suppose that is?' Dunbar asked.

'Some kind of waste pipe?'

They continued along the back wall, still without finding any means of access. The same applied to the end wall. They backed off to see as much of the roof as possible. There were no skylights or unshielded ventilation shafts.

'I told you,' said Douglas.

'Let's take a closer look at the waste pipe,' said Dunbar.

The pipe comprised riveted metal sections and was about two feet square. Scraping away the earth round its base, Dunbar uncovered two metal drain covers. Douglas saw what he was about and gave him a hand to raise one of them. The smell that emanated made them both gag.

'Jesus!' exclaimed Douglas.

'Pig slurry,' said Dunbar. 'Let's have the torch.'

Douglas handed him a long rubber-shielded torch and he inspected the pit. The end of the pipe was clear of the slurry. He reached down to check that there was no grille over the end. It was clear. He straightened up and said, 'I think we could get up the inside of that pipe.'

Douglas screwed up his face at the thought but had to agree it was possible and there appeared to be no other option. He looked down at the slurry pit and asked, 'How deep do you think it is?'

'Only one way to find out.' Dunbar eased himself over the edge of the pit and lowered his legs into the foul morass. It had just covered his knees when he said, 'I've touched bottom.'

'I'll have to stash this,' said Douglas, taking off his rucksack.

Dunbar squatted down so that he could get into the end of the pipe. The smell threatened to overpower him in the confined space as he entered, arms first, then his head and shoulders. He straightened up and tried to find hand-holds on the slimy interior walls. It was difficult, but he found that there was enough space for his fingers to curl over the inner portion of the box joints. If he could pull himself up another three feet, he'd be into the horizontal section of the pipe and could crawl up to the end.

'Are you okay?' asked Douglas.

'So far.'

Dunbar pulled himself agonizingly upwards, using only the tips of his fingers, then managed to scramble in ungainly fashion into the flat section. He crawled slowly along to the far end and found himself up against a wire grille; but he was inside the building. He pushed hard against the grid and it sprang off, enabling him to crawl out into a wide, shallow metal basin. The noises all around him said that he had pigs for company. He turned round to encourage Douglas, who emerged a few moments later, seemingly using a curse for each foot of the way.

'This is where they keep the pigs,' said Dunbar.

'You don't say,' replied Douglas sourly.

Douglas turned on his torch. They were standing in the sluice for pig waste. There were two large taps on the wall beside the pipe exit. Dunbar turned one on and started to wash himself down, then waited while Douglas did the same.

'We'll probably die of pneumonia now,' said Douglas, wringing out as much water as he could. 'But it's better than smelling like that.'

The two men made their way out of the pig-house and into the main corridor of the building. The lack of windows meant they could use the torch freely, although they didn't risk turning on any of the main lights. There were several small laboratories, one large one and finally what Dunbar was looking for, an office equipped with computer facilities. He turned on a desk light and started looking for useful information. There were several letters on the desk addressed to James Ross, so he knew he was in the right place. He searched the desk drawers that were unlocked, but there were no disk storage boxes there. The bottom drawer was locked. He asked Douglas for help.

Douglas knelt down to examine the lock and smiled. He brought out what looked like a series of metal spikes and selected one. He looked up at Dunbar as he twisted and turned the spike, all the time feeling for what was going on inside the lock.

'And . . . Abra . . . cadabra!' he announced as the lock turned and clicked.

Dunbar pulled open the drawer and found a plastic computer disk box. Each disk was meticulously labelled, something he put down to Ross's nature and something he was extremely grateful for. He put to one side those concerned with accounting and record-keeping and kept the ones marked 'Experimental Data' with relevant dates. He turned on the computer.

'How long are you going to be?' asked Douglas, anxiety in his voice.

Dunbar reached inside his jerkin and brought out a plastic bag containing several blank disks. 'Not long,' he replied. 'I just have to copy these.'

'I'll take a look around,' said Douglas.

'Don't move anything,' cautioned Dunbar. 'We don't want anyone to know Santa's been.'

Dunbar made copies of the three data disks, switched off the computer and put everything back as he'd found it. 'That's it,' he said when Douglas had returned. 'Can you lock the drawer again?'

Douglas looked at him as if it was the strangest request he'd ever heard, but complied. He had slightly more trouble locking the drawer than he'd had unlocking it, but it eventually clicked and everything was as it had been.

'Let's go,' said Dunbar.

As they left the office and started to make their way back down to the pig house, Douglas said, 'Do you notice anything strange?'

'What?'

'Take a good look, then think back to how the building looked from the outside.'

Dunbar did as he was bid, shining the torch all over the walls. 'What?' he asked.

'Part of the building is missing. I twigged it while I was having a nose around. Look at the length of the place.' Douglas swung the torch to and fro. 'Now think about the length from outside.'

'You're right,' said Dunbar. He pointed the beam straight ahead. 'That must be a false wall.'

'If there's no access from the outside, there has to be a door in here.'

They walked over to the end wall and started searching for a way through.

'Strange,' muttered Dunbar, running his hands over the wall. 'Seems unbroken.'

'Crazy,' agreed Douglas. Suddenly something he had touched caused a panel in the wall to slide back. It startled him and he dropped the torch, which went out, leaving them in darkness.

'Christ! What's that?' exclaimed Douglas as the sound of grunting filled their ears.

'More pigs, I suppose.'

'Don't smell like pigs,' replied Douglas, cautiously entering the new part and reaching to the side to feel for a light switch. 'Where is the bleeding thing?' he murmured as he failed to find one.

Dunbar inched his way along the wall, guided only by the sound of Douglas's voice. He froze suddenly as Douglas let out a scream that rent the air.

'What the hell . . . ? Where are you?' gasped Dunbar. He reached the entrance and felt for a light switch. He found it and clicked it on. Douglas's face was contorted with pain. He had unwittingly reached into the steel-barred cage of a large female ape. She had grabbed his arm and bitten it and was now trying to tear it off. Douglas's eyes pleaded for help; blood was streaming down his arm.

Dunbar attacked the ape as best he could, punching at it through the bars, shouting at it, trying to distract it, but the animal kept hold of Douglas. Dunbar looked around for something to use as a weapon. He saw the torch that Douglas had dropped just outside the opening in the wall and retrieved it. One particularly good blow to the animal's head made it release its grip and stumble backwards. Dunbar was able to pull Douglas away.

Douglas sank to the floor, shivering with shock.

Dunbar did his best to staunch the flow of blood, using two towels that he retrieved from a wash-basin at the far end of the room. As he was applying one as a tourniquet, he became aware of his audience. There were five apes in the room. All were female and all were pregnant. Despite the distraction of the moment, he couldn't help but notice that all of them had scars across their bellies as if they'd had Caesarian sections, yet they were all still swollen in pregnancy.

Douglas clutched weakly at his neck and muttered something Dunbar couldn't make out. He leaned closer.

'Omnopon,' murmured Douglas.

Dunbar suddenly realized what he meant. He reached inside the man's shirt and found a little bag of the painkiller Omnopon hanging from a leather thong round his neck. 'Old habits die hard,' he said. Douglas must have served with a Marine Commando unit at some time: this was standard operational practice. He administered the drug to Douglas and took off his jerkin to make it into a pillow for his head while he thought what to do next. At that moment he heard the front door open. 'I'll be right back,' he whispered. He stood up and clicked off the light.

'I'm telling you, I heard a bloody scream,' said an animated male voice.

'It was your imagination,' replied a calmer voice. 'It was something on the radio.'

'It was James fucking Last on the radio.'

Dunbar pressed himself against the wall, trying to decide what to do. Both security men had come to have a look, so there was still some doubt in their minds. It sounded as if only one man had heard something, so the chances were that they hadn't yet reported anything. If he could close the wall panel, the guards might go away without finding anything amiss; unless, of course, they decided to search the whole building routinely. He was feeling for the button when Douglas tried to move and let out a loud moan. The game was over; the guards came running.

Almost without thinking, Dunbar pulled down his balaclava and ran towards them as the main lights came on. The two men were taken by surprise. One had hardly opened his mouth when Dunbar hit him sharply on the left side of his chin and he went down like a felled tree. The other turned to run for the door, but Dunbar caught him and dropped him with a blow to the side of his neck. He lowered him to the floor and dragged him back to lie beside his companion. He had been as restrained as possible. He wished them no harm.

Dunbar ran back to see to Douglas. The painkiller was doing its job, and Douglas was conscious and calm, sitting up, holding the towel against his arm.

'Can you stand?' asked Dunbar.

'Sure.' Douglas tried to get up, and succeeded with some help from Dunbar. Dunbar put his jerkin back on. 'Put your good arm round my neck.'

Dunbar half carried Douglas to the front door, then turned out the lights before pressing the door-release button. The door slid back letting them breathe in fresh night air.

'Where did you leave the rucksack?' Dunbar asked.

Douglas seemed sleepy. He hesitated before saying, 'Behind the pipe.'

They made painfully slow progress along the back of the building till they reached the waste pipe. Dunbar retrieved the rucksack and started to put it on, but Douglas stopped him.

'Inside . . .' he said. 'Paint . . . Spray paint . . .'

Dunbar's first thought was delirium, but then he understood. Despite his pain and shock, Douglas was still thinking about their mission.

'In case . . . things went wrong. Someone . . . to blame.'

Dunbar searched the sack and found a can of spray paint.

'Will you be okay for a minute?' he asked.

'Go . . .'

Dunbar went up to the wall of the building and started spray-writing. 'No to Vivisection . . . Free the Animals . . . Scientist Bastards . . . Stop the Experiments . . . Evil Bastards'. The can was empty. He ran back to where Douglas lay and put the empty can in the sack before slinging it on his back and helping Douglas to his feet. 'We've got to get you to a hospital,' he said.

It seemed to take forever to cover the three hundred yards or so to where they'd left the Land-Rover, but there was still no commotion behind them. The security guards must still be unconscious. Dunbar took the keys from Douglas's pocket and eased him to the ground while he unlocked the vehicle. He manoeuvred Douglas into the front seat and strapped him in securely. Douglas's head rested on his chest but he was still conscious.

'Are you okay there?'

'I'm okay,' grunted Douglas.

Dunbar started the vehicle. He considered briefly the idea of driving across country to avoid the possibility of meeting the police on their way out to Vane Farm, but decided that Douglas could not take the rough ride. He'd have to risk the road.

He glanced to the right as they passed the farm entrance. The gate-house was empty. He turned to Douglas and asked if the Omnopon was still working.

'Still floating,' said Douglas but he was clearly in shock.

When they reached the station yard, Dunbar parked the Land-Rover next to his own car and transferred Douglas. While they were outside he took the opportunity to relax the tourniquet on Douglas's arm for a few moments. He didn't want any problems arising from cut-off circulation.

'We'll have to leave your car here,' he said. 'I don't want to leave mine in case they trace it and connect me with Vane Farm. They'll be less suspicious of a Land-Rover.'

'I'll have one of the lads pick it up,' said Douglas.

'The sooner we get you to hospital the better,' said Dunbar.

'No hospital,' croaked Douglas.

'You need proper treatment,' insisted Dunbar. 'That's a bad wound.'

'No hospital,' repeated Douglas. 'They'll ask all sorts of questions and I want to work again. I need it. There's nothing else for me, man.'

'If you don't get proper treatment you might never work again anyway. You could lose your arm.'

'That serious?'

'That serious,' confirmed Dunbar.

'You a doctor, then?' asked Douglas, expecting a negative reply.

'I am.'

Douglas shook his head as if in disbelief. 'Then what the . . . You fix it, then,' he said.

'With what? A car jack and some tyre levers? You need a hospital.'

Douglas let out a sigh. 'Get me back to the Crane,' he said.

'The Crane closed hours ago.'

'I live in the flat above it. I can call up help from there. He's done it before.'

'You mean some struck-off old lush who stitches wanted heads for beer money?'

'Something like that. I'm not going to hospital.'

'I'll make a bargain with you,' said Dunbar. 'We'll go to your place but I call up my people. I'll tell them it's vital that you be treated in secret.'

'Do you think they'll play?'

'They'll play, but it might not be a substitute for a hospital.'

'No hospital.'

They had just entered the built-up area when two police cars shot past in the other direction. Dunbar felt relieved, not just because they had passed them by but because it meant that at least one of the security men had come round.

They reached Salamander Street without incident and Dunbar parked outside the pub, which he had trouble finding in the dark without the tell-tale spillage of light from its windows. Its inconspicuous frontage merged perfectly into the long, dark stretch of unoccupied tenements. Douglas himself couldn't help much. The painkillers were starting to wear off and increasing pain was occupying all his attention. He sat with his head back, his eyes tight shut.

'I really think—' began Dunbar.

'No!' snarled Douglas.

Dunbar shrugged. 'How do we get in?' he asked.

'Door . . . to the left. Keys . . . side pocket of the sack.'

Dunbar found the keys and got out to unlock the heavy door to the left of the pub. He returned to the car, helped Douglas out and supported him across the pavement and into a long, dark entrance hall. Sounds of scuttling feet reached them from the blackness.

'Which flat?' Dunbar asked.

'First . . . and first door. It's the only one occupied.'

Dunbar helped him up spiral stone steps, feeling his way in the dark. The narrowness made it difficult, as did the fact that the steps were badly worn in the centre. It was a relief to reach the landing. Still supporting Douglas, he felt his way along the wall to the first door, found the lock and unlocked it with the second key he tried. He clicked on the hall light and helped Douglas, who was now only semi-conscious, into a room where he half collapsed on to a couch.

'Where's your phone?' Dunbar asked but didn't wait for a reply; he saw it on a small table to the left of a gas fire. First he closed the curtains and lit the fire. Douglas was shivering badly, partly from cold but mainly through shock.

Dunbar called Sci-Med and told the night duty officer that he needed urgent medical help for an injured man. 'Severe upper arm trauma inflicted by a laboratory primate,' he reported. 'Biting involved. No known disease implicated in the animal, although it can't be ruled out. Blood loss severe.'

It occurred to Dunbar that Douglas, as an ex-Marine, would know his own blood group. He asked him and repeated the answer down the phone: 'A – positive.' He gave details of their whereabouts and asked how long help would be.

'Can't say. We'll do our best.'

After ringing off, Dunbar undid the tourniquet and dressing and took a look at the wound. 'I'm going to clean your arm up a bit,' he said. 'Do you have any whisky in the flat?'

'You're not going to pour that over it are you?' demanded Douglas.

'No, I'm not,' agreed Dunbar. 'This isn't a John Wayne film. You're going to drink it because this is going to hurt like hell.' He re-applied the tourniquet, poured out the liquor and foraged in the bathroom cabinet for anything useful. Back in the main room, he handed the half-full tumbler to Douglas and removed the tourniquet again, substituting finger pressure while he examined the wound and dabbed at the torn flesh with cotton wool and antiseptic.

Douglas took a gulp of the whisky and gasped, 'What do you think?

'Hard to say.'

Douglas threw back his head in anguish. 'Christ,' he exclaimed. 'Pigs! I was expecting pigs!'

'I'm sorry. I didn't know,' said Dunbar guiltily.

'Not your fault,' said Douglas. 'I'm grateful. You saved my life back there. That fucking ape was all for turning me into a Lego set. Did you see she was pregnant?'

'I did,' agreed Dunbar. 'They all were.'

Time passed. Douglas dropped into a state somewhere between sleep and unconsciousness. Fitfulness and occasional moans said that he wasn't at peace but he had achieved some respite from the pain through the combination of alcohol and painkillers, sometimes an unholy alliance that ended in tragedy but occasionally in other circumstances, as now, a blessing. Dunbar had to disturb him at fifteen-minute intervals to loosen the tourniquet so that circulation was maintained. Two hours went by before he heard a car draw up in the street and then a knock on the front door.

Two men stood there. In the first grey light of dawn, he could see that they were dressed in surgical tunics and trousers and each had the words Bladen Clinic on the left breast of his tunic. One carried a folded stretcher, the other a black equipment box.

'Dr Dunbar? We've come for your patient.'

Dunbar led them up to where Douglas was lying along the couch.

'Is he stable enough to be moved?'

'He'll do. I've been unable to do anything apart from stem the blood flow,' said Dunbar. 'He had Omnopon about four hours ago and a fair amount of alcohol since for the pain. Maybe you should get some fluid into him before you move him, and if you have some proper dressings there I'll change them.'

The attendants put up a saline drip for Douglas and Dunbar changed the dressing.

'What the hell did this?' asked one of the men when he saw the state of Douglas's arm.'

'An ape.'

'Jesus!'

'The clinic's ready for him?'

The attendant nodded. 'There's a theatre on stand-by. Surgeon's on his way.'

Douglas was transferred to the stretcher and Dunbar held up the saline drip bag as they worked their way downstairs, with great difficulty on the spiral turns. Mercifully, Douglas was still only semi-conscious. Dunbar took hold of his good hand and gave it a squeeze. 'Good luck, Jimmy,' he said as the attendants prepared to close the doors of the ambulance. Dunbar watched its lights disappear before returning to the flat to lock up. 'What a mess,' he whispered as he came downstairs again. 'What a fucking mess.'

217

FIFTEEN

Dunbar was close to both mental and physical exhaustion when he got back to the hotel and parked the car, but he smoothed his hair, straightened his clothing and steeled himself to walk briskly up to the desk and ask for his key. He then turned away smartly and headed for the lifts. He didn't want the desk clerk taking in too much detail of his appearance. As soon as he'd closed his room door, he got out of his muddy, wet clothing and stowed it away in a hotel laundry bag, before stepping into the shower and letting the warm water soothe his aching limbs for a good ten minutes. He put on fresh clothes and followed up with a large gin and tonic. Then he called Lisa. It was six thirty.

'Steve? Are you all right?' she asked at the sound of his voice.

'It all went wrong,' said Dunbar. 'I'm okay but Jimmy Douglas was badly hurt.'

'You were caught?'

'No, we got away. I even got what I wanted, but it was a hell of a mess. I'm not long back. I haven't had a chance to look at anything yet.'

'Why don't you come over? I'll make you some breakfast and you can tell me about it.'

Dunbar said he'd be over in half an hour.

'God, what a nightmare,' said Lisa. 'What on earth is he using apes for? I thought those days were over.'

'The apes were all heavily pregnant,' said Dunbar. 'They also all had recent Caesarian scars on their bellies.'

'I don't understand. How could they still be pregnant if they had section scars?'

'I don't think the section was performed to deliver the baby. It was done to operate on it,' said Dunbar.

'*In utero* surgery,' exclaimed Lisa, her eyes widening. 'I read about that in the *Nursing Standard*. They say it's the coming thing, but it's difficult. It's easy to induce premature labour and lose the foetus. Why would Ross be interested in that?'

'I don't know,' admitted Dunbar. 'But it must have something to do with what he's up to. He went to a lot of trouble to conceal it.'

He told her about the false wall and how finding the opening in it had led to Douglas's injury.

'Do you really think he'll lose his arm?' she asked.

'It was badly damaged. His chances can't be better than fifty-fifty.'

'Poor man,' said Lisa. 'And what a mess. You said the security-men were injured too?'

'I had to knock them out so we could get away.'

'Then they saw you?'

'I had my face covered.'

'Maybe this has made the early-morning news,' said Lisa. She turned on the television and tuned to STV for the breakfast programme. Ten minutes later, it was the third item on the regional news bulletin.

'Last night animal rights activists broke into the laboratories of Glasgow transplant surgeon James Ross and attacked two security men. They daubed slogans over the walls, and are believed to have caused considerable damage to the premises. The security men were taken to hospital, but a spokesman said later that neither was seriously injured.'

Dunbar let out a sigh of relief.

'Dr Ross, speaking to us earlier by telephone, condemned the break-in as an act of wanton vandalism. He said that the research at Vane Farm was vital to his transplant work. These people were doing no good at all; they were endangering the lives of sick children.'

'Go on, hit the cuddly bunny button,' said Dunbar under his breath.

'What d'you think?' asked Lisa when the piece had ended.

'Looks like they bought the animal rights angle,' said Dunbar.

'A bit hard on them,' said Lisa.

'Don't feel too sorry for them,' said Dunbar. 'They don't exactly play by the rules themselves.'

Lisa raised her eyebrows but said only, 'More coffee?'

Dunbar held out his cup.

'You said you got what you went for,' said Lisa.

'I managed to copy the disks with Ross's research data on them.'

'The evidence you need,' said Lisa.

'That's what I'm about to find out,' said Dunbar, getting to his feet a bit unsteadily. 'I'd best get started.'

'You're exhausted!' Lisa protested. 'You need rest. You can't possibly go in just yet.'

Dunbar started to argue but Lisa was insistent. 'It's still very early,' she said. 'At least put your head down for a couple of hours. You'll feel all the better for it. I'll wake you, I promise.'

Dunbar hesitated but then conceded he was very tired. He was asleep within seconds of his head touching the pillow in Lisa's bed.

She woke him at ten.

'I'd like to check on Jimmy's condition before I go,' said Dunbar as he was preparing to leave. 'It would be safer if I did it from here.'

'Of course,' said Lisa.

Dunbar called Sci-Med. He didn't ask to speak to Macmillan but the director came on the line anyway.

'What went wrong, Dunbar?'

'Just bad luck,' replied Dunbar. 'An unfortunate series of events, something that no one could have foreseen.'

'What's the fall-out liable to be?'

'With a bit of luck there won't be any,' said Dunbar. 'Scottish Television carried the story on their regional news programme this morning. Animal rights activists are being blamed for the break-in.'

'And did you get what you were after?'

'I did, but I haven't had time to analyse it yet.'

'Keep me informed.'

'Yes, sir. I actually phoned to ask about the condition of the man assigned to me, James Douglas.'

'Hang on a moment. I'll transfer you.'

'Operations manager.'

'Steven Dunbar here. I'm trying to find out about the condition of James Douglas. He was injured last night on a job with me.'

'I've just been reading the night duty officer's report. Ambulances in the middle of the night, hush-hush operations, surgeons called from their beds. God knows how I'm going to put all this through the books.'

'How's Jimmy?' asked Dunbar with an edge to his voice that said his temper was fraying.

'Let's see . . . report in from the Bladen Clinic, Glasgow, at 09.00 hours. Patient reported as being comfortable after an operation to repair severed tendons and tissue damage to his right arm. He's expected to make a good recovery, but it will take time.'

Dunbar closed his eyes. 'Thank God,' he whispered.

'Friend of yours?' asked the operations manager.

'We were on a job together. It went wrong.'

'Happens.'

'News?' asked Lisa who had come back into the room on hearing Dunbar put the phone down.

'Jimmy's going to be okay.'

'You must be relieved.'

'I'll say. I felt responsible.'

'From what you told me, it was just one of those things.'

'Neither of us is particularly good at accepting that explanation,' said Dunbar. He kissed her lightly on the forehead.

'Call me later?'

'Sure.'

* * *

Kate was on her knees in front of the oven, scrubbing it out with a scouring pad. It was a job she normally hated, but this morning she was singing as she worked. Amanda had been doing so well recently that everything seemed much brighter. Life was worth living again. She hadn't said anything to Sandy, for fear of tempting fate, but inside she felt that quite soon the possibility of Amanda coming home and changing over to home dialysis would be raised. In the meantime she had persuaded Sandy to go hill-walking at the weekend with his friends. It was something he enjoyed and something he hadn't done since Amanda's illness started. He had almost finished her doll's house – complete with lights in every room; it would do him good to get away and do his own thing for a while.

Kate had her head half in, half out of the oven and was launching into a lusty, if tunefully suspect, chorus of 'Love is All Around Us' when she stopped. She was not mistaken; the phone was ringing.

'Was it ever different?' she thought as she got to her feet, stripping off her gloves as she skipped through to the living room.

'Mrs Chapman? It's Dr Hatfull here at Médic Ecosse. I've got some good news for you. We've had notification that a kidney is likely to become available for Amanda very soon.'

Kate couldn't speak for a few moments.

'Mrs Chapman? Are you there?'

'Sorry, yes, I'm here. That's absolutely wonderful news. Excuse me, I think I'm . . .' Kate searched for her handkerchief. 'Oh dear, now you'll think I'm a stupid, over-emotional woman.'

'Not at all. We're all delighted here, too.'

Kate did her best to sound composed. She took a deep breath and asked, 'Can you say when, Doctor?'

'We think some time in the next few days.'

'That soon?'

'As I understand it, the putative donor has been declared brain-dead but is currently on a life-support machine. Permission for organ removal has been obtained, so it's just a question of completing certain formalities. The donor isn't in a British hospital, so there will be transport details to arrange. I'm afraid I can't give you any more details; I don't have that information to hand.'

'I think I'd rather not know any more,' said Kate.

'Of course. Why don't you call us later on? We'll be able to tell you more about dates.'

Kate put down the phone. Her hands were shaking and her pulse was racing. She didn't know what to do first. Sandy! She had to tell Sandy! Her fingers were all thumbs as she dialled the number of the local hospital. 'Get me the lab, please.'

'Ringing for you now.'

'Lab.'

'Sandy, it's me. A kidney's going to become available for Amanda in the next few days!'

'You're kidding!'

'No, I'm not. I've just had Dr Hatfull on the phone. They've identified a donor and they've got permission. It'll be coming from abroad so they have transport to arrange but he sounded confident. It's going to happen!'

'That's absolutely wonderful! I can't believe it. I thought we'd have to wait for God knows how long.'

'Me too. I thought the best that could happen would be that she would be allowed home, but this is even better.'

'I still can't believe it,' stammered Sandy. 'This is just so good, I . . .' Words failed him.

She heard the sob in his voice. 'I know,' she said gently. 'I feel just the same.'

All thoughts of the oven disappeared from Kate's head. She wanted to tell absolutely everyone. She phoned her mother and father, and then Sandy's mother and father, before putting on her coat and running down to the school to see Isa Jenkins. She met the janitor at the door.

'Hello, Mrs Chapman,' he said. 'Coming back to us then?'

'Soon, Joe, soon,' Kate replied as she hurried along the corridor to Isa's classroom.

Isa was teaching but Kate gestured to her through the glass door panel and she smiled and came outside.

'Amanda's going to have her transplant,' said Kate, her eyes bright with excitement.

'Oh my dear, I'm so happy for you,' said Isa, putting her arms round Kate and hugging her.

'I can't believe it,' said Kate. 'It's a prayer answered, a dream come true.'

'And kidney transplants are really just routine these days,' said Isa. 'She'll be back at school in no time and so will you, I hope. We all miss you.'

'I can't wait,' replied Kate. 'I just want everything to be as it was before this awful business started.'

'I'm sure it will be,' said Isa. 'Now I'd better get back to the geography of the Amazon delta and you've probably got a thousand things to do.'

'I don't know where to start,' laughed Kate. 'I just had to come and tell you and thank you for your support through all this.'

'No need,' said Isa. 'I'll pray that everything goes well for her.'

When she got home Kate decided to phone Clive Turner at the Children's Hospital and tell him the news.

'What a piece of luck,' he said. 'That's absolutely marvellous. I'm so pleased for you all. You hardly had to wait any time at all.'

'I can't believe it myself,' said Kate. 'I just wanted to thank you for suggesting the referral in the first place. I shudder to think what might have happened if it hadn't come about.'

Turner wanted to point out that the Children's Hospital might have been equally successful in stabilizing Amanda in the long run, but he didn't. He realized that Kate was euphoric and excited and meant no slight to his own hospital. He simply said, 'I wish her all the luck, Kate, not that I think she'll need it.'

Lack of proper sleep almost caused Dunbar to make a serious mistake. He wanted to start work at once on analysing Ross's research data disks and had loaded the first one into the computer in his office when he remembered the monitoring cable. He hit the eject button with a thump, and the disk popped out into his waiting hand. The blood started pounding in his temples. Had the disk registered its presence on screen before he'd hit the button? He hadn't seen it come up in the corner of the screen but then he hadn't been looking closely.

Fear had now made him very wide awake indeed. He had to act quickly. He brought out his notebook computer and quickly loaded the disk into it. He needed to know its title. The disc was named simply 'Research Data One'. This was a bit of luck. He ejected it and replaced it with a blank disc which he initialized as 'Research Data One'. There was no reason why he couldn't have a disk of his own with that title. He'd leave it lying around on his desk, just in case anyone had seen Ross's disk register when he'd put it in. He quickly transferred some accounts data to it, then, satisfied that he'd covered his tracks as well as he could, put Ross's disk into his notebook computer and started to work through the data.

True to character, Ross was meticulous with his experimental records. They made straightforward reading to someone with a medical background. Dunbar found out exactly what he wanted to know, and quickly. That was the good part. The bottom line said that Ross and his colleagues had made much progress in altering the genetic make-up of experimental pigs to contain elements of the human immune system. The bad news was that they were still a very long way from being able to transplant pig organs into human subjects with any hope of success.

The records showed that immunological problems had plagued the programme from the outset. Ross and his team were struggling with a lack of stability in the transgenic pigs' make-up which had brought progress practically to a halt and showed no sign of resolution in the near future. They had not even started to address the problems associated with the possibility of viral transfer from pigs to humans, the objection that was currently the main stumbling-block as far as government licensing was concerned.

This all meant only one thing to Dunbar. His recent doubts were well founded. He'd been on the wrong track all along. With things the way they stood, Ross would not have dreamed of attempting pig-to-human transplants.

After checking that she was still at home, Dunbar drove back to Lisa's place to tell her the bad news in person. 'There's been no big research breakthrough,' he said dejectedly. 'Ross is nowhere near being able to transplant animal organs successfully. There'd have been no point in even trying. We were wrong.'

'But the kids still died,' said Lisa. 'And I'm still certain they were given incompatible organs.'

Dunbar nodded.

'And you actually saw them removing organs from a pig at the hospital.'

'I've no doubt that Ross is up to something,' agreed Dunbar. 'But it's not as straightforward as we imagined. Ross is just too clever a man. I tried making a list of everything out of the ordinary I'd seen at Médic Ecosse, to see if I could fit more pieces into the puzzle, but no success so far.'

'What sorts of things?' she asked.

Dunbar shrugged. 'Little things. There's a kid in at the moment, Amanda Chapman. She's waiting on a kidney transplant. Médic Ecosse gave her a marrow puncture she didn't really need – all her blood stats were known already. Everyone seemed to know that except the people in charge of her treatment.'

'A marrow puncture?' exclaimed Lisa as if it meant something to her.

Dunbar felt a chill across the back of his neck. 'Yes. Why?'

'Amy had that done as well,' said Lisa.

'Amy Teasdale had a marrow puncture she didn't need?'

'I remember one of the housemen pointing out that it wasn't necessary, but Dr Ross insisted she had one anyway.'

'Tell me about it,' said Dunbar. 'I want to know everything that happened to Amy.'

'You know most of it. She was a difficult case. She'd been ill almost from the time she was born, and appealing to Médic Ecosse was a last resort for her doctors.'

'So no one was too surprised when she died,' said Dunbar thoughtfully.

'Put that way, I suppose not,' agreed Lisa. 'People were more surprised that the hospital took her on in the first place when things hadn't been going too well for them financially and Amy seemed a bit of a lost cause anyway.'

'A bit like Amanda.'

Lisa looked questioningly at Dunbar but he chose not to elaborate. Instead, he said, 'Then you rocked the boat when you started saying that Amy died because she'd been given the wrong organ?'

'I suppose so. You see, she was only a lost cause when they couldn't find a suitable kidney for her, but within weeks of coming in to Médic Ecosse they did. By rights she should have been perfectly okay after her transplant.'

'There was an Omega patient in the hospital at the time, wasn't there?' said Dunbar, still half preoccupied with his own thoughts.

'Yes. How did you know?'

'I checked the dates of free transplant patients before Amanda Chapman against those of Omega patients.'

'Why?'

'I thought at first that the hospital might be using income from Omega patients to cover the costs of expensive free referrals.'

'And now?'

'There's more to it. I wonder if Kenneth Lineham was a free transplant patient too?'

'Couldn't you check?'

'The list of free referral patients didn't include names. I suppose I could—' He broke off in mid-sentence.

'What is it?'

'I've just remembered something,' said Dunbar excitedly. 'Sheila Barnes, in her journal, got quite upset at one point because an Omega patient seemed to be getting more attention than her patient. That means there *was* an Omega patient in the hospital at the same time as Kenneth Lineham. He must have been the first free trans-plant patient, Amy was the second and now Amanda Chapman is number three. All apparently hopeless cases taken on out of the goodness of Médic Ecosse's heart and always at the same time as an Omega patient.'

'But surely that means—'

'That Amanda Chapman is in great danger,' interrupted Dunbar. 'Just like the others.'

'What are you going to do?'

'We need more than just suspicion,' said Dunbar, exasperation showing on his face. 'We need hard evidence and we haven't got any. We don't even have a clue what they're really up to.'

Lisa looked alarmed. 'We can't just do nothing,' she said.

'I'm going to talk to Clive Turner. He might have an idea.' She nodded.

Dunbar called Turner at the Children's Hospital. 'I'm sorry I didn't get back to you sooner,' he began. 'The truth is, I haven't been able to find out discreetly why Amanda Chapman was given an unnecessary marrow puncture.'

'As it happens, I don't think anyone is going to be too upset, even if it was a mistake,' said Turner.

'What's changed?'

'A kidney's become available for Amanda. Hadn't you heard?'

'No, I hadn't,' said Dunbar slowly. 'That is good news.' He said the words but his head suddenly seemed full of broken glass. It was happening all over again. It was happening to Amanda just as it had to the others. She was going to die. She was going to reject her transplant.

'Amazing luck really,' continued Turner. 'She's a very fortunate young lady.'

'Clive, could I come over there? I need to talk to you.'

'Why . . . yes, I suppose so. Is something the matter?'

'I'm not sure. How about now?'

'If you like.'

'I'll be there in fifteen minutes.'

He found Turner in the duty room, talking to a colleague.

'Clive? I'm Steven Dunbar.'

Turner broke off his conversation and turned to shake hands. 'We can talk next door,' he said. He ushered Dunbar into a small, sparsely furnished room and offered him coffee from a half-full flask that sat on an electric heating plate. This and a computer terminal were the only furnishings in the room, apart from two hard chairs and an old Formica-topped table. It said something about modern-day priorities.

'Thanks. Black, no sugar.'

Turner handed Dunbar his coffee and sat down opposite him. 'You sounded a bit concerned on the phone?'

Dunbar nodded. 'The truth is I don't quite know where to begin. I know you're going to find this hard to believe, but something very wrong is going on at Médic Ecosse and I think Amanda Chapman is about to be caught up in it.'

'Go on,' said Turner, now looking serious.

Dunbar told Turner who he really was and why he had been sent to Médic Ecosse.

'So you think Amanda is at risk like the previous two,' said Turner.

'I do. I don't know how or why exactly, but I do feel she's in great danger.'

Turner moved his hands in a gesture of confusion and tried but failed to find words.

'I'm sorry to have sprung this on you like this, but I need your input. You're a transplant expert,' said Dunbar.

'There's rather a lot to take in,' said Turner. 'James Ross has an international reputation. It's difficult to believe he's mixed up in anything shady. On the other hand, if what you say is true . . . What is it you want from me?'

'I'd like to be able to call on you if it proves necessary at any point. I'd also be interested in any suggestions you might care to make as to why the kids died.'

'You say both previous patients were given ostensibly compatible transplants yet they rejected them strongly? That would be unusual in itself.'

'The computer agrees with you,' said Dunbar. 'I checked. They were the only two in the country to die with compatibility ratings as high as they had.'

Turner nodded. 'You know that Ross has been experimenting with animal organs but you say you don't think he risked trying them on the patients?'

'I've seen his research data. There was no hope of success with pig organs the way they are at the moment. There would have been no point in attempting it.'

'What about a mistake in the compatibility ratings given to the donor organs?' suggested Turner.

'Checked at both ends in Amy Teasdale's case,' said Dunbar.

Turner made a face. 'They agreed?'

'To within five per cent.'

'Maybe we should check up on the kidney they've found for Amanda?'

'Good idea,' agreed Dunbar.

Turner logged on to the computer terminal in the corner of the room and asked for access to the donor database. While the machine was considering his request, he suddenly swore as if he'd just remembered something and got up to go next door. He came back clutching Amanda Chapman's old notes. 'We're in luck,' he said. 'I thought they might have been taken down for filing. I need to know her tissue type.'

He thought for a moment, then went on, 'It won't be any good asking for a kidney match if the kidneys have already been booked for Amanda, but it might still be possible to ask about the availability of the liver.' He entered the request for a liver, along with Amanda Chapman's tissue type.

There was a delay of about thirty seconds before the screen filled with information. 'There we are,' said Turner quietly. 'There's our donor. Eighty-four per cent homology. A first-class match. Amanda should have no problem at all. All straight and above-board.'

Dunbar stared at the screen without emotion. 'You'd better decline the liver,' he said. 'They're holding it for you.'

Turner was about to enter the cancellation when Dunbar put a hand on his arm. 'Before you cancel, can you find out where the organ is coming from?'

'Sure.'

Turner requested the information, still under the pretext of searching for a liver for someone with Amanda's tissue type. 'Here it comes,' he said as the screen blinked and changed. 'The organ is available through the Kohl Clinic.'

'Where's that?' asked Dunbar.

'Geneva.'

'Sweet Jesus,' muttered Dunbar.

'Something wrong?'

'Ross has some connection with Geneva, a consultancy, something like that.'

'Switzerland is full of private clinics,' said Turner. 'I don't think you can read anything too sinister into that.'

Dunbar held up his hands in defence. 'I know, I know,' he said. 'It's just that everywhere I turn I find little clues like that. I just can't fit all the pieces together yet.'

Turner looked at him in silence for a few moments before saying, 'I wish you luck. I feel sort of responsible for Amanda; I suggested the referral in the first place.'

'And I didn't raise any objection,' said Dunbar with a wry smile. 'That makes me equally guilty. You said the organ was "available through the Kohl Clinic". What exactly does that mean?'

'I'm not sure,' confessed Turner. 'I suspect it means that the patient isn't actually in the clinic but the clinic is handling the arrangements.'

'I see,' said Dunbar thoughtfully. He sensed that Turner wasn't telling all he knew. 'Handling the arrangements?' he prompted.

'All right, I have my suspicions,' said Turner. 'There's a black market in human organs just like there's a black market in anything else that there's a demand for. I suspect this Kohl Clinic may be a front for that sort of thing.'

'I've heard stories of healthy people selling a kidney to make money in places like India,' said Dunbar. 'I didn't realize how wide-spread it was.'

'It goes on. I've heard tell that they even have a tissue-type register of people who are prepared to do this so they can call them in when a request comes through.'

'God, what a world,' sighed Dunbar.

'That's just a guess,' insisted Turner. 'And these organs don't come cheap. It wouldn't make any sense in Amanda's case if Médic Ecosse are doing the paying.'

'No, it wouldn't,' said Dunbar. 'But not making sense is par for the course.'

'I'm sorry, I'm not being much help.'

'You've given me something else to think about.'

'You really are worried about this transplant, aren't you?' said Turner.

'I've got such a bad feeling about it. But on the face of it, Amanda's in a top-class hospital under the care of a world-famous surgeon and she's about to receive a kidney with an eighty-four per cent compatibility rating. What can I do?'

'Not a lot,' said Turner.

'Incidentally, they did a marrow puncture on Amy Teasdale too. It wasn't a mistake. Ross knew she'd had one done before.'

'He must have wanted stem cells,' said Turner. 'Wonder why? Maybe something to do with his immuno-preparation work.' He shrugged and asked, 'Is there anything else you'd like me to do?'

'Just be available,' said Dunbar. 'Right now, I don't know why or what for.'

'I'll give you my home number and a mobile as well.'

Dunbar returned to Médic Ecosse. He supposed he felt better for the chat with Turner, but he was far from easy in his mind. As he parked his car and walked round to the front of the hospital, a taxi drew up outside the front entrance and two men got out. They were well-dressed and had the aura of successful profes-sional men, Dunbar noted as he passed that one was carrying a very expensive alligator-skin medical bag. Both had American accents.

Out of curiosity, Dunbar lingered near Reception, pretending to look for something in his briefcase.

'We're expected,' said one of the men as they reached the desk.

'Dr Ross left word,' said the receptionist. She rang the bell for the porter and said to him, 'Show these gentlemen up to the Omega wing, will you?'

Dunbar waited until the three men had disappeared before approaching the receptionist.

'Dr Dunbar, what can I do for you?'

'Those two men. Who were they?'

'I couldn't rightly say, Doctor. Dr Ross just advised me that two medical gentlemen would be arriving sometime this afternoon. Sounded American, if you ask me.'

SIXTEEN

Dunbar sat at his desk and embraced the silence. He took slow, deep breaths as an aid to thinking clearly and rationally; mounting frustration had been preventing this. He knew exactly what he wanted to do. He wanted to put a stop to Amanda Chapman's transplant operation, but he couldn't. This was the unpalatable bottom line that was making him so uncomfortable. He couldn't because he had no good reason to. If he tried, he would be seen by all and sundry as some kind of interfering lunatic, at best suffering from a sudden nervous breakdown, but more probably reviled as a madman of the sort who mowed down the innocent.

No one would listen and they couldn't be blamed. There was really nothing of substance to consider. For that reason they would all be against him, the hospital, the transplant unit, Amanda's parents, Sci-Med, everyone. Even if he were to succeed in stopping it, the chances were that Amanda would still die because she couldn't get a transplant in time when – as others would not be slow to point out – one had been available. He would be seen as her murderer and all because he suspected things weren't going to turn out well for her.

He knew that unless he worked out exactly what Ross was up to by the time the donor kidney arrived from Geneva, he was going to have to sit still and do nothing. If, as he suspected, Amanda should reject her transplant, like Amy Teasdale and Kenneth Lineham, it would still be his fault because he hadn't done anything to stop it. Talk about the devil and the deep blue sea. Damned if you do, damned if you don't. He cursed and got up to start pacing the room.

Once more he juggled the pieces of information in his head, trying to make a coherent picture, but they still wouldn't fit. Maybe there weren't enough or maybe there were too many and not all of them relevant.

He was distracted by the sound of a taxi's diesel engine as it drew to a halt and idled noisily at the front door. He looked down to see another person carrying a medical bag had arrived. There was certainly lots of activity surrounding the Omega patient. Soon, he reflected, there would be lots of activity surrounding Amanda Chapman. He frowned and asked himself again: what's the connection?

Amanda had been taken to the Omega wing for her unnecessary marrow puncture. He hadn't been able to come up with a reason for it but at least he knew that the test itself wasn't a simple mistake of duplication. Amy had been subjected to the same procedure. Ross had insisted on it. What was it that Turner had said? He must have wanted stem cells for his immuno-preparation work.

Dunbar suddenly saw the light. The tests hadn't been performed for the benefit of the patients at all. Ross hadn't wanted duplicate tests done. He'd needed stem cells from the patients for a purpose other than the obvious one of checking their immunotype. There was no repetition of unnecessary tests at all. There never had been.

He felt a frisson of excitement. He was getting somewhere at last. Immuno-preparation work? Where had he come across that term recently? Turner had used it but he had seen it somewhere else. If only he could remember . . . The phone rang and broke his train of thought. He cursed and answered it. It was nothing important.

Dunbar tried to recover his concentration but failed. The moment had gone. He decided to cut his losses and waste no more time wondering. He connected his notebook computer to the phone line to call up Sci-Med. He wanted the latest information they had about James Ross.

His interest quickened at once: they'd found out something about Ross's Geneva connection. Their earlier problems had been due to an inability to trace a Médic International hospital or clinic in Geneva. The reason for this was simple. There was no such place and Médic International had no interests at all in Geneva. Ross had been going there for other reasons; he also owned a house there, a villa overlooking the lake. He had paid $2 million for it three years ago.

'Jesus,' muttered Dunbar. So money was involved after all. Big money. You didn't buy a house like that on eighty grand a year. He saw that there was more information to come and scrolled down the screen. Ross had an interest in a Swiss medical recruitment agency called Roche Dubois. It specialized in the recruitment of high-grade staff for private clinics all over Europe. Doctors, nurses, technicians of all sorts, could find highly paid work if they were good enough. The agency was above-board and had a good reputation. It specialized in finding positions for American nursing and medical personnel wishing to work in Europe for whatever reason, although exchanges for European nationals were also arranged.

Dunbar wondered if this was relevant. Did Ross have reason to recruit medical staff on his own behalf? He thought about the American doctors being shown to the Omega wing. Could all the secrecy, stone-faced guards and strange medical people coming and going really be ascribed to a need for confidentiality? No, there had to be more to it.

The Omega patients were the key to the whole damned thing, Dunbar decided. It wasn't that the money they brought in was being used to subsidize NHS charity patients. Quite the reverse. The NHS patients were being used in some way for the benefit of Omega ones. That must be why Ingrid had feigned ignorance when he had mooted a connection between them and Omega patients over funding. She knew what was going on. He had thrown her by making the connection but for the wrong reason.

This still didn't help. The only connection he was aware of was the marrow puncture done on Amanda Chapman in the Omega wing and the fact that there had been Omega patients in the

236

hospital when Amy Teasdale and Kenneth Lineham had been patients.

Just who the hell were these Omega patients? he wondered angrily. What were they really there for? He had the hollow feeling that he was running out of time. He needed information and he needed it fast. It was time to change tactics. No more pussy-footing around. He would cause a fuss by asking questions openly. Maybe he couldn't stop Amanda's operation, but he could certainly create the illusion that he knew much more than he did. That might scare someone in the know; it might scare them enough to achieve the same end. It was a dangerous game to play, though. Ignorance was never a position of strength.

He picked up the phone and called Ingrid's extension. 'Ingrid, would you come over, please?'

Ingrid arrived and smiled. 'You have something for me?'

'I want to know who the current Omega patient is. I want her name and I want to know why she's here. I also want to know where she was before she came here and who referred her to Médic Ecosse.'

Her smile faded. 'I'm not sure I can do that,' she stammered. 'The strict confidentiality surrounding—'

Dunbar interrupted her. 'I need that information. I need it now, please.'

Ingrid tried to recover her composure. 'Are you absolutely sure?' she asked tentatively. 'If you'll forgive my saying, it doesn't seem to be strictly relevant to the investigation and monitoring of accounts.'

Dunbar had anticipated such opposition. 'On the contrary,' he said, 'I have reason to believe that the true income from Omega patients is not being declared.'

'But you've seen the figures,' said Ingrid, taken aback. 'The profit for the hospital amounted to many thousands of pounds.'

'I've seen the declared profit,' agreed Dunbar. 'I'd like to see for myself how the figures are arrived at. For that reason I want to know all about the current Omega patient, who she is, why she's here, and I need verification of her condition from an outside source, preferably the hospital or clinic that referred her to you.'

'I see,' said Ingrid. 'I very much doubt if Mr Giordano or Dr Kinscherf will agree to this.'

'If they don't, I will lodge a formal complaint of obstruction with my colleagues at the Scottish Office and suggest that an investigation be mounted immediately by the Serious Fraud Office.'

Ingrid tried to maintain eye contact with Dunbar, by way of a challenge, but she failed after a few moments. 'I'll see what I can do,' she said quietly; she was obviously unnerved at seeing a side to Dunbar she hadn't encountered before.

The door closed behind her and Dunbar remained in his chair, sitting perfectly still, wondering how well he'd played his hand. Would they give in and tell him what he wanted to know or would they try to delay as long as possible? He had to admit that the latter would be the bright thing to do. They were vulnerable only as long as the Omega patient was in the hospital. Once she'd gone they'd be safe. She'd be lost in the mists of secrecy. His only hope lay in Ingrid relaying his threat to call in the SFO as being imminent. They might just believe that his interest was still financial and gamble on giving him the information he asked for. After all, no figures had been declared for the current Omega patient. They had nothing to worry about on that account. He decided to help matters along by exploiting the fact that his computer screen was being monitored. He sat down at it and started drafting a letter requesting that the Scottish Office consider calling in the SFO on the grounds that he'd been denied access to files he thought might be concealing fraud.

After nearly half an hour, Ingrid returned, carrying a file. 'Here are the notes you asked for, Doctor,' she said without emotion. 'I'm asked to remind you of their strictly confidential nature. Please inform me as soon as you're finished with them.'

'Of course.'

Dunbar felt a thrill of excitement as he flipped open the cover and started to read.

The patient was a thirty-year-old Saudi Arabian woman, the wife of a sheikh with extensive oil interests and an income to match. She was pregnant for the third time. Her first two babies had been stillborn from a congenital heart defect. The sheikh, who doted on his wife, was anxious that she be monitored every step of the way through her current pregnancy. The Mayo Clinic in Rochester, Minnesota, had been given the task but after it was diagnosed at an early stage, through the use of the latest foetal monitoring equipment, that the foetus was suffering from the same cardiac defect as the others, the woman had been removed from the Mayo and flown across the Atlantic to Médic Ecosse. Corrective surgery was planned immediately after a successful birth.

Dunbar noted the name of the attending physician at the Mayo Clinic, Dr Gordon Hasselhof, and closed the file. There was certainly more to it than just a difficult birth, but did it help him at all? It was difficult to see how little Amanda Chapman could be involved in the obstetric care of a thirty-year-old Middle Eastern woman. He phoned Ingrid and told her he was finished with the notes. They were collected within minutes and without comment.

There was one question that sprang to mind though – although it might not be relevant, thought Dunbar. Why had the woman been transferred to Médic Ecosse? The Mayo Clinic was one of the most famous medical institutions in the world. A transatlantic flight and the trauma of moving to yet another strange country and hospital could not have been the most restful experience for the patient. What had precipitated it? Had there been some kind of disagreement over her treatment at the Mayo? Some undisclosed problem?

It had not been Dunbar's intention at the outset to contact the referring doctor or hospital; he had made his request for their identity purely as a safeguard against being fobbed off with anything Médic Ecosse cared to tell him. But now he decided he would make inquiries. In his present state of ignorance, no detail should be overlooked. He looked at his watch. Making adjustments for the time differential, it would be around 10 a.m. in Minnesota. He asked the switchboard to make the call.

'Good morning. Mayo Clinic. How may I help you?' said a robotic female voice.

'I'd like to speak with Dr Gordon Hasselhof, please.'

'May I ask who's calling?'

'Dr Steven Dunbar. I'm calling from Glasgow in Scotland.'

'Please hold.'

For a few moments the line was left open and Dunbar could hear the everyday sounds of a hospital in the background; then music cut in as he was put on hold. 'Greensleeves' coming from the wrong side of the Atlantic seemed slightly bizarre.

'Hello, caller.'

'Yes?'

'Dr Hasselhof is currently in conference. Would you care to leave a message or call back later?'

'I'll try later,' said Dunbar.

'Have a nice day, Doctor.'

'You too,' said Dunbar. He cautioned himself that it was better to be told to have a nice day by someone who didn't mean it than to get lost by someone who did.

He put down the phone and started to tidy up the papers on his desk. He saw that his letter to the Scottish Office was still on the screen of his computer and decided to copy it to disk rather than cancel it. He picked up the disk he had initialled earlier and inserted it. He saw it come up as 'Research Data One', the title he'd given it when covering up the mistake of inserting one of Ross's disks. Looking at it and thinking of Ross's research reminded him where he'd seen the term 'immuno-preparation' before: in the title of one of Ross's research papers, the one he had put aside while he read the others. He grabbed his jacket and briefcase and made for the car park. The paper was in the file in his hotel room.

There was a laundry bag sitting on his bed when he got there, with a note pinned to it. Dunbar feared it would be a complaint from the hotel about the state of the things he'd sent for cleaning, the clothing he'd used on the ill-starred expedition with Jimmy

Douglas. He opened the envelope. It wasn't a complaint. They were returning a set of car keys that had been left in one of the pockets. Dunbar looked at them. They were the keys to Jimmy's Land-Rover. He'd have to find a way of returning them.

When he retrieved Ross's paper from the Sci-Med file, Dunbar noticed that it was over three years old. This was not encouraging. Could what Ross had been working on over three years ago really be relevant to what was going on at the moment? If it had been a successful line of research, why had he not published any more about it in the intervening period? He sat down and started reading.

He had to struggle with the immunological jargon at the beginning but it soon began to make sense and he jotted down the major points as they emerged.

Fact number one was that the human foetus did not start out with an immune system of its own. If biological material from a foreign source were to be introduced to it before its own system developed, it would be accepted. More importantly, when the baby finally did develop its immune system, it would continue to accept material from that source throughout its life. Animal experiments using stem cells . . . Dunbar swallowed as he read the words . . . had shown this to be the case. Unborn mice, surgically infused with human stem cells before development of their immune system, had subsequently been born with a human immune system as well as their own.

Using this technique, it was possible to 'prepare' a foetus by surgically introducing stem cells from a putative donor into it while still in the womb, making a subsequent transplant after the baby's birth problem-free. There was no need for steroids or any other kind of immuno-suppressants to overcome rejection problems. There simply wouldn't be any. The tissue would be one hundred per cent compatible. The perfect transplant, in fact.

The limitations to this strategy, as Ross pointed out in his paper, were obvious. Such transplants would have to be restricted to organs that the donor could afford to lose, such as a half or whole kidney. If the foetus needed a heart or liver then, of course, there could be no human donor. It was suggested, therefore, that the development of this technique of 'immunizing' foetuses against rejection of a future transplant would best be pursued with animals in mind as the donors. Improvements in foetal surgery would also have to be achieved if stem cells were to be introduced without a high risk of premature labour induction.

Dunbar felt a chill down his spine as the picture became clear. He had discovered something so awful that his mind almost rejected it. He looked back over the text and picked out the the words 'there could, of course, be no human donor'. He was mesmerized by them. In his head he started to modify the text: there could, of course, be no human donor unless . . . the stakes were high enough . . . to include murder as part of the procedure. And that's what the ape experiments were all about. Ross was practising foetal surgery because he needed to introduce stem cells into unborn foetuses. Christ! It all fitted now. Kenneth Lineham, Amy Teasdale and now Amanda Chapman had not been admitted to Médic Ecosse as transplant recipients at all. They were the donors.

Dunbar rubbed his forehead as he struggled to come to terms with the discovery. Amanda's marrow puncture had been carried out to obtain stem cells for surgical introduction into the unborn foetus of the Omega patient. That's why she had been taken up to the Omega wing. In the intervening weeks, the Omega baby had been developing Amanda's immune system and it must now be ready to accept Amanda's tissue as its own. Dunbar guessed at an operation timed to coincide with a Caesarian delivery when the baby was large enough to receive a child's heart.

It also seemed a fair guess that Ross had put out a request to the black market for a suitable kidney for Amanda, knowing that if the price were high enough one would be found. At some point before or during Amanda's operation, he would substitute an incompatible kidney, an animal organ, knowing that she would reject it and die. He would then steal her heart for the Omega baby. At autopsy he would put the correct donor kidney into Amanda to make everything neat and tidy. Her death, like those of Amy and

Kenneth before her, would be just another one of those things . . . unless two nurses said otherwise!

Dunbar thought back to McVay's report on Amy Teasdale. He'd said that not only her kidney but also her heart had been removed; they had both assumed at the time that this had been part of a routine earlier autopsy. McVay had been asked to examine Amy's transplanted kidney. If only he'd been asked to examine the heart too. He would almost certainly have discovered that it was not her own but the previous Omega patient's baby's heart. It was odds-on that Amy's heart was currently beating inside the offspring of some unknown Omega patient in a foreign land. This could be proved with a second exhumation of Amy, but Dunbar prayed that that wouldn't be necessary. In the meantime, the prime objective was to save Amanda Chapman's life.

His immediate thought was to inform Sci-Med and call in the police. That would put an immediate stop to everything. The problem was that 'everything' included Amanda's chances of a transplant in time. Despite everything, it was true that a real, compatible kidney had been found for her. It just wasn't Ross's intention to use it until after her death. There must be some way of allowing things to continue so that the kidney arrived safely and was given to Amanda. He'd contact Clive Turner at the Children's Hospital but first he'd tie up a last loose end. He'd call Hasselhof at the Mayo Clinic again.

'Who is this?' asked an American voice after a short wait.

'My name is Steven Dunbar. I'm calling from the Médic Ecosse Hospital in Glasgow, Scotland.'

'You've got a nerve!' retorted Hasselhof.

'I'm sorry?' said Dunbar, recoiling slightly from the earpiece.

'The medical profession has enough problems without carpet-baggers like you in it.'

'I'm sorry, there must be some kind of mistake. I really don't understand what you're talking about, Doctor. I'm calling about one of your patients who was transferred here from the Mayo Clinic.'

'I figured that,' said Hasselhof. 'You people promised that man

243

and woman something that can't be done. There is no operation that could save that woman's baby. The malformation is far too great for corrective cardiac surgery to be of any value, but you people obviously convinced them otherwise. That, sir, is fraud in my book. And you now have the nerve to call me for advice!'

Dunbar was about to explain to Hasselhof that he hadn't called for advice and that he wasn't part of the Médic Ecosse set-up, but he changed his mind. There wasn't time. He simply asked one question. 'What if the baby were to have a heart transplant, Doctor?'

'A transplant? The child wouldn't survive long enough for a donor to become available. Even if one did, the necessary steroid suppression of the immune system would lay the child open to every infection under the sun. It's just not possible.'

'Thank you, Doctor,' said Dunbar. 'I'm obliged.'

He put down the phone, muttering to himself, 'Oh yes it is, Dr Hasselhof, if you know how to make sure the baby accepts the heart as its own flesh and blood so you don't have to use steroids and if you're prepared to murder the donor for her heart.'

Dunbar called the Children's Hospital and asked to speak to Clive Turner.

'Dr Turner's in theatre at the moment,' he was told.

'Damn!' said Dunbar as he put down the phone. A voice inside his head urged caution. 'Take it easy. There's no need to panic. Think it through. The first thing to establish is when they plan to operate on Amanda.'

He would simply go back to Médic Ecosse and inquire, which would be in keeping with his new up-front policy of asking things outright. As he prepared to leave his room, Dunbar wondered if there was anything he'd overlooked. He had the unpleasant feeling that there was but for the moment whatever it was eluded him. He had his briefcase and his computer. He had his notebook in his pocket. As soon as he'd established when the kidney from Geneva was going to arrive, he'd devise a plan of action to intercept it and inform Médic Ecosse. He closed the door with an air of finality and set off to play out the last act in a nightmare.

He got no further than the car park. As he inserted his key into the car door lock he felt a sharp pain in his thigh and the world started to swim. Nausea . . . a falling sensation. His last conscious thought was the realization that Médic Ecosse knew he'd contacted the Mayo Clinic. He'd phoned the first time from the hospital, and the call would have been logged. He'd given away that his interest in the Omega file was not confined to financial matters.

Dunbar woke up in complete darkness. He had a splitting headache and felt sick but this was partly due to the smell in the room, a strange mixture of excrement and . . . wet grain was the best he could come up with. It was the smell of harvest time in the fields, a throwback to his childhood. But no, it wasn't that . . . It was the smell of animal feed. And animals.

Despite his muzziness it took him only a moment to figure out that he must be back at Vane Farm. He tried to sit up but the pain in his head soared to new heights so he slipped back down again. As long as he lay still he could think clearly. He ran his hands over his body. He had clothes on, shirt, trousers, shoes. One of the sleeves of his shirt, the left one, had been torn away and his upper arm ached. Oh God! They'd been giving him more injections. That meant there was no way of knowing how long he'd been unconscious. It could have been days or even weeks. Amanda Chapman could be dead by now.

His next thought was to wonder why he'd been allowed to regain consciousness at all. Was it deliberate or a mistake? The human body quickly developed a tolerance to narcotics, which meant dosage had to be increased to maintain the effect. Was that it? Had he come round before his next injection was due? If so he probably didn't have much time. He rolled over on to his stomach and began to drag himself over the floor to explore his surroundings.

The first thing he came into contact with was a sack made of coarse hessian; it was full. He stretched up, put his hand inside the neck and pulled out a handful of small hard round pellets.

He smelt them; it was animal feed. He also found a metal scoop inside the sack and put it in his pocket. It was a weapon of sorts, he supposed.

The room was a food store. The only thing other than sacks of feed-stuffs in the room was a floor-standing machine which, judging by feel, was some kind of processor. It had a large loading hopper on top and an exit pipe with a grille over its front lower down. There was a control panel on the front with two buttons on it, one raised and one recessed. The recessed one must be the On switch. It always was on industrial machines; a safety measure.

Dunbar froze as he heard voices. They were quite loud but he couldn't make out what they were saying. He put this down to his wooziness until he realized that they were not speaking English. The throat-clearing sounds suggested Arabic. There were two of them and they were probably coming to give him his next injection – or worse. Feeling as ill as he did, and armed only with a pellet scoop, he could do little to stop them.

A mobile phone started to bleep and the men's talk stopped, to be replaced by one side of a phone conversation, again in Arabic. When it ended it became apparent that one man had been called away. Both voices receded and Dunbar heard the front door open and close. He waited for returning footsteps and did not have long to wait. At least with only one opponent the odds were a little more even. He lay down again, hiding the metal scoop in his right hand behind the small of his back. He wished his head would clear. He felt as if he were in a drunken stupor.

He opened his eyes fractionally so he could see something when the door was opened. The lock turned, the door swung open and he saw the silhouette of a tall, well-built man with a syringe in his right hand. He seemed to stand still in the doorway for ages, like an executioner contemplating his victim's neck on the block as some announcement ceremony went on around him.

Dunbar desperately wanted to swallow but did not dare. He closed his eyes completely as the light was clicked on. The next few moments were going to decide whether he lived or died. The light on his eyelids dimmed as the man's shadow fell on them. Dunbar sensed him kneel down to his left. He could hear his breathing, smell a suggestion of foreign food on his clothes.

He felt his arm being grasped firmly but not with undue roughness. The man suspected nothing. Timing was all-important now. At the first touch of the needle point Dunbar rolled smartly away to stop it piercing his skin. He brought the metal scoop from behind his back and swung it at his assailant's head. It connected with a dull clunk and threw the man off balance, but Dunbar knew the blow wasn't heavy enough to knock him out. The man was already recovering and soon Dunbar was going to be in real trouble. He'd used up his adrenalin in fighting the effects of the drug.

Fuelled by panic, he struggled to his knees and swung his right fist at the Arab but his arm felt like lead and the punch carried no weight at all. The Arab evaded it with ease and grinned as Dunbar slumped back to the floor. There was no point in trying to throw any more punches; he hadn't the strength to make them count. He backed away instinctively, now just hoping to survive as long as possible. The Arab recovered his syringe and checked it leisurely before coming after him.

As Dunbar retreated, he stumbled against the sack of animal feed, which spilled over. He grabbed a handful of pellets and flung them across the floor under the Arab's feet. It seemed odds against, but for once he got the luck he needed. The Arab lost his footing and pitched forward, saving himself from falling by reaching into the hopper of the processing machine. Instinctively, Dunbar groped for the On switch on the control panel – it took only a second but seemed like an eternity – and pressed it.

The machine sprang to life and drew the Arab's arm into the blades. Mercifully, he fell into unconsciousness as the scream died on his lips. The machine jammed. Dunbar hit the Off switch and was enveloped in silence.

'Your kind of justice, I believe,' he murmured. 'An arm for an arm.'

SEVENTEEN

Dunbar knew his only chance of survival was to get out of the building before the other man returned or the security men came across from the gate-house. What about the staff? He decided they couldn't be here. Research must have been suspended while Ross and the Arabs were using the farm as a prison. He was totally disorientated. He didn't know what day it was or even whether it was day or night. He dragged himself to the front door and then stopped when he realized that he couldn't go out this way. The door faced the gate-house. He would be seen. It might even be broad daylight out there. There was only one alternative and it wasn't an attractive one. He would have to go out through the slurry pipe he and Jimmy Douglas had used.

He balked at the idea. He wasn't at all sure he had either the stamina or the courage for it in his current condition but there seemed to be no alternative. But then what? There'd be no car waiting three hundred yards up the road this time and he didn't have the strength for a prolonged cross-country run. Despair was on the horizon when he remembered Jimmy Douglas's Land-Rover and the keys the hotel laundry had returned to him. Please God he had them with him and please God they were the only set of keys for the vehicle. Jimmy had said something about having it picked up. He felt in his pocket and found the keys.

If the police hadn't taken the Land-Rover away, and there was a good chance that they hadn't, he could use it . . . but only if he could reach it. His stomach turned over at the thought of the slurry pipe. Going out through it posed a whole new set of problems. It was going to be even worse than coming in. At least last time he'd been able to open the drain covers from the outside and step down into the pit. This time he'd have to open the covers from below. For that he would have to submerge himself completely in the sump.

Dunbar started to prepare mentally for the nightmare ahead. He imagined himself outside in the fresh air, heading for freedom across the open fields; but reality kept intruding. If he made it to the outside he'd emerge from the pipe like the creature from the black lagoon and there'd be no water or clean clothes available. He had a sudden thought. There must be some kind of clothing kept in the building for research workers. If he could find a change of clothing and some plastic to wrap it up in . . .

He found what he was looking for in a linen cupboard in the hallway leading to the staff locker room. He helped himself to a surgical tunic and trousers and added a towel to his bundle. A further search uncovered a roll of plastic bin sacks. He tore one off and put the clothes and towel inside, making the package as flat as possible. He tucked it inside his shirt against his chest and smoothed it as best he could.

He was getting stronger by the minute as the effects of the drug in his bloodstream wore off, but the thought of the slurry pipe still filled him with dread. If he failed to raise the drain covers from below, the ultimate in claustrophobic nightmares would become his, followed quickly by his death.

Dunbar removed the inside grille with slow deliberation and eased himself feet first into the pipe. It was only fear of the consequences of being recaptured that drove him on. The pigs round about grunted their approval. The horizontal section of the pipe was easy; then came the turn into the vertical drop. Dunbar could feel the blood pounding inside his head as he resolved not to stop and think. He closed his eyes and held his breath as he wriggled slowly backwards until gravity took over; his rate of slide accelerated and he fell straight down into the slurry, landing with a jolt that travelled up his spine and rattled his teeth. He was now standing in the slurry pit. Next he had to wriggle down and out of the mouth of the pipe and raise the drain covers, and then he would be free.

He couldn't hold his breath any longer. He raised his face as far as possible from the slurry and took in a breath of air from above. He gagged and knew that he couldn't do that again. He writhed and wriggled down into the pit and immersed himself in its contents before slamming his back and shoulders up against the drain covers. They didn't budge. Nightmare thoughts of their being padlocked filled his head as he strained up at them again. This time they gave with a loud sucking sound. Recent rain had sealed the edges with mud and water, creating a vacuum seal. He took in a huge breath of night air and tried to clear the filth from his face and eyes. The sky was black as pitch and it was raining.

Fighting the urge to retch, he replaced the drain covers . . . and remembered the electric fence. The realization made him sink to his knees and brought him close to tears. There was no question of trying to go over it or dig a way under it and he certainly didn't have anything to cut and bridge it with on this occasion. He'd have to leave by the front entrance.

He wriggled up to the corner of the building on his belly and decided on his route. It wasn't going to be as difficult as he'd first imagined. The gate-house was designed mainly to monitor people coming in rather than leaving. If he could cross the twenty metres of open ground between the main building and the gate-house without being seen, he could get round the back and into the neighbouring field at the corner where the electric fence ended. He got up on to his haunches and prepared for the short sprint. He was still a little unsteady so he took his time in composing himself. A stumble could be fatal.

The men inside the gate-house seemed to be moving around a good deal. Dunbar waited until none of them was near the window facing the main building, then sprinted across the tarmac and into the welcoming shadows. He paused, motionless, for a few moments before continuing round the blind side of the gate-house and squeezing through into the neighbouring field where the electric fence ended.

Dunbar started out on his journey towards the abandoned rail station where his hopes were pinned on the Land-Rover still being parked. The night was so dark that he kept stumbling and losing his footing as he made his way diagonally across the first field to follow the line of the road. The icy rain was doing something to clear the mess from his head and face but he desperately wanted to find water flowing in one of the many ditches he had to cross. It wasn't until he was on the far side of the second field that he found a small stream running down the side of a pine wood. The water was freezing cold, but sluicing himself down with it was preferable to carrying on in his current condition.

It seemed as if every muscle in his body went into shivering spasm as he stripped off his contaminated clothing and knelt down in the water to clean himself. When he'd finished, he scrambled out on to the bank in ungainly fashion and brushed off excess water with the palms of his hands as best he could before extracting the towel from the binsack and rubbing himself down vigorously to maintain circulation. He put on the surgical tunic and trousers, cursing the fact that it was difficult because he wasn't properly dry and his movements were jerky because he was shivering. He emptied the pockets of his old clothes and then stuffed them as a rolled-up bundle under a stone below the bank. He started running as fast as he dared in an effort to work up some warmth. He was still shivering all over when he finally reached the car park and saw that Jimmy's Land-Rover was still there.

The engine rattled into life. Dunbar willed it to heat up quickly so that he might have the warmth of the heater to fight against threatening hypothermia. He crunched the vehicle into gear because the shivering of his leg made holding down the clutch pedal difficult. He bumped a little too fast over the broken surface, bouncing himself off the seat as the vehicle lurched out on to the road. He had to get to a phone box.

Although he was trying to travel as fast as he could he had the feeling of being trapped in a slow-motion world. Every gear change seemed to take for ever as the revs fell, the gears crunched and the build-up suggested he was towing a juggernaut. He resorted to staying in low gear and screaming the engine as he fought his way along the twisting country road back to town.

There was a woman dialling in the first phone box he came to. Dunbar screeched the Land-Rover to a halt beside her and got out. The mere sight of him, staggering from exhaustion, hair soaking wet and wearing medical attendant's clothing, made the woman change her mind about the urgency of her call. She stumbled out of the box and took to her heels, looking anxiously behind her at what she obviously saw as an escapee from a lunatic asylum.

There was an awful moment when Dunbar couldn't remember the number of the Sick Children's Hospital but it came back to him. He then failed to dial it properly because the trembling in his hand made him hit two buttons together no fewer than three times. He took a deep breath, calmed himself and succeeded at the fourth attempt. He asked for Clive Turner, praying that he'd be there. He had no idea of time or date for that matter.

'Dr Turner.'

'Thank Christ,' stammered Dunbar.

'Who is this?' asked Turner.

'Clive, it's Steven Dunbar. Has Amanda Chapman had her operation yet?'

'Steven? Where the hell are you? What's happened? You sound strange.'

'Just tell me. Has Amanda had her operation yet?'

'It was scheduled for eight this evening. Her father phoned me this morning. What's happening? Where are you?'

Dunbar's heart sank. 'What time is it now?' he asked.

'Ten past nine. What is it? Where are you? What's wrong?'

'Listen! They're deliberately giving Amanda the wrong kidney. They want her to die so they can steal her heart and give it to another patient.'

'You can't be serious,' exclaimed Turner.

'Believe me, it's true. We've got to do something to save Amanda if there's still time.'

'What can we do? If you say they're giving her the wrong kidney . . .'

'They've had the matched kidney sent from Geneva. It must have arrived by now if they're doing the operation, but they only plan to give it to Amanda after she's dead. If we can get there in time we can see that she gets it instead of the bloody animal organ they're giving her!'

'I just can't believe this is happening,' stammered Turner.

'Clive, just trust me. It's true. Can you get a surgical team together and meet me in the car park at Médic Ecosse as soon as you can? I'm going to call in the cavalry.'

'There's only a surgical houseman and one theatre technician on duty at the moment.'

'Do what you can. I think I can get you a theatre nurse.'

Dunbar called Lisa next.

'Where have you been? I've been worried sick about you!' she exclaimed. 'It's been two days!'

'I'm sorry. There's no time for explanations,' said Dunbar. He gave her the briefest of summaries of what was happening and said, 'They may need all the help they can get tonight. You're an experienced theatre nurse. Will you help?'

'Of course. What do you want me to do?'

'Get over there as quick as you can. Meet us in the car park.'

Next Dunbar called Sci-Med in London. He had to reverse the charges. His money had run out. Luckily his call was accepted automatically.

'This is Steven Dunbar in Glasgow. I need help urgently. Everything will have to be done from your end. Understood?'

'Understood,' said the duty officer. 'But I may have to call for authorization.'

'Do what I ask first!' insisted Dunbar. 'Then call anyone you like. I'll take full responsibility. I need police back-up at the Médic Ecosse Hospital as fast as you can get them there, and some of them should be armed. They've not to do anything until I get there but I won't be long. Tell them to wait outside the car park and out of sight. Okay?'

'You're sure about the arms?'

'I suspect at least two of the opposition are carrying.' Dunbar was thinking of the Arab guards on the Omega Wing. Hopefully they wouldn't be involved but it was better to be safe than sorry.

'Anything else?'

'I need a couple of WPCs in the squad.' Again, he was thinking of the Omega wing.

'Anything else?'

'I need a forensic pathologist to examine a kidney biopsy.'

'We'll ask the police. Is that it?'

'Those are the priorities but the police might like to take a trip out to a place called Vane Farm; it's north of Glasgow on Lomond Road. I've been held there for the last two days by some Arab gentlemen, one of whom might have been admitted to hospital by now with severe hand and arm injuries.'

'I'll pass that on. Sounds like you're having a busy time.'

'Just get on to it right away.'

'Will do.'

Dunbar got back in the Land-Rover and headed for Médic Ecosse as fast as he could. He couldn't help but imagine Amanda lying on the operating table, being ever so precisely and carefully murdered.

As he got to within a mile of the hospital he was passed by a speeding police car on a long downhill section of the road. He snatched the opportunity and put his foot to the floor to take advantage of the swathe it was cutting through traffic. This was fine going downhill and even on the following straight section once his speed had built up, but the Land-Rover wasn't built for cornering like the police car. Every sharp turn was a white-knuckle ride on two wheels before clattering back down on to four again.

As the two vehicles screeched to a halt in the street outside the hospital car park, Dunbar allowed himself to slump forward momentarily on to the steering wheel in deference to mental exhaustion. He needed a moment to calm himself and regain composure. Both policemen from the car in front were at his doors before he knew it.

'What the hell d'you think you were doing back there?' demanded one. 'Bloody idiot! Get out the vehicle.'

'I'm Steven Dunbar,' replied Dunbar. 'You're here to assist me.'

The two men exchanged uncertain glances and looked at Dunbar's appearance and clothing with some suspicion.

'Get me whoever's in charge,' snapped Dunbar, putting an end to their uncertainty. 'Now!'

He saw Clive Turner and Lisa coming to meet him. They were joined, before they reached him, by a police superintendent.

'Look at the state of you,' said Lisa putting her arms round him.

'You look all in,' said Turner.

'Dr Dunbar? I'm Superintendent Renton. What is it you want us to do?'

'There's a transplant operation going on in there. We're going to interrupt it. They're murdering the patient, not curing her. I'd like you to escort us wherever we go and generally smooth the way.'

'What opposition can we expect?' asked Remton.

Dunbar told him about the Arab guards on the Omega wing and that he suspected they might be armed.

'We'll deal with them first. Just tell us where to find them.'

Lisa told the policeman where the Omega wing was, while Dunbar asked Clive Turner how many people he'd managed to recruit at short notice.

'Two medical, one theatre technician.'

'Lisa's a qualified theatre nurse,' said Dunbar.

Turner and Lisa acknowledged each other.

Dunbar walked over to join Renton, who was standing with his radio held up at face level. 'Every second is important,' he impressed on him.

'I'm waiting to hear from the armed response team. They've just gone in.'

The seconds seemed like hours. A car drew up and a man in civilian clothes got out.

'Farrow, police pathologist,' said Renton. His radio crackled into life and the disarming of the Arab guards was confirmed. 'All right,' said Renton. 'Lead on.'

Dunbar led the run along the corridors and up the stairs to the transplant unit. Questions from bemused staff were brushed aside as he led the way to the scrub room and asked the policemen to wait outside for the time being. He didn't want them intruding in a surgically clean area. He warned the others that he didn't know what to expect from those in theatre. 'Be prepared for anything,' he advised. 'Now let's scrub up.'

Médic Ecosse staff in the scrub facility were ushered out of the room into police custody while Dunbar and the others took over. Dunbar was the last to be ready, having had to shower before going through normal scrub procedure. When they were all gowned and masked, he turned to Turner and asked, 'All right?'

Turner nodded nervously and adjusted his mask.

Dunbar entered the theatre first and met the eyes of the lead surgeon across the table. It wasn't Ross. It was Hatfull.

'What the . . . Who the hell are you?' asked Hatfull.

'Steven Dunbar, Dr Hatfull. I'm here with the authority of the Sci-Med Inspectorate and the backing of Strathclyde Police. What stage are you at?'

'What the . . . What the hell is this all about?' stammered Hatfull.

'What stage are you at?' demanded Dunbar.

'About ten minutes from the exchange. What do you think you're doing? Don't you realize what we're involved in here?'

'You're about to give this child the wrong kidney,' said Dunbar, watching Hatfull's eyes.

Hatfull was almost apoplectic. 'The wrong kidney!' he stormed. 'The damned thing has come all the way from Geneva. It's as near a perfect a match as you can possibly get.'

'It's been switched.'

'Have you taken leave of your senses? What the hell are you talking about?'

'Not by you,' conceded Dunbar, accepting that Hatfull seemed to know nothing of the affair. 'Don't remove her own kidney just yet. We're going to take a biopsy of the donor organ. We'll have to wait for the result.'

Hatfull ran the back of his forearm along his brow in frustration. 'Will somebody please tell me what's going on?' he asked. He'd given up blustering; he said it quietly.

'Our one chance of saving Amanda Chapman's life is to find the kidney that came from Geneva. Any ideas?'

Hatfull looked at the ice-filled container beside him. Turner was taking a sliver of tissue from the kidney in it.

'That's not it, I promise,' said Dunbar.

'Then . . . I've no idea,' said Hatfull.

'Do your best to keep her stable,' said Dunbar. 'Any idea where Ross is this evening?'

'He left for Geneva earlier today.'

Dunbar's eyes widened over his mask. 'Geneva?' he repeated. This was a show-stopper.

The tissue sample from the donor kidney was bottled and handed over to Farrow.

'Quick as you can,' said Turner.

Dunbar went out of the theatre and out into the corridor where he pulled down his mask.

'How's it going in there?' asked Renton.

'Badly,' confessed Dunbar. 'Our main suspect ran off to Geneva this afternoon. The surgical team in there know nothing about the scam, so Ross is the only one who knows where the real donor organ is. Shit! What a mess.'

Dunbar was berating himself for not having considered that Ross wouldn't be doing Amanda's operation himself. He hadn't done Kenneth Lineham's or Amy Teasdale's either. He probably thought it wise to distance himself from these operations once he'd switched the human organ for an animal one. But Geneva? The more he thought about it, the less sense it made. If Amanda reacted like the others, she'd be dead within twenty-four to thirty-six hours. Ross would have to be on hand to do the heart transplant with his own surgical team, the Americans he'd seen arriving two days ago. If the Omega surgical team were already here, it didn't make any sense for Ross to be in Geneva. He wasn't, Dunbar concluded. It was a lie. He was locked away in the Omega wing with the others.

Dunbar told Renton what he thought.

'If that's so, I don't think anyone's been alerted up there. The armed response team took the two men on the door without any trouble. They're holding them downstairs.'

'Then we go in,' said Dunbar.

'Armed?'

'Maybe one armed officer. We don't know who's inside,' replied Dunbar.

Renton, Dunbar, three constables, including a WPC, and an armed response unit officer wearing full protective gear and carrying an automatic weapon moved quickly up the stairs to the Omega wing and entered through its now unguarded doors. Everything was quiet inside. They moved along the main corridor in silence, listening outside doors as they went. They stopped when they heard women's voices coming from one of the rooms. They were speaking Arabic.

'The patient's room,' whispered Dunbar.

They had just started to move off again when a door ahead opened and an Arab woman stepped out into the corridor. She saw them and let out a scream. A door on the other side of the corridor opened and Leo Giordano looked out. He saw Dunbar and quickly backed in again.

'In there!' said Dunbar leading the charge.

Giordano failed to get the door closed in time. Dunbar put his shoulder to it and kept the stalemate until two of the constables added their weight and it crashed open.

'This is an outrage!' said Giordano.

'Save your breath,' said Dunbar looking round the room. Ross was there, along with Kinscherf, Ingrid, two Arab men and the American medics.

'I've stopped Amanda Chapman's transplant,' said Dunbar, looking directly at Ross. 'I know what's been going on. Where's the real donor kidney?'

'I don't know what you're talking about,' said Ross calmly, meeting Dunbar's stare. 'This is an outrage. Explain yourself!'

'It's all over, Ross. You must see that. Where is it?' demanded Dunbar.

There was a moment of silence before Ingrid suddenly shook her head and said, 'He's right. For God's sake tell him!'

'Shut up!' snapped Ross but the westerners started showing signs of unease too. One of them got to his feet and said to Dunbar, 'I don't know what's going on here but it's nothing to do with me. I've just been contracted to be part of a surgical team for one transplant.'

'Me too,' said another getting up to join his colleague. 'I don't know anything about anything.'

'Sure,' said Dunbar sourly.

Both men looked down at the floor.

'Sit down,' said Dunbar. He turned back to Ross.

'They exhumed Amy Teasdale and examined her heart,' he lied.

A flicker of doubt appeared in Ross's eyes.

'For God's sake tell him!' pleaded Ingrid.

Ross turned to the younger of the two Arab men and said, 'Will you please tell the sheikh that these men have come to stop the operation to save his son.'

The man did as he was bid in Arabic. The sheikh listened, then looked up very slowly at Dunbar and his colleagues. His eyes, which had been calm, were now hard and full of anger. He rasped something at the younger man, who pulled out a pistol and pointed it at Dunbar. The armed policeman swung the butt of his weapon and caught him on the jaw. The Arab collapsed in a heap and the policeman recovered his weapon. Dunbar had to step over the Arab to get to Ross.

'It's all over, Ross. Where is it?' demanded Dunbar.

'For God's sake tell him!' said Ingrid again; she was now almost hysterical.

Dunbar nodded to the policemen to take her away.

'Where is the kidney, Ross?' Dunbar repeated, his voice betraying his urgency and frustration.

'I've nothing to say. I demand to see my solicitor.'

'Does anyone else know where the real kidney is?' asked Dunbar looking around. 'The child is going to die, for God's sake!'

The others in the room, looking pale, shook their heads.

'Jesus,' said Dunbar. 'Nobody.'

'We could search the building,' suggested Renton.

Dunbar looked at his watch. 'We're already out of time,' he said. Then, looking with loathing at those in front of him, he said, 'Get them out of here.'

He rapped his knuckles against his forehead as he tried to think what Ross might have done with the missing organ. 'Come on . . . think, man . . . think,' he muttered.

Suddenly it was obvious. It would be near where Ross would need it next. The post-mortem suite! He raced out the door past the mêlée of policemen and prisoners and down the stairs to the basement corridor. He sprinted along to the PM suite and crashed the door open. The lights seemed to take for ever to stutter into life. 'A fridge . . . a fridge,' he repeated as he pulled open cupboard doors all round the room. Then suddenly he found it. The fridge interior light clicked on to illuminate a metal container sitting there. It was similar to the one sitting beside Amanda on the operating table upstairs. Dunbar removed it carefully and undid the lid to look in. There was a kidney sitting there in crushed ice, scarlet on white.

Praying all the way that it wasn't too late, Dunbar rushed back up the stairs and along to the transplant theatre. He held the container in two hands in front of him.

'You got it!' exclaimed Lisa as he burst into the scrub room.

Dunbar was out of breath. He handed over the container to Turner who, like Lisa, was waiting there in surgical dress in case they were needed.

'What's happening?' Dunbar gasped.

'You were right. The path report on the kidney they were going to give to Amanda says it's an animal organ.'

'How is she?'

'We're just about to find out,' replied Turner.

As Turner entered the theatre, one of the theatre nurses came out, obviously distressed. 'I just can't believe what's been happening,' she sobbed. 'I'm sorry . . . I can't . . . I just can't.'

Dunbar looked at Lisa and nodded. 'Good luck,' he said.

Not having been through the scrub procedure, Dunbar couldn't enter the theatre himself. He went upstairs to watch from the teaching gallery. He turned on the sound relay so he could hear what was said.

'Dr Turner, would you assist?' he heard Hatfull ask. Then Hatfull turned to Lisa and said, 'Staff Nurse Fairfax, I'm obliged to you . . . If everyone's ready?' There were nods all round. 'Good, let's get on with it.'

Dunbar sat down and felt exhaustion sweep over him like a fast-running tide. It was over. It was finally over. If there was any justice in this world, Amanda Chapman's new kidney would give her back her childhood. Her family would be restored . . . Her family? Dunbar suddenly realized that Sandy and Kate would be waiting downstairs for news of their daughter's operation. He wondered what, if anything, they'd been told. He took it upon himself to go down and sit with them.

Sandy and Kate stood up as soon as he entered the family waiting area. 'Any news?' they asked in unison, before realizing who it was.

'The operation is progressing,' said Dunbar. 'The surgeons encountered a little difficulty at the outset, but everything's going well now.'

'We've been worried sick,' said Sandy. 'There seems to have been an awful lot of to-ing and fro-ing in the hospital tonight.'

'There were police cars outside,' added Kate.

'You didn't forget to tax Esmeralda, did you?' asked Dunbar in an attempt to change the subject.

'Probably,' answered Sandy with a smile.

* * *

Dunbar woke with wintry sunshine streaming in the window and playing on his eyelids. It took him a moment to realize that he was in Lisa's flat.

'You're awake are you?' said Lisa. She was standing in the doorway, smiling down at him.

'God, I slept like a log.'

'You deserved to.'

'What's the time?'

'Eleven thirty.'

'Good Lord. Amanda! What about Amanda?'

'She's doing fine,' said Lisa. 'I phoned earlier this morning. Her new kidney's working well and she's making a more than satisfactory recovery.'

'Thank God,' sighed Dunbar.

'No. Thank you,' corrected Lisa.

'Thank a lot of people, including you.'

'Is the whole Médic organization crooked?'

Dunbar shook his head. 'No, just the four of them. Ross, Kinscherf, Giordano and Ingrid, and, of course, the fifth element.'

'Fifth element?'

'Mindless, pitiless greed.'

'Frightening,' said Lisa quietly. 'What people will do for money.'

'And the medical profession is no exception.'

'Well, Dunbar, you're to be congratulated,' said Macmillan. 'A job well done.'

'Thank you, sir.'

'We've come out of this rather well, I fancy. The Home Secretary was pleased when I told him. I think he's finally decided that Sci-Med was a good idea after all.'

Dunbar smiled.

'And now you'll be ready for some leave, no doubt?'

'Yes, sir.'

'Good to be back in London eh?'

'Actually I'm going back to Scotland, sir. I've taken a cottage on the west coast for a few weeks.'

'Alone or with friends?'

Dunbar smiled again. 'With a friend.'